Mobilize!
Reassembling Forces with the World in Chaos

John A. Harper
Captain USNR (Ret.)

AuthorHouse™
1663 Liberty Drive
Bloomington, IN 47403
www.authorhouse.com
Phone: 1-800-839-8640

© 2010 John A. Harper. All rights reserved.

No part of this book may be reproduced, stored in a retrieval system, or transmitted by any means without the written permission of the author.

First published by AuthorHouse   11/17/2010

ISBN: 978-1-4520-9140-2 (sc)
ISBN: 978-1-4520-9141-9 (hc)
ISBN: 978-1-4520-9142-6 (e)

Library of Congress Control Number 2010917087

Printed in the United States of America

This book is printed on acid-free paper.

Certain stock imagery © Thinkstock.

Because of the dynamic nature of the Internet, any Web addresses or links contained in this book may have changed since publication and may no longer be valid. The views expressed in this work are solely those of the author and do not necessarily reflect the views of the publisher, and the publisher hereby disclaims any responsibility for them.

DEDICATION

I dedicate *Mobilize!* to my dear, departed wife of sixty-five years, Margaret Green "Peggy" Harper for her unflappable patience, encouragement, and at times, contribution to content, during the fourteen year writing process.

Contents

Confluence	*1*
Challenge	*6*
The Hajj	*13*
Shaqra	*20*
Pax River	*24*
Gulf Chaos	*27*
il-Dauli: The Empire	*31*
The Agony and the Ecstasy	*37*
Israel	*42*
Orders	*44*
Boxer	*50*
Istanbul	*55*
What Reserves?	*59*
Eisenhower Sacked	*63*
Ottoman Revisited	*66*
AMARC	*70*
Sea Duty	*76*
The Admiral	*80*
Command	*84*
The Bosnia Trigger	*88*
Terror at Sea	*95*
Sarajevo Sortée	*99*
Commissioning	*107*
Surge	*115*
Wings	*121*
Point Mugu	*127*
Deploy	*139*
Protocol	*146*
Taiwan	*149*

Kinmen Tao	*157*
Diversion	*165*
Reunion	*171*
Balkan Surprise	*177*
Pirates	*179*
Havens?	*185*
Prep	*189*
Day And Night	*195*
Epilogue	*198*

PROLOGUE

The year is 2015. Al-Qaeda, its senior leadership decimated, has been reduced to small, ineffective bands of extremists scattered across the Muslim world with no central authority or leadership.

Afghanistan is a full fledged democratic republic with a fully functioning central and provincial governments all continuing to work toward the achievement of a modern infrastructure following the establishment of a broad based multilevel education system. Some warlords still cause trouble.

Iraq has grown into a free democratic republic whose economy dominates the middle-east and whose influence has brought gradual change in the governments of its neighbors from Islamic theocracies and Arab monarchies to a semblance of social and economic freedom for their peoples.

The United States Congress, with growing concern over the federal deficit, used the aforementioned developments in 2012 as an opportunity to reduce the deficit by voting draconian reductions in our armed forces.

The force realignment begun in 2012 and exacerbated by the severe cuts in the armed forces has resulted in force levels in Germany and on the Korean peninsula lower than at any time since the end of World War II. The U.S. Air Force has been forced to move out of Okinawa and Qatar but was able to move back into Prince Sultan Air Base southeast of Riyadh due to improved relations between the United States and Saudi Arabia. Meanwhile, the Navy has been reduced to less than four hundred ships.

Events proceed nearly simultaneously in California on Pacific Standard Time (PST), Greenwich Meridian Time minus eight hours (GMT-8), and in Saudi Arabia on Arabic Standard Time (AST) GMT+3, an eleven hour difference.

1
Confluence

The coincidence of events in this week of the Muslim pilgrimage to the **Hajj** in Mecca begins the rude conversion of the life of one Naval Reserve captain and his family as the forces of Islamic extremism reorganize.

*

FRIDAY, 02 Oct 2015, 0100 Arabic Standard Time - AST - Jiddah, Saudi Arabia

A rusty old Kaiser class escort carrier of World War II vintage lies at the pier in the Red Sea port of Jiddah, the open waist curtains revealing a jumble of crates and vehicles on the hangar deck. Silence is broken only by the remote purr of the ship's electric generator. The scarlet, black and green flag with crescent and star flying from the yard arm reveals her Libyan registry.

An Army type jeep in the standard olive drab paint and soiled with the reddish mud of the desert slows to a quiet stop at the ship's gangway. A man, dressed in traditional Arabic white flowing robe and red and white Ghutra - head scarf - folded in the style of his hereditary tribe, steps out of the passenger side, says a few words to the driver, and eases toward the gangway, surveying the dock area carefully before proceeding. The man's swarthy complexion, large straight nose, and narrowly trimmed black beard suggest a princely Bedouin heritage. His steel blue eyes and tall, lithe physique demand respect, if not fear. The agile Arab glides up the ladder two rungs at a time without inducing vibration or sound and steps onto the quarterdeck to surprise the watch stander, a powerful man of six-foot-two weighing two hundred fifty pounds or more.

"I must see your captain." The Arab demands, in a hoarse whisper. "Tell him Abdul is here."

"Your papers?" The implied threat is conveyed through a thick German accent.

"Never mind 'papers'." Abdul growls, undaunted. "Say 'Abdul'. That will be enough."

The seaman looks doubtful but turns to disappear into the nearest passageway. In a few moments a short stout man wearing a navy pea coat over a white turtleneck sweater and blue denim dungarees emerges from the same passageway. His soiled white officer's cap is reminiscent of a German U-boat captain's. He wears a four day white stubble to match his shaggy white hair.

"Abdul." The captain shows an evil smile and extends his hand. "I vait since yesterday."

"Yes, Otto." Abdul acknowledges with a glare, ignoring the hand. "We come with others as our pilgrimage to the *Hajj* - You have the shipment - yes?"

"And you have ze money, ja?" Noting Abdul's nod he counters: "viz you?"

"The money is near." Abdul growls. "But first, I must inspect the shipment."

A frown wrinkles the captain's forehead and his eyes become slits. "Ja, Vee go to ze hangar deck - Helmut, kommen Sie mit uns!"

With a slight bow from the seaman the captain leads down three ladders to the cavernous hangar deck where aircraft were parked and repaired during the ship's World War Two service with the U.S. NAVY. Abdul heads directly toward a pile of crates at the aft end of the hangar deck. After a quick visual inspection, he turns to glower at the captain.

"These crates have been opened - explain that!"

The captain recoils a couple of steps. "Ve vere inspected vile ve enter Suez." He raises both hands, palms to Abdul. "Zey open some crates und find only your farm implements.

"How can I be sure?" Abdul demands, moving menacingly toward the captain.

Helmut steps between Abdul and his captain.

"I assure you, Abdul." Otto offers with a patronizing smile. "Only ze farm implements." Abdul thinks: *What if this German pig is lying? If INTERPOL knows the contents of all those crates our mission is destroyed. Ugh, We will find out!* "And what of the vehicles?"

"Kein problem." Otto spreads his hands and shrugs. "ze inspector just noted 'Four Humvee civilian type vehicles' und released us."

Abdul strides to the most aft Hummer and stops. "Which vehicle did he inspect?"

"Er . . . uh . . . zis one." The captain tries to appear certain . . . Then: "What was that gurgle sound forward? Go, Helmut, und find out!"

"Ja wohl, mein Kapitan." The clatter of Helmut's boots on the steel deck echoes through the hangar deck. Then . . . the sound of a brief struggle . . . and another gurgle . . . and a dull thud.

"Allahu Akbar, Abdul . . ." Comes the shout from up forward. Then more in Arabic language.

Abdul eyes the captain ominously. "Now Captain, we are alone . . . except for my four comrades who eliminated your crew . . . quietly." He pins the terrified captain against the Hummer. "Now! The truth about the 'inspection' Otto." He slams the captain against the vehicle and growls. "There is no inspection at Suez . . . IS THERE CAPTAIN?"

"Ja . . . ja wohl, Abdul . . . zere IS! I tell you as it vas!" The captain tries to shrink into the Hummer as two men dressed in black join Abdul.

"Amr, show the captain we are serious."

One of the men steps forward and strikes the captain on the right knee with a heavy wrench handle. "Owww! You broke my leg." The captain moans.

"It is not broken, Otto." Abdul says softly . . . "But it WILL BE . . . if you continue lying." He slams the captain against the side of the Hummer. "Now! The truth about the open crates."

Otto is whimpering. "Ja, ve open zem." sweat pours from his face. "You didn't tell me you had rifles, rifle grenades, RPGs, and . . . argh . . . ugh." A trace of white spittle drips onto Otto's chin and his eyes bug out as Fazul's garrote does its job and the captain sinks to the deck, motionless.

"You have the heroin, Amr." Abdul eyes Amr. It was not a question.

Amr nods the affirmative and pats his pocket.

"Return the captain to his cabin, be sure he is comfortable." Abdul shows a sly grin. "And leave him some 'Horse'."

*

THURSDAY, 01 Oct 2015, 1400 Pacific Standard Time (PST) - El Segundo, CA

Just back from a luncheon appointment with Colonel Isaak Barshewski, NAVSTAR Program manager at USAF Space Division, Karl Wilhelm Swenson sits at his mahogany desk reading the morning mail and exchanging e-mail messages. Karl's angular frame fits poorly in the standard black leather executive chair as he exceeds six foot two when

Confluence

standing and weighs in at about one hundred-eighty-five pounds. His full head of auburn hair is clipped to a military length, a holdover from his many years as a Naval Reserve officer and Naval Aviator, in and out of active duty in response to world conditions, and his civilian pursuit as Boeing test pilot. His square forehead, high cheek bones, blue-gray eyes, and small, straight nose emphasize his Swedish heritage. He is the director of the Los Angeles office of the Boeing Company.

"Mr. Swenson." Comes the soft voice of his secretary on the intercom.

"Yes, Jill." Responds Karl Swenson.

"Mr. Sherman in Seal Beach is on line two." Bill Sherman is Vice President, General Manager of the Boeing Seal Beach plant with responsibility for the launch vehicle business unit, among others.

"Thanks." *I think.* "Yes sir, Mr. Sherman, Swenson here." "I'll put him on, sir.". *God! the arrogance of the man.* "Hello . . . Yes sir . . . Swenson . . . you called." . . . "You heard right, sir. I am going on my fourteen day annual training duty in my mobilization billet with the Naval Air Systems Command, leaving Saturday." . . . *He says call him Bill - Okay* . . . "Hey Bill." Exasperation shows. "I'm not the only guy in this office, you know. I'm just the director . . . There are actually three of us covering *NavStar* at the Air Force Space Division and, as you know, Kevin Davidson is . . . ". . . *Jeez, he knows Davidson. He came right out of his engineering department* . . . "Yes sir. I DO know the importance of phasing in *SparLaunch* to cut off Lockheed Martin's threat to our *Delta VI* on the *NavStar* program, but please keep two things in mind." *Whew! This is a tough sell.* "First; Kevin Davidson is the lead on this program and, as you know, is recognized and very well respected by Colonel Barshewski. Kevin has coordinated all elements of your meeting with Colonel 'Bar' tomorrow . . . and I'll be there . . . just in case General Klein shows up . . . and we hope he does. Kevin will do all the follow-up, as usual, and I'll be back on Monday the twelfth - no problem." A deep breath. "Second; my leave for annual training duty is fully supported at corporate." . . . "Yeah, Gil Tarteki." *Should I tell him the whole story . . . yeah.* "Gil says corporate will pick up all my expenses for the trip in return for my complete report covering Boeing programs from Navy P-8 *Poseidon* to F-18F, G and H." A wry smile curls Swenson's lips. "and to *SparLaunch* for *NavStar* over at Air Staff, and within the Navy . . . don't forget that Navy has a big stake in *SparLaunch*." . . . *Damn! I wish to hell he wouldn't talk that way about Gil* . . . "No sweat, Bill." Swenson grins. "I'll just slip over to the *NavStar* office while I'm in the Pentagon on my Navy business. Hell, I know all those guys well enough to just drop in on them." *That ought to pacify him . . .* "Well, thanks for your confidence, Bill." Karl smiles. "I hope I can confirm it on this trip." *I hope I hope.*

On the way out the door of his office, Karl says: "I'm going home to hear our new president's first speech since his ascension to the presidency."

2
Challenge

FRIDAY, 02 Oct, 2015, 1730 PST - Pacific Palisades, California

Karl Swenson steps through the front door of the modest stuccoed residence on Alma Real. "Hi Mush." He calls to his wife Marcia. "Where are ya."

Marcia Churchill Swenson was called "Mush" by her little brother Geoffrey, six years her junior. Her father, James W., claims Winston Churchill as a distant cousin. Marcia is a trim five-foot-seven with honey blonde hair and an athletic figure. She shows her English heritage with her straight nose, liquid green eyes, and a fair complexion showing a touch of sun tan.

"In the kitchen, honey." Marcia calls as she quickly takes off her apron and checks her hair and lipstick in her little magnetic mirror on the refrigerator before rushing to the entry hall to Karl's enthusiastic embrace. They kiss. After a breath, Marcia sighs: "Mmm! . . . er . . . how are things at the office, honey?"

"Same-o, same-o." Karl shrugs. "Lockheed-Martin's got a new launch vehicle to threaten our Delta VI monopoly on the GPS satellite launches so Seal beach is trying to phase in *SparLaunch* to replace Delta VI and hold on to the business. Bill Sherman and his gang are coming up tomorrow to brief Space Division and Aerospace - big bucks involved in this one."

Marcia raises an eyebrow. "So what does Sherman say about you being away on active duty for two weeks?" She queries with a sly smile.

"You got it, honey. He's already bitchin' to Corporate." Karl grins like a chessie cat. "Hey! Corporate's payin' all my expenses for the trip . . . and Gil Tarteki wants a complete report on anything and everything of interest to Boeing." He heads for the bar. "And what isn't" A shrug. "It'll be a long report." Ice tinkles in the glasses. "Scotch for you, honey?"

"Perfect."

Karl pours. "Besides, Kevin can handle these appointments just fine - he's been in on the *SparLaunch* drill from day one." Karl hands Marcia a drink and they click glasses. "Lets have a drink, relax, and watch our new president react to the assassination of his predecessor."

"I was wondering what brought you home so early." Marcia giggles.

Karl wraps his free arm around Marcia and gives her a big kiss. "I couldn't resist your charm." Ushering Marcia into the family room Karl asks: "What station d'you like? it's on all of them."

"Well, I guess FOX would be as good as any. They've got Paul Jensen . . . I kinda like him." The TV clicks on and the drumbeat of an automobile commercial shatters the quiet of the Swenson home.

Karl instinctively grabs his ears. "Mute that damn thing, will you?"

"Okay." Marcia clicks the mute. "Oh! here's Jensen now." Click.

". . . the cabinet files into the house chamber, shaking hands with Representatives and Senators as they move slowly to their seats in the well of the House." Jensen intones. "Oh! and here come the justices of the Supreme Court." .

"It will be interesting to hear how our new president handles this appearance before a joint session of Congress just one week after the assassination of President Downs in Jakarta in a terrorist coup which also claimed Indonesia's president." Jensen begins. "What sort of background can he bring to this challenge, Bill?"

"Well, you know that he was picked by Downs because he would bring to the ticket some strength in defense matters and in foreign policy, both Downs' weaknesses. Wyatt - William Webster Wyatt, that is - was born and raised in conservative Webster Groves, Missouri, and is revered for his service as a Navy fighter pilot, known as 'Woolly' Wyatt by his squadron mates during action in Iraq and Afghanistan."

"Who's this guy, Honey?" Marcia interjects.

"Bill Crawford, FOX's guy in the White House Press Corps."

Jensen is continuing: ". . . but what does he know about governing?"

"Well." Crawford continues. "He was Lieutenant Governor of Missouri for one term and served two-and-a-half terms in the House before he was tapped for Veep."

"Wasn't he a complete unknown, nationally, at that point." Jensen leads.

"Oh yeah." Crawford agrees. "Except in Defense circles . . . Oh! here comes the Sergeant at Arms."

Challenge

"THE PRESIDENT OF THE UNITED STATES." Is announced in a voice that fills the chamber and the martial strains of "Hail to the Chief" greet President Wyatt as he descends the stairs amid subdued applause from both sides of the aisle and vigorous hand shakes with leaders of both parties. The president is a barrel chested five-foot-ten with balding dark red hair, a ruddy round face, a small straight nose, and blue eyes. After the somber yet extended greetings the president makes his way to the podium just below the seats occupied by Vice President Aikin and the Speaker of the House of Representatives, Howard Keitel.

"This is an historic twist for both the Vice President and the Speaker." Jensen begins. "Boyd Aikin was plucked from his position as Speaker of the House to be Veep when Wyatt assumed the Presidency and Speaker Keitel was only recently elected by the new Republican majority."

"Well." Karl begins. " Now that Republicans have firm control of both houses of Congress, perhaps Wyatt can get something done."

"Don't count on it." Marcia whispers as the Speaker begins.

"It is my singular honor and privilege to present President William Webster Wyatt."

Standing ovation.

"Thank you." The president shakes hands with both and hands them each a manila envelope. "You will excuse me If I speak from the podium in the well of the house used by members of this body." He starts down the stairs to the well. "I'll feel at home speaking from there."

"But sir." The speaker interjects. "You won't have TelePrompTers down there."

"I won't need those damn things." Wyatt tosses over his shoulder. "I know what I'm going to say."

A small commotion erupts in the well as ushers clear the area, replace the podium, and check the sound system while Wyatt descends the stairs. Whispers and muffled laughter are heard.

"UNPRECEDENTED!" Jensen groans.

"UNBELIEVABLE!" Crawford exclaims.

"I can't remember the last time a president ad libbed an address to a joint session of Congress."

That's because you weren't born yet, Jensen." Karl sneers. "Hell, this is really gonna be good." He snaps his fingers. "Hot Damn! A Nasal Radiator in the White House . . . GO WOOLLY!"

"Ladies and gentlemen assembled. I regret that I must first appear before you on such a solemn occasion as the death of President Downs so I ask you to join me in a brief moment of silence to honor his life and contributions to our Union."

President Wyatt resumes: "Thank you. I thought it best to recognize the forces that brought about President Downs' assassination and address actions that will be required to repel their recent assaults upon our interests. I'll be brief and to the point." President Wyatt begins. "I report to the American people tonight that our ability to identify and neutralize these renegade forces is SERIOUSLY DIMINISHED."

Jeers from the Democrats and stunned silence from Republicans.

"I'm sorry. Those are the words most descriptive of our current predicament." He glowers as he surveys the Senators and Representatives seated comfortably. "Oh, yes. The economy is still going strong, stock market full of bulls, the average wage higher than ever, crime and drug use on the wane, and trade relations continue to improve with the European Union, Mexico, Japan, and even Russia and China . . . Indonesia is a different story."

A universal sigh of relief fills the chamber.

"BUT!" He waves a clenched fist. "There is a serious and growing threat to our security that most of us have too long ignored while pumping up domestic handouts."

A grumble ripples through the audience of Senators and Representatives.

"God!" Karl crows. "It's about time someone noticed."

"We thought we had eliminated the terrorism of radical Islam when we killed or captured most of al-Qaeda leadership and its foot soldiers scatterd to the wind . . . **WRONG!** All the young Arabs and other Islamists trained in bin Laden's training camps back in the nineties have come of age with the same deep hate and resentment for the western, Judeo-Christian world - especially the United States and Israel. The fury of this new threat was demonstrated last week with the assassination of President Downs and Indonesian president Harrudman in Jakarta, Indonesia, a new hotbed of radical Islam. Until now we viewed this threat as small, splintered, disassociated, groups - just ineffective remnants of al-Qaeda. But in recent months we have recognized an ambitious revolutionary calling himself Süleyman the Third, The Modern Magnificent, and claiming the mantle of the sixteenth century Sultan of the Ottoman Empire, Süleyman The Magnificent. This charismatic disciple of al-Qaeda teachings has been reported rallying al-Qaeda remnants across the Islamic world from Kurdish Iraq to Zamboanga with a fanatic commitment to eradicating the

Challenge

American presence in the middle east and the East Indies. We still haven't identified the terrorists who gunned down President Downs and President Harrudman of Indonesia in a daring ambush in the center of Jakarta. Intelligence sources identify them as Islamic so the fact that Harrudman is a Muslim suggests that President Downs was the real target as a signal to the United States to **GET OUT!**" Wyatt slams his fist on the podium.

"Our complacency vis-a-vis this burgeoning terrorist threat has already cost us our president and poses a clear and present danger to our citizens and institutions here at home. And our healthy economy remains an attractive target of this terrorist in emperor's clothing.

"There is a reason for this renewed aggressiveness and growing unity among Islamic extremists from Bosnia to East Timor. It is the continued weakening of our armed forces through escalating Defense budget cuts to the point where world trouble makers are emboldened by our waning strength and inaction. They know we are powerless even to protect our interests, much less to retaliate."

The president is greeted with rapt silence as he takes a drink of water.

"Wow!" Marcia exclaims. "He paints a pretty bleak picture."

"It's true." Karl exclaims. "Trouble is, President Wyatt is the first to tell the truth about it . . . Hey d'you want another drink, honey?"

"Yeah, thanks."

The president continues. "I haven't even mentioned the Chinese occupation of the islands of Quemoy and Matsu in a threatening move against Taiwan, and North Korean testing of a nuclear tipped long range missile and armed incursions into the south. Our serious draw-down of U.S. forces in Korea and the absence of a Japan based carrier battle group has encouraged these aggressive actions."

Another groan and some subdued mumbling issues from the seats.

"A stark example of the folly of the continuing reduction of our armed forces is the premature decommissioning of aircraft carriers *Vinson,* and *Eisenhower,* and the severe reduction of funds for the next CVX class carrier, postponing its introduction indefinitely, all of which leaves us with just eight carriers of which two are currently in the yard for periodic maintenance and modernization, and we're down to just two Expeditionary Strike Groups. We no longer have a carrier battle group based in Japan, inviting mischief from China and North Korea, and it is impossible to maintain a battle group in the Persian Gulf full time, emboldening the Islamic extremists. The deep cuts in the Army bring similar problems to our commands in the western Pacific and the Middle East - CinCPac and

CinCCent. The Marines are better off but cannot be effective without naval support and Army backup. Compounding the problem is the serious erosion of our intelligence capability, mostly in the 'HumInt' (human intelligence) category - we just can't find out what these trouble makers are doing... and anonymous computer "crackers" have already demonstrated an ability to disrupt our Command and Control functions. The upshot of all this is that this so-called super power is viewed as a paper tiger world wide, easy prey for any ragtag armed gang. We are unable to foresee attacks on our interests and haven't the resources to beat back these incursions."

A scattered applause rises from both sides of the aisle amid some more grumbling while Wyatt takes a sip of water and Jensen comments: "Aha! He's playing to the Republicans who took back control of both houses in the last election."

President Wyatt spreads his arms as a question. "What do we do?"

Bits of quiet conversation ripple through the chamber and Karl shouts: "Rebuild the Navy, that's what!"

"Strange you'd say a thing like that, Karl." Marcia snickers.

"Here's what we do!" Wyatt claps his hands. "As you know, the new Fiscal Year budget you are approving this month was predicated on the assumption that the relative peace we have enjoyed would continue into the indefinite future. We now know that the status quo is unrealistic so today I am sending you a supplemental request for seven hundred billion dollars to begin rebuilding our forces: The Army in the image of a fast reaction fighting force with emphasis on strengthening CinCPac, CinCCent, and CinCSO, special operations; For the Navy, accelerating construction of the next CVX class carrier, to permit its commissioning next year, a full six years behind schedule, recommissioning three aircraft carriers and two Amphibious Assault Ships now in moth balls, reactivating support ships, cruisers, Destroyers, etc.; At the CIA, enhancing the Human Intelligence function by emphasizing Arabic language training; and building robust computer security elements in the Department of Defense and each of the armed services. I **IMPLORE** you to approve this supplemental request to give me the tools to reestablish the United States as the world's super power. To do otherwise would be to surrender to those forces who would **BURY US!**"

A thunderous standing ovation comes from the Republican side and even from some Democrats.

Crawford comments: "By God! There's a bold stroke."

"I wouldn't have believed it." Jensen intones. "He's got them eating out of his hand.

"Hey!" Karl crows. "He might bring back *Boxer*, my old ship."

"You'd like that wouldn't you." Marcia grins.

"Hell yes." Karl smiles. "I've had three deployments on amphibious assault ships, including one on *Boxer*."

"Don't I know it." Marcia frowns. "I'm the one who stayed home with the kids."

Jenson replys to Crawford: I guess he thinks he can get away with it since the Republicans took back control of both houses." Jensen mumbles.

"Never happen, Honey." Marcia whispers. "Not even with a Republican congress."

"Well. We can dream, can't we?"

3
The Hajj

Saturday, 03 October 1200 PST - Pacific Palisades, CA

 Karl Swenson bursts into his modest California style home followed by his son Harm. Both are dressed in tennis whites and dripping perspiration, fresh from the father-son tennis tournament at the municipal tennis courts. Karl, at six-foot-two and a hundred and ninety pounds, is a strong physical specimen. Harm looks more Swedish than his father with platinum blonde hair, blue eyes and high cheek bones. He carries his one-hundred-eighty pounds very well on his six-foot-four frame.

 "I'm getting a coke - with ice - dad." Harm announces. "D'you want one?"

 "Yeah, tall, with a lime . . . Please." Karl calls while collapsing in the family room easy chair.

 "Well, boys." Marcia Swenson sings, sweeping into the family room. "How'd it go."

 "Great!" Harm blurts out as he delivers the iced coke to his dad. "Our final match was against Mister Kimball and his son Ben."

 "We whipped 'em good." Karl interjects proudly.

 "Does that mean you won the tournament?" Marcia persists.

 "Yeah, yeah!" Harm gloats. "The Swensons are the tennis champs of the Palisades."

 "Just a one day tournament." Karl comments. "Good thing too, since I have to leave for San Diego post haste, and on to PAX River tomorrow . . . So I'd better get moving." He gets up and heads for the master bedroom. "Hey Harm, when are you going back to Palo Alto?"

 "I've got a flight at ten . . . uh . . . Something." Harm scratches his head. "Ten-twenty I think. I don't have a class until Monday afternoon though."

Karl turns to face Harm. "Well, keep up the good work. We're looking for top grades this semester." He turns to disappear through the door. Then the sounds of the bedroom TV are heard, followed by the rush of water in the shower.

"It's going to be mighty lonesome here for the next two weeks, honey." Marcia comments as Karl emerges from the shower, wrapped in a towel.

The TV Fox News anchor, Sharon Brown, is saying: "Looks like drug related killings . . ."

"Hey!" Karl turns up the sound. "I wonder where that was . . . Yeah, honey, it'll be lonesome where I am too. I'll miss you . . . a LOT."

Sharon Brown again: "Let's go to Don Kirschner in Jiddah, Saudi Arabia . . . Don?"

Satellite delay . . . "The bodies were found garroted and . . ."

"Uh-huh." Karl slips into his shirt. "That's become a druggie favorite."

". . . Three kilos of heroin were found in the captain's cabin . . ."

"Yeah, but where'd it happen?" Karl turns up the volume again.

". . . Bodies were found aboard an old World War Two jeep carrier in the Red Sea port of Jiddah . . . The ship, with Libyan registry, was apparently used to transport outsized cargo items such as large boats, airplanes, special vehicles, and drugs."

"Well, it's not in the U.S. anyway." Karl sighs. "We don't need any more of that."

"Honey." Marcia pleads. "Why don't you give up this reserve stuff. You said you've got enough points to retire when you get to be sixty . . . You don't really have to do it any more."

"Wait. I want to hear the TV."

Sharon Brown asks Don Kirschner: "Don, how did this old ship . . . You called it a 'jeep' carrier get in this dirty business?"

"Well, I'm told." Kirschner begins. "That the ship was one of many escort, or 'jeep' carriers built by the Kaiser shipyard during World War Two and preserved for possible future use in the mothball fleet near the mouth of the James River, near Norfolk. As a result of the severe budget cuts in two thousand, eleven, most of the mothball fleet was sold at auction. I am told the Greek shipping magnate Apollo Odysseus got it for a song, put it in operating condition at considerable cost, rechristened her *Odyssy II,* and began operating her under Libyan registry.

"Sounds pretty shady to me." Sharon interjects.

"Yes." Kirschner responds. "But the *Odyssy II* has never been cited before."

"Well, thanks for the report, Don." Sharon turns a page of her notes. "After the break . . . ."

"Back to your question, Mush; If I can make admiral I'll have a lot better retirement." Karl reasons.

"Yeah . . . Fat chance." Marcia sulks.

"Come on, Honey." Karl soothes. "It won't be much longer . . . And you'll know it's worth it when we retire with good retirement pay." *And I have the pride of being a Rear Admiral.*

*

MAP OF SAUDI ARABIA
ROUTES FROM JIDDA AND MECCA TO
RIADH AND PRINCE SULTAN AIR BASE

Saudi Arabia map courtesy of the University Libraries, The University of Texas at Austin

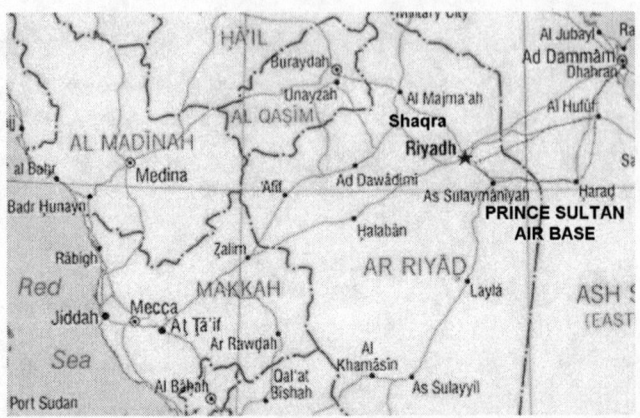

Follow the routes of Abdul and his raiders from the acquisition of their vehicles and weapons in the Red Sea port of Jiddah to Mecca under cover of the Muslim pilgrimage to the Hajj; thence via their separate routes as described in Chapter 3 to the staging point at Shaqra. Then, following the description in Chapter 4, trace the groups' separate routes to the Saudi royal palace in Riyadh and Prince Sultan Air Base, the U.S. Air Force operating base.

Mecca, Saudi Arabia

Abdul stands on a small sand dune facing east where the brilliant red sunrise silhouettes the minarets of the Great Mosque of Mecca. Sitting cross-legged in the sand before him is the small band of his closest followers. A group of men may be seen in the dry wadi one hundred yards down the hill to the east. among the four Hummers and the Jeep.

Nine Arabs - ostensibly pilgrims to Mecca - wear the simple white robes of the Hajj and Ghutra in the styles of eight different Islamic tribes and nations - from Sunni to Shi'ah and from Palestine to Iran. But all are unified in their dedication to the eradication of Americans from the Arab land and the destruction of the Arabic regimes that harbor them.

Abdul raises his right hand, palm forward. "Comrades! We are a small elite force of twenty-eight men, trained in unconventional warfare. But today we must appear as pilgrims returning from the Hajj, celebrating our achievement in the sight of Allah." He holds a Michelin road map of Arabia in his left hand and uses his right to point. "Today, we travel across the desert to Shaqra - here, just a few kilometers south of the main road turn-off at Al Majma'ah. Here is where we prepare our thrust against the infidels." He points to a spot two hundred kilometers northwest of Riyadh. "It is just a village, dominated by a small mosque." He holds up an enlarged photograph of a drab warehouse building bearing a large Arabic sign translated to 'OIL FIELD SUPPLIES' under the Arabic. "Seven kilometers east on the road to Washm you will see this warehouse on the south side of the road." He hands the photo to Amr and signals for him to pass it around. "Drive around to the back of the building and knock on the first garage door you come to. You understand!" It is not a question. "I will be there to meet you."

"We each go by a different route, departing at different times, to avoid suspicion." Abdul speaks carefully and eyes each man intently as he directs: "Here are maps, one for each vehicle. You must all arrive in Shaqra no later than 1800 hours." There is nodding and a murmur of assent from the group. "As you know, each vehicle carries weapons and explosives in concealed compartments and farm implements in the cargo bed. If you are stopped along your route you must not . . . you WILL NOT . . . allow inspection of the weapons cache. If action is required, make it quiet . . . knife or garrote. Clean up any evidence of a fight and take the bodies with you to dispose of them where they will not be found." The group acknowledges with more nods. "Another thing: Change drivers once or twice so you will all have time for some sleep en-route. There will be no time for rest at Shaqra and we will need all our alertness tomorrow morning."

Abdul continues: "Omar. You will drive the jeep and I will ride with you. The jeep has Saudi plates. We will depart at 0700, as soon as everyone has their instructions."

"I am proud to be your driver, excellency." Omar responds proudly. "We will have two other men."

"Good . . . now." speaking to each driver individually, Abdul begins. "Yousef, you and Bassam have volunteers with you. Correct?"

Yousef stands. "Yes, excellency. We have four more men, faithful to Süleyman, standing ready . . . there, by the vehicles."

"Good! But never mention Süleyman again on this mission!" Abdul turns to the group. "Pass that along, all of you. Never mention Süleyman!" More nodding and mumbled assent.

Again addressing Yousef and Bassan. "Take the off-white soft-top Hummer with Palestinian plates and travel north to Medïnah, here." He points to Medïnah on the map, then traces another road eastward. "You will turn eastward toward Buraydah." He pokes the map for emphasis. "As soon as you can, after leaving Medïnah, pull into a secluded area and change to the Kuwaiti plates and replace the Palestinian papers with the Kuwaiti registration - burn the Palestinian papers, bury them with the license plates, and smooth out your tracks . . . That's what the rakes are for." Abdul allows himself a sly smile as subdued laughter spreads through the group. "Drive and walk over the raked area before you proceed eastward. When you reach Burayadah turn south through Unayzah down to the main road, turn northeast about forty kilometers to Ushayqir, and turn right. It will be about five kilometers southeast to Shaqra. This route is about twelve hundred fifty kilometers so it should take you a little over ten hours at one hundred twenty kilometers per hour and with good road conditions. At worst it may be twelve hours." Abdul points toward the vehicles. "Go now!" Yousef and Bassam slog down through the sand toward the vehicle park.

"Amr!" Abdul calls. "You and Fazul have the next longest route - about nine hundred eighty-five kilometers." He traces the route on the map. "You will depart eastward past At Tä'If, continue northeast to Zalim and bear right. You continue on past Halabān to Al Muzāhimïyah. Turn to the northwest and it will be one hundred, fifty kilometers to Shaqra. Remember, the rendezvous is about forty kilometers past Washm, on the left. Your route is nine hundred, eighty-five kilometers. You will depart at 0800 hours in the green Hummer wagon with Saudi plates."

"Ismael and Salem."

"Yes, excellency, our other four men await at the vehicles."

"Good." Abdul is pleased. "You will take the same route - via Zalim and Al Muzähimïyah. Depart at 0900 in the white, hard top Hummer with the Bahrain plates.

"Rashid." Abdul calls. "You and Tariq take the silver Hummer and follow the direct route, via Zalim and Afif. Depart at 0930 hours." He examines his notes. "Your vehicle has Irani license plates."

As the group breaks up and begins the descent to the vehicles, Yousef's Hummer stirs a cloud of desert dust as it speeds westward toward the main highway to Medïnah.

*

Sunday, 04 October - San Diego, California.

Karl Swenson boards American flight 284 at Lindbergh Airport bound for Reagan National Airport, Washington, D.C. with one stop in Dallas-Fort Worth.

4
Shaqra

Now that Captain Karl Swenson is on his way to the Washington D.C. area his activities will be on Eastern Standard Time (EST) GMT-5 yielding just eight hours difference from Arabic Standard Time (AST) GMT+3.

*

Shaqra, Saudi Arabia

Abdul stands on a table before three large posters taped to the concrete block wall. "Allahu Akhbar!" Abdul's call to Islam echoes off the bare walls of the oil field warehouse.

"ALLAHU AKHBAR!" Shouted by all twenty seven of Abdul's small band rattles the corrugated roof of the building causing some dust to fall softly on the men, seated cross legged on the bare concrete floor.

"We come here to support Süleyman III, the Modern Magnific . . ."

"SÜLEYMAN - SÜLEYMAN" The accolade from the group interrupts Abdul, again shaking more dust from the ceiling.

"Praise Allah!" Abdul begins again. "We are the initial thrust to support Süleyman's vision of the modern Islam, Il-Dauli, the Empire, stretching from Morocco in the west to the Philippines in the east and to Bosnia and Croatia to the north." His lips curl in an evil grin. "The modern Ottoman Empire"

"ALLAHU AKHBAR!" Again the corrugated roof shakes.

Abdul has the group motivated. "Our mission tonight is the initial step in creating a strong air force which will spearhead Süleyman's campaign." The excitement in the crowd is quieted by Abdul spreading his arms, hands down. "We have three objectives: To rid Saudi Arabia of the American presence, capture U.S. aircraft in Saudi Arabia for the Il-Dauli Air Force, and assassinate the Saudi king and his court to gain dominion over Saudi

Mobilize!

Arabia and command of her armed forces. In support of our action, Saudi Air Force officers who share our concern over American presence have built a cadre loyal to Süleyman III who are immediately ready to take over Saudi fighter wings at Tabük, Dahran, and Kamis Mushayt upon our command. Other units will follow. Most Saudi Fighter pilots and ground crew at Tabük Air Base have revolted and sworn allegiance to Süleyman III. Those who didn't were executed. Within an hour after you have secured the base and neutralized the air defense a detachment of Saudi pilots and crew will be airborne in a C-130 en route to Prince Sultan Air Base to commandeer the USAF F-35s and F-22s."

"As you see." Abdul waves his arm toward the four Hummers and one jeep parked on the shop floor. "Our vehicles have been painted U.S. Air force camouflage." He permits himself a wry grin. "They will be driven in the mud outside before we depart."

We strike our two objectives simultaneously, exactly at 0200 hours tomorrow." Abdul announces as he holds up his left arm and points to his watch. "Stand by to set watches at 1944 hours, zero seconds . . . Stand by . . . MARK!"

"Amr." Abdul calls.

Amr stands and bows ceremoniously. "Excellency!"

"You will lead Ismael and his group to destroy the American forces at Prince Sultan Air Base just east of As Sulaymanïya." Abdul hands Amr, Ismael, and Omar each a packet. "Here is the detailed plan for your attack along with road maps, air base plat, detailed plans of the U.S. Air Force barracks, the headquarters building, and the maintenance depot, and photographs of those buildings and the Patriot antimissile site. Study them carefully with your men before you depart. Your time to Prince Sultan Air Base is about two hours, forty minutes." Abdul looks at his watch. "Amr, you will depart at 2245 hours. Start north toward Al Majma'ahr, turn to the East on the road to Riyadh and proceed through Riyadh to Prince Sultan Air Base - understood?"

"Understood, excellency."

Abdul turns to Ismael who stands to attention. "You will depart at 2300 hours and follow the road Southeast via Washm through the Al Muzähiymïa junction and around this loop . . ." Abdul traces the route with his pointer. ". . . to the road to the air base."

"Yes, excellency."

"And Omar."

Omar prostrates himself as in prayer, then stands to attention. "Sir!"

"Take the jeep and your three commandos and follow just ten minutes behind Amr, on the same route . . . via Riyadh to the air base. You will carry no weapons to avoid suspicion. You will pick up the weapons you need at the rendezvous point from the concealed caches in the Hummers.

"Time your trips to rendezvous here at 0140 hours." Abdul points to a road intersection on the wall map of the air base and environs. "About one kilometer from the main gate." He then points to the main gate. "Omar, you will proceed at a leisurely pace toward the main gate and at about fifty meters short of the gate, and without stopping, drop two of your men off to scale the fence and approach the gate house on foot to neutralize the sentry or sentries quietly by garrote and knife at 0145 and open the gate."

Abdul draws the extended fingers of his right hand across his throat. "Silence is paramount."

Amr, Ismael, Omar, and their men show fierce grins, and some imitate Abdul's throat cutting gesture and shout. "ALLAHU AKHBAR!"

"Amr, you and Ismael will approach the gate from opposite directions at a moderate speed and drive both Hummers quietly through the gate, followed by Omar, picking up his two men on the go." Abdul almost whispers. "Amr."

"Yes, excellency."

"Drive your vehicle quietly along this road toward the Patriot missile battery, here." Abdul points to an emplacement on the map. "The Americans have removed all but one of their Patriot batteries in an economy move, and there is no conventional antiaircraft battery." Pointing to another spot between the main gate and the *Patriot* battery Abdul turns to Amr. "You have a man trained in the *Dragon* shoulder fired Antitank missile." It is not a question.

"Yes, excellency." Amr signals for one of his men to stand. "Hassan, here, served with Hamas as *Dragon* missile gunner against Israeli army tanks."

"Good. Hassan will station himself on this high point about 300 meters from the *Patriot* battery while you and the rest of your men deploy at Rocket Propelled Grenade (RPG) range. Hassan will open the attack at exactly 0200 hours with a *Dragon* missile into the Patriot launcher and the rest of you will follow with RPGs, finally eliminating any survivors with rifle fire." Abdul permits himself a slight smile as he contemplates the carnage.

"After the *Patriot* battery has been neutralized, you will move directly to the flight line to secure the area and await the arrival of our pilots and ground crew from Tabūk Air Base.

"You, Ismael, will dr . . . "

"Aye, excellency." Ismael's eagerness is palpable.

"You will drive to the barracks of the Americans." He points to a building on the wall map. "Here. At exactly 0200 hours attack with rocket propelled grenades to blast these structural points." Abdul points to the vulnerable spots on his photograph of the barracks. "If our estimates are correct the building will collapse and there will be few survivors. Any escaping survivors will be shot. Do you understand?" Abdul stares into the eyes of Ismael to cement his point.

"I understand, excellency." Ismael draws the fingers of his right hand across his throat. "No prisoners!"

"Good." Abdul turns to his wall map. "Omar, you will drive the jeep directly to the headquarters building, here." He points to a building on the map. "To attack exactly at 0200. Plan your assault with the building plan in the packet I gave you and take control of all command functions. You may expect assistance from the Saudi base managers who are in revolt against the Saudi king. They will meet you in front of the headquarters building."

5
Pax River

Sunday, NAS Patuxent River, MD

"Captain Swenson reporting for training duty in NavAir." Swenson wears a blue blazer over gray slacks - his travel outfit. "Here are my orders." He adds, tossing the manila envelope on the counter behind which a large blue wall plaque with gold lettering screams: "NAVAL AIR SYSTEMS COMMAND".

"Yes sir, Captain." The yeoman replies, stowing the envelope. The small plaque on the counter announces: Y2 Frank J. Donnelli. "The duty officer's expectin' you. Please go right in." He points to his right. "First door on the right. I'll take care o' your orders, sir."

"Thanks." The placard on the office door reads: "Command Duty Officer" with an insert reading CDR Isaac J. Collins. CAPT Swenson knocks.

"Come on in." Comes the answer from behind the door, in a voice tinged with a hint of Boston accent.

Swenson enters to find CDR Collins rising from his chair and skirting the desk to greet his visitor. He is a well built five foot eleven at about one hundred sixty-five pounds, bald on top and shaved on the sides. His light blue eyes twinkle with excitement as he extends his hand. "Welcome Captain." A firm handshake. "I'm Ike Collins but I'll answer to 'ICE'."

"Karl Swenson here. I was known as 'KARLO' when I had a *Harrier* detachment on *Boxer*."

"How was your trip over from Reagan Airport?"

"Just fine." Swenson replies with a smile. "Car and driver were right there when I arrived, thanks."

"Have a seat." ICE waves at the couch against the wall opposite his desk. "But we don't have any time for chit-chat. Admiral Brewster wants you to join him in the JCS conference room over in the Pentagon ASAP." ICE enjoys the urgency.

Swenson drops his six foot two frame onto the couch. "What's that all about. Last I heard before I left home was that I was to report to Admiral Brewster in his office tomorrow morning."

"Some rag-head's gone ape." ICE comments with a silly grin. "Says he's gonna take over the world. Screamin' headlines in all the evening papers . . . Now! What do you need for your fourteen day stay?"

"Wow! That must've just happened. Nothin' in the news this morning." Then shifting to needs: "I'll need quarters for the two weeks . . . oh . . . and a car.

"Donnelli has reserved quarters for you at the VOQ. I think you'll find them comfortable." Ice grimaces. "No cars for O-6s though . . . Sorry."

"God Damn!" "I knew things were tight, but this is too much." Swenson sputters. "So how the Hell do I get to the Pentagon?" *I guess I'll just have to rent a car.*

"Gotcha covered!" Punching the intercom button on his phone he calls. "Donnelli!"

"Yes SIR."

"Get a car for Captain Swenson . . . ON THE DOUBLE! He's got to get to JCS **ASAP**."

"Aye Aye, Sir." Donnelli answers. "Car and driver waiting out front."

"Do you have your gear with you Cap'n?" ICE inquires.

"Yeah. Out in the lobby, why?"

"Tell the driver to fall by the VOQ and you can drop your gear in your room before you head for the Pentagon. Go in the River Entrance and . . ."

"Whoa!" Swenson holds up his right hand. "I'd better change into my uniform before I go to JCS."

"No time for that." Ice advises. "The briefing's supposed to start at nineteen hundred." He checks his watch. "You'll be a little late as it is. Don't worry. A lot of people will be in mufti . . . Sunday night, you know. Hell, you'll be more formal than most . . . Oh! JCS is just inside the River entrance."

"So how do I get back . . . No tellin' how late it'll be."

"Just call the Pentagon motor pool." ICE twirls his rolodex. "Uh-huh . . . here's the number." He scribbles on a Postit, rips it off, and hands it to Swenson. "You can use the motor pool any time you're in D.C."The door opens and Donnelli's head appears. "Your car is waiting Captain."

"Good." Swenson rises and extends his hand. "Thanks for your help, ICE."

"You mean, 'thanks for nothin'." ICE frowns. "Sorry about the shortages."

"Oh. You did the best you could . . . See you around . . . I suppose."

6
Gulf Chaos

Sunday, 2000 EDT - The Pentagon
"Thanks for the ride." Swenson calls as he steps out of the official car into a slow drizzle at the Pentagon River entrance and hops up the stairs two steps at a time.. Inside, he announces himself: "Captain Swenson, Navy, Admiral Brewster is expecting me in the JCS conference room."

"ID please." Is the impassive response from the guard. "Tighter security lately, sir."

"I'm attached to NavAir over at Pax River." Swenson begins. "I just checked in an hour ago so I don't have a badge yet." He fumbles in his wallet. "Here's my regular ID."

"A reserve, huh?" The guard fingers the ID card. "I'll have to call for clearance . . . Admiral Brewster you said?

"Yeah, that's right."

The guard keys in the number. "This is the guard at River Entrance . . . yeah . . . I've got a Captain Swenson here . . . Yeah, Navy Reserve, supposed to see Admiral Brewster he says." He puts his hand over the phone mouthpiece. "She's gone to look for him."

"You said 'tighter security'. How long's that been goin' on"

"Just went on a couple hours ago . . . some big blowup in the . . . Oh! . . . Yeah . . . Okay, I'll send him in . . . yeah, I'll give him a temporary badge . . . JCS ONLY."

"Here's your badge, good for today only. It's that door right over there. just knock . . . the sergeant said she'd meet you at the door."

"Thanks." *I guess I'll find out what happened when I get in there.*

Knock, Knock . . . The quiet clatter of a dead bolt being withdrawn and the door opens about six inches. A round female face with grey-blue eyes and dishwater blonde hair in a short shag appears. She whispers

"Captain Swenson?" Then, with a nod and a show of his badge by Swenson, she opens the door just far enough for him to enter. "The briefing has started, sir, but you haven't missed much. This is Admiral Goodman, JCS intelligence speaking now." She then turns to lead him into the auditorium. She wears staff sergeant's chevrons on her Air Force uniform. *Hmm, Admiral Goodman is in uniform - one broad stripe - must have had the Sunday duty. Hey, that must be the JCS Chairman, General Victor "Ski" Skwarkowski, sitting quietly to the left of the podium wearing Army fatigues with four black stars on his collars. His scowl speaks volumes.*

"This was a very well planned and coordinated attack executed simultaneously at 2300 Zulu today by a combination of forces from the territories of Iran and Iraq, conducted either BY those nations or by extremist elements within." The red arrow of the admiral's LASER dances about the huge wall map of the middle east.

The sergeant directs Swenson to a row of seats where he recognizees Admiral Brewster next to an empty seat five seats from the aisle. "Thank you Sergeant."

Admiral Brewster is dressed in a gray wool crew neck sweater over a blue oxford cloth button down shirt. His flowing white hair contrasts with his florid complexion as he turns to greet Swenson with a wink of a pale blue eye and a gesture to the chair next to him. Swenson squeezes in and takes his seat. "What's goin' on, sir?" He whispers to Admiral Brewster..

"*Stennis* has been severely damaged in the Gulf - let's listen."

"The brief report we have from the battle group commander before our satellite was jammed describes multiple *SCUD*s launched from southern Iraq near Salman, a swarm of *SILKWORM* cruise missiles from near Bandar-e-Deylam in Iran, and torpedoes fired from one or more submarines which must have been sitting on the bottom to avoid detection." Goodman sips water from a glass on the podium, then continues. "The Office of Naval Intelligence believes the submarines were of the Russian Kilo class supplied to Iran in 2006, probably armed with wake homing torpedoes - carrier killers. *Stennis* has sustained serious damage to the flight deck from one *SCUD* that got through, superficial damage to the island by a *Silkworm* cruise missile, and crippling damage to her propellers and steerage by one or more torpedoes. She is dead in the water at last report while *Port Royal* and *Lake Champlain* are preparing to take her under tow for our naval base in Bahrain. Airborne aircraft are all bingo to Bahrain. So far, we have no report of casualties or damage to aircraft on board *Stennis* nor damage to other ships of the battle group." Admiral Goodman steps back and looks to

General Skwarkowski who rises to his full height of about six-foot-six, the ceiling lights glistening off his balding pate and prominent Slavic nose, as Goodman closes his remarks. "That's all we have for the moment, sir."

The buzz of conversation spreads quickly through the room as General Skwarkowski steps to the podium, raising both hands as a request for quiet. "Gentlemen . . . gentlemen . . . er and ladies." He pleads and the room quiets. "As Admiral Goodman reported, we currently have no direct communication with the *Stennis* Battle Group but communications is working alternate channels for more reports. Please do not leave the room." He points to the back of the room. "We have coffee. Make yourselves comfortable. We may be here for a while."

At the coffee counter we are greeted by a small man with sloping forehead, sparse curly hair and large nose, dressed in taupe corduroy pants and green sweater over a red plaid flannel shirt. "Hi Brian." He extends his hand to Admiral Brewster. "Surprised?"

"Not really, sir." Brewster replies. "We've been worried about such a threat from Islamic extremists . . . Oh! I want you to meet Captain Karl Swenson, who just reported in for his reserve annual training duty . . . Karl, this is Admiral Massey, CNO."

"Honored to meet you, sir." Karl gives just a hint of a bow as he shakes the admiral's hand.

"Well. A reserve eh?" The admiral is expansive. "What's your specialty, son."

Hmm. First time I've been called "Son" for a long time. "My MOB billet is as Director Air Warfare Programs, sir."

"What do you do in civilian life?"

"I'm Director of the LA office for Boeing." *Should I quit while I'm ahead? Naaw.* "I came out of Boeing St. Louis where I was a test pilot for six years interspersed with two years active duty as CO VMF-153 detachment on *Boxer* involving heavy participation in the Afghan and Iraq wars."

"How'd you ever get command of a Marine squadron." Massey is flabbergasted.

"Not a squadron, sir, just a detachment." Karl responds modestly. "But at the end of my tour in Carrier Suitability at Pax back in 1995, including Harrier tests, I requested and got exchange duty with the VMF detachment aboard *Belleau Wood*." Karl stated proudly.

"Well." Exclaims ADM Massey. "You certainly have had an exposure to the *Harrier* carriers."

"There's more, sir." Karl suggests. "I was flight deck officer on *Belleau Wood* for a year before I went to Post Grad school at Monterey."

"Goood!" Admiral Massey smiles broadly. "Be ready, Swenson. I think we're going to need people like you . . . soon." Then to Brewster. "Well, President Wyatt called it. Sounds like the radical Islamic threat he mentioned in his speech to the congress is comin' out to bite us. We may have to expedite the carrier recommissionings he called for . . . stand by for a budget battle." He allowed himself a sly grin. "Hell. we may need more carriers than he called for . . . and we can't forget the Amphibious Assault ships like *Boxer*." He pins Swenson with an intense gaze. "Swenson, how would you like to serve on one of the commissioning details?"

"I'd love it, sir." Karl replies cautiously. "But my wife would hate it."

"Well." Massey grins. "If this thing heats up we may need you anyway . . . Stand by!"

7
il-Dauli: The Empire

Sunday, 2100 - The Pentagon

The quiet conversation in the JCS conference room is interrupted by Admiral Goodman at the podium. "Ladies and Gentlemen, please take your seats." He confers with two staff personnel as the room settles and General Skwarkowski steps off the stage to take his seat in the front row.

"Must've gotten something new." Brewster comments as he and Swenson return to their seats.

Goodman raises his arms, palms forward, calling for quiet. "Please . . . Thank you." Now a deep breath. "FOX News Channel is reporting some terrorist action in Saudi Arabia that fits well with the attack on *Stennis*. The crew is putting up FOX News on the big screen now . . . er . . . in a minute."

"Isn't this ridiculous." Brewster fumes. "We've gotta get our intelligence from cable news . . . Tells you something . . . our new president was right the other night about the loss of a 'HUMINT' capability in the CIA."

"Ah . . . Here it is." Goodman sighs with relief as the huge screen fills with a picture of Barney Hall and Trudy Landsford in the FOX studio. Hall is introducing the piece: " . . . Here is Armand Bashur reporting from Riyadh, Saudi Arabia . . . Are you there, Armand?"

The scene shifts to the Saudi Royal Palace, the reporter in the foreground speaking into his microphone: "I'm here, Barney . . . At exactly two AM local time the Saudi Royal Palace, behind me, was the scene of a bloody coup perpetrated by a small band of Islamic extremists who assassinated the Saudi king and murdered everyone else in the building."

"Hey." Brewster calls. "That's 2300 Zulu. Exactly the same time that *Stennis* was attacked."

"And 1800 here." Swenson comments.

Bashur continues: "They have taken control of the government and, in particular, the Saudi armed forces." He hesitates as he is approached by a man who hands him a sheet of paper. "Now we have a report that Prince Sultan Air Base has been captured by another small band of terrorists and that . . . "

"Just a minute, Armand." Trudy Landford interrupts. "We have a report from Anna Christiani, reporting from Tabriz in northern Iran.. . . Anna, are you there?"

The scene shifts to a map of the middle east with accents at Riyadh, Prince Sultan Air Base, south of Riyadh, and Tabriz in northern Iran with a still picture of Christiani in the upper left corner, a leopard print scarf accenting her sultry beauty, a beauty combining a straight Arabic nose, Italian coloring, and the deep black eyes typical of both.

"I'm here, Trudy, thanks." Christiani's voice comes in with a scratchy telephone quality. "We have been told to expect the appearance of the new leader of Islam here at the town square where carpenters are still constructing a small speaker's platform while two men string wires to strategically placed speakers. There are already a few thousand followers in the square and hundreds more are streaming in."

"Hold right there, Anna." Hall calls. "I've got to get back to Armand in Riyadh . . . Sorry, Armand, Anna Christiani has a breaking story in Tabriz . . . awaiting an announcement by some Islamic leader at any moment . . . now, back to you, Armand."

"Thanks Barney. This report from Prince Sultan Air Base indicates that all command functions have been taken over by . . . "

"Wait a minute, Armand." Trudy calls. "Christiani's Tabriz story is breaking NOW . . . What's happening, Anna?"

"Yes, Judy, They're just getting started . . . A small, lean, clean shaven man in a deep red cape, or 'Kaftan', and an outsized white turban has just been introduced as 'Süleyman the Third, the Modern Magnificent'." She hesitates . . . "I wish we had a cameraman here to capture this new self-styled leader of Islam . . . As I said: Small, lean, handle bar mustache, a classic Arabic nose and a sloping forehead. I am informed that this Süleyman got his early education in madrassas in his home town in Turkey and went to Harvard during the 1990s so he is probably in his mid forties. If that sounds quite ordinary I must tell you that his piercing black eyes practically hypnotize his listeners, even at hundreds of meters . . . AMAZING!" Christiani hesitates . . . "I think you will be able to hear the speech through my cell phone, here, he's speaking now."

"We gather here in Tabritz, the eastern extent of Ottoman Empire conquests under Süleyman the Magnificent in the sixteenth century as a symbol of our determination to rule Islamic lands East to the Philippines while reestablishing Islamic rule northwest to Vienna and control all commerce throughout the Mediterranean. We have begun our drive to unite Islamic peoples and to rid our territories of the colonial grip of the United States and her lackeys in the UN and NATO."

"ALLAHU AKHBAR." Is heard in unison from the cheering mob, punctuated by a few rifle shots.

Christiani's voice again: "That was the mob of Süleyman Third fanatics numbering about two thousand, waving signs supporting this 'Modern Magnificent'."

"Ana!" Trudy calls. "Was that the sound of jet engines we heard?"

"Yes, Trudy." Christiani replies. "That was two U.S. Air Force F-35s buzzing this seething mob on their way to the air base . . . Oh! I think the U.S. Markings have been obliterated . . . The crowd has responded with a loud roar."

Christiani continues as the crowd's roar subsides. "This speech is obviously intended for Western consumption as Süleyman Third is speaking English while an aide translates into Arabic for the clamoring mob . . . Oh! He's speaking again now."

"Our il-Dauli . . . uh, empire, consolidating the power of the Jihad in Iran, Iraq, and Syria, will move rapidly to incorporate Muslim nations from Morocco in the west to the Philippines in the east, and north to Bosnia, Hungary, and beyond. We will build a modern day OTTOMAN EMPIRE, devoid of western influence!"

"Oh!" Christiani exclaims. "An ugly stir sweeps through the crowd as they chant 'SÜLEYMAN . . . SÜLEYMAN. Now Süleyman Third continues."

"This morning il-Dauli forces have achieved three objectives: One; They have neutralized the American aircraft carrier *Stennis* in the Gulf of Arabia with coordinated salvo attacks by *Scud* missiles from Iraq, *Silkworm* cruise missiles from Iran, and submarine launched torpedoes; two, our commandos eliminated the Saudi royal family and replaced the Saudi government with a temporary military regime until we can fill political positions with our own appointees, and we've taken control of the U.S. Air Force Facilities at Prince Sultan Air Base; and three, Islamic defectors in the Saudi Air Force have delivered the Saudi Air Force to il-Dauli along with captured American aircraft at Prince Sultan and Jiddah Air Bases."

Christiani again: "Oh! Look! This Süleyman is firing short bursts from his AK-47 into the sky and his followers, almost to a man, are obeying by firing their weapons skyward. I must tell you Barny . . . The noise is deafening! Now a military jeep is weaving its way through the crowd carrying two standards topped with round symbols of some kind . . . Oh No!" Christiani gasps. "Those are human heads carried on fifteen foot poles . . . aaarrgh."

Süleyman Third spreads his arms in a welcoming gesture. "I introduce you to Saudi King Faisal bin Abdul Aziz al-Saud and Crown Prince Fahd bin Abdul Aziz brought to us by a captured American F-35."

"Oh!" Christiani reports breathlessly. "Süleyman is bowing deeply to each head, enhancing the drama of this scene as the crowd erupts with thunderous approval and the sound of automatic weapons fills the square."

"Yeah, We can hear it." Hall says. "But what's the symbolism of the severed heads?"

"It harks back to the original Süleyman's barbaric custom of celebrating victories with a display of enemy heads." Christiani replies with a palpable shudder. "Sometimes hundreds of them."

"Whooooa!" Admiral Brewster whispers. "This Süleyman certainly has that mob eating out of his hand with that gruesome demonstration." And grimacing: "I wonder how broad his support is."

Barney Hall is saying: "This Süleyman seems able to attract a small crowd of dissidents in Tabritz, Anna. Tell me, Does he have any other support in the Arab world?"

"Barney, this is NOT a small crowd, and when I applied for my broadcast permit I asked the same question of the local officials." Christiani begins. "They tell me that he has drawn large crowds of supporters preaching in Azerbaijani towns from Baki on the Caspian Sea to Naxçivan near the Iranian border, in the Georgian capital Tblisi, and in the Kurdish towns of Mosul and Irbil in Iraq. He is seen by some as the new prophet of Allah with the charisma to inflame the masses against perceived injustices. Listen." She pauses to allow the full volume of the chanting and gunfire to come through her phone. "It appears that he is recruiting here and in Kurdish areas of Iraq and Turkey for a new major attack somewhere soon. The 'where' is presently unknown."

"But the weapons used in the attack on *Stennis* were launched from both Iraq and Iran." Landsford remarks. "How could this Süleyman join Sunni and Shi-'a nations in a common effort."

"There was a stir in Tehran back in December." Christiani reports. "But that seemed to settle down after the progressive Saradi government was violently deposed and replaced with one supported by radical mullahs . . . Oh! We did have a report of a January conference of Irani and Iraqi extremists in Basra but we couldn't get any information on the subject of the meeting. Perhaps that's where they planned the coordinated attack . . . gee, I don't know."

"So." Landsford begins. "Do you think he has enough support to pull off this modern Ottoman Empire?"

"Hard to say, Trudy." Christiani muses. "But he certainly has made a good start, and it seems he will make it very difficult for the U. S. and her allies in the near future."

"Thanks Ana, an now back to Armand Bashur in Riyadh . . . Are you there Armand?"

"I'm here, Barney." Bashur reports as the huge screen again fills with the Riyadh scene. "As I said, The report I got from Prince Sultan air base states that the base was overrun this morning about two AM by a small band of terrorists who have taken over all command and communication functions and destroyed the Patriot battery. . . many American casualties reported."

"Armand, do you have any information on the disposition of the aircraft at Prince Sultan?"

"Yes. This report says that all U. S. aircraft have been commandeered by renegade Saudi Air Force pilots."

"Anna, are you still there?" Judy asks.

"I'm here."

"Can you tell us who Süleyman the Magnificent was?"

"Have you got five minutes?" Christiani replies with a giggle.

"No, but go ahead anyway - this is a big story." Hall interjects.

"Well - Süleyman the Magnificent succeeded his father, Selim the Grim, early in the sixteenth century as a young man of twenty-six at a time when the Ottoman Empire, founded in Turkey in the tenth century, had battled European monarchs to build an empire covering the Balkans and Hungary, the Crimea, and what is now Syria, Israel, and Iraq. Süleyman seized Constantinople, now Istanbul, as his capital, and spread the Empire westward to Algiers to control Mediterranean commerce and southward into the Red Sea to protect the Islamic shrines of Mecca and Medina. He died in the campaign to extend his control further north into Hungary . . ."

Judy interrupts: "And can you tell us what 'Dauli' means?"

Without hesitation Christiani replies: "*il-Dauli* means 'The Empire'. Does that give you a hint?"

Barney comes in: "And who, really, is this Süleyman the third?"

Christiani: "This Süleyman was born Dogan Ürug in the small Black Sea fishing village of Agva near Istanbul. In high school he became obsessed by the stories of Süleyman the Magnificent in books and magazines. He had a charisma by which he found he could sway his classmates who elected him class president. As a young man he envisioned himself as a modern Süleyman and began gathering followers in areas previously part of the Ottoman Empire, thus the name il-Dauli.

General Skwarkowski suddenly leaves his seat to mount the stage and take the microphone from Admiral Goodman. "That's enough. Turn that thing off. Give me the map of the eastern hemisphere on the big screen." The general turns to address the screen. "We've got lots of work to do and damn little time to do it." His red laser arrow dances across the screen. "It appears that this 'Dauli' has united extremist forces in Iran, Iraq, Syria, and Palestine against the United States presence in the region and with the addition of renegade Saudi forces to the mix forms an overall force that could . . . I say COULD, accomplish this Süleyman's announced objectives." The red arrow sweeps across the map from Gibraltar to Manila. "We may soon be fighting this unholy alliance of Islamic Jihad and surviving al-Qaeda in three of our area commands: CinCLant in support of NATO, CinCCent covering the tinderbox middle east, and CinCPac watching the Philippines and Indonesia." He circles the areas targeted by Süleyman III.

"I want each service to develop urgent mobilization plans to meet this threat. You will present your draft plans here on Saturday at 0900 hours. This conference is concluded."

8
The Agony and the Ecstasy

Sunday, 18 October 2015 - Pacific Palisades, CA

"Whew! It sure was nice to get a little rest for a change." Karl Swenson exclaims as he sits down at the breakfast table on their cozy east facing patio brightened by the late morning sun. "Eighteen hours a day for two weeks and then the red-eye from Washington last night . . . home at oh-dark-thirty."

"Well." Marcia begins with a coquettish smile. "You seemed to have plenty of pep when you got home," Then: "What were you doing for eighteen hours a day?"

"You heard about the big flap in the gulf." Karl begins between bites of grapefruit. "*Stennis* disabled, Saudi king assassinated, and both U.S. and Saudi air forces captured by this "il-Dauli, which means 'The Empire'." He looks up to see his wife nodding. "The Chairman - Joint Chiefs you know - considers this a major threat and ordered an intense all services mobilization planning effort on the Sunday night I arrived . . ."

Marcia gets up to clear the fruit plates and slips through the French doors into the kitchen.

". . . and he demanded a review of the plans the following Saturday." Karl is shouting now so Marcia can hear him in the kitchen.

Marcia brings the tray with two plates of poached eggs and rye toast. "Well, how did that involve you, Honey? She asks, sitting down. "I thought you were in Air Systems Command, not plans."

"Well! I want to tell you, Honey." Karl takes a bite of poached egg. "They drafted every able bodied officer who wasn't nailed down, so I spent the whole time in the Navy Aviation Plans office."

"I understand the Army activated the draft." Marcia mumbles.

"Yeah, that could affect Harm." Karl sighs. "We'll have to talk to him this evening."

"I just talked to him last night." Marcia takes a bite of toast spread with Roses Lime Marmalade.

"What'd he say?" Karl sips his coffee.

Marcia hesitates, then sips her coffee. "You won't like this."

"Try me."

"Well . . . Harm says he won't let himself be drafted."

"So what's he going to volunteer for?"

"Huh!" Marcia laughs stiffly. "He says he won't serve . . . says he's been accepted at the University of British Columbia."

"DAMN! (Agony) I've got to talk to that kid." Karl drops his fork.

"I don't blame him." Marcia intones. "Who wants to be in the Army. It's uncomfortable and it's dangerous."

"It's all dangerous, but we've got to do it. He's physically and mentally qualified to be a Naval Aviator and if he doesn't like the Navy he can get in the Air Force. That's a hell of a lot better than being a defector. That'll ruin his life. I've got to stop him."

"You'll have to hurry, Karl." Marcia sighs. "He says he's leaving this week."

"I'll get up there tomorrow, damn it . . . he just can't do this." Karl frowns and takes a gulp of coffee. " is there any good news? How about Karen. What's she doing?"

"God! You'll never guess." Marcia exclaims. "She wants to be a Naval Aviator . . . what do you think of **THAT**?

"Wow!" Karl chokes on his coffee. "Where did she ever get that idea?"

"Are you kidding?" Marcia breaks another piece of toast. "You've been bugging Harm since he was in diapers to "FLY NAVY", obviously some of that rubbed off on Karen."

"Well, What did you tell her?"

"What do you mean, 'tell her'. She told **ME**!" Marcia shakes her head. "She's already applied!"

"Hot damn!" Karl slams the table and his coffee spills. "That's great." (Ecstasy).

"Wait a minute, Karl." Marcia puts up her hand. "You're the one who said women shouldn't serve in the armed services . . . much less fly airplanes off carriers." She angrily takes another bite of toast.

"Karen'll be fine."

"Sure, sure." Marcia is exasperated. "That's dangerous business Karl."

"You're telling ME?" Karl shrugs his shoulders. "What do you want me to do?"

"Talk her out of it."

"That'll be a trick . . . but I'll try . . . just for you, Mush."

"Thanks." *I know he'll only make a token effort . . . he's proud of her.* "But what happened to the big mobilization plan." Marcia smiles wryly.

"Can't tell you much, Honey." Karl begins cautiously. "You remember President Wyatt's speech where he proposed recommissioning three aircraft carriers and two amphibious support ships?"

"Yeah, I remember that part." Marcia sips her coffee.

Karl scratches his head. "That would be Vinson, *Nimitz,* and *Eisenhower* . . . A-AND . . . two amphibious ships, one of which could be *Boxer,* my old ship."

'You'd like that, wouldn't you, 'Captain'? Marcia sneers. But they'll never get money for that."

"I don't know." Karl muses. "Secretary of Defense Kolb is going to the president with it and the Congress is demanding immediate action." Karl stands up and heads for the door with his plate.

"Whoa, Karl." Marcia stands up to stop him. "I get the idea that there's something else you need to tell me . . . huh?"

"Er . . . Oh yeah." Karl stammers. SecNav has ordered a beefing up of the Naval Reserve . . . back to its strength of the mid eighties." *I hope that'll satisfy her. I know what she's fishing for, knowing my inclination toward volunteering.*

"I hope you're not going to volunteer, Karl." Marcia eyes him with suspicion. "We've done enough of that."

"I may not have a choice, honey." Karl offers, defensively. "They want me to be executive officer of the commissioning party for one of the amphibious ships . . . I may just get orders."

*

Monday - The Boeing office, Los Angeles

Good morning, Jill.

Good morning Mister Swenson." Jill stands. "Nice to have you back. . . . uh, your mail and messages are on your desk. I tried to sort them and indicate repeat calls.

"Thanks." Karl strides into his office. "Come on in, Jill, we've got to get moving . . . Please sit down."

"Wait'll I get my book." Jill pleads as she rushes out he door.

Jill returns to see Karl gazing at the pile of mail and notes. "We've got a problem, Jill."

"What's that sir."

"Oh, it's our son Harm. You know, he's a sophomore at Stanford." Karl says with pride. "He says he's going to evade the draft and not serve in this emergency. He says he's going to Canada." Karl sighs visibly. "I've got to talk to him . . . ASAP!"

"Oh! You and Marcia must be at wits end . . . I'll get him on the phone, right away."

"That won't do any good, Jill. We talked to him last evening and he wouldn't budge. I've got to go up there and talk turkey to him . . . TODAY!" Karl slams his desk and some of the papers scatter. "I'll need reservations on the first flight out of here to San Fran, a car at the airport, and a return flight around four-thirty or five." He reaches for his wallet. "And charge it all to my credit card."

"Yes sir, I have your credit card number . . . but . . ."

"But what, Jill" Karl's impatience shows.

"Er . . . Mister Sherman's secretary called last Friday. He wants a meeting in his conference room at ten o'clock this morning to discuss *SparLaunch* . . . he wants you and Mister Davidson to be there."

"Well, I've got a bigger emergency than *SparLaunch*." He turns to his telephone on his credenza. "Get those reservations! I'll call Sherman."

"Hello, Maria?" Karl calls into the phone. "This is Karl Swenson . . .Yeah, thanks, glad to be back . . . I need to speak to Mr. Sherman . . . yes, I understand that he is busy . . . *He always is* . . . Please tell him it is very urgent that I speak to him as soon as possible. I'll hold."

Karl fumbles through the mail in the "urgent" pile . . . *Hmm, what's this from Tarteki.*

Yes, I'm here . . . Thank you, Maria . . . Mr. Sherman, Swenson here . . . yes sir, I know you have a meeting scheduled today . . . Yes sir, my report on *SparLaunch* contacts is in the word processor . . . Yessir, talked to both the Navy *SparLaunch* guys and Air Force *Navstar* program office . . . No sir. That's what I called about. I've got a serious family problem . . . I've got to talk to our son Harm out of defecting to Canada . . . Yeah, up at Stanford - I'm flying up this morning . . . I really appreciate that, sir . . . Tomorrow at ten? . . . Right! I'll be there." He hangs up the phone. *Whew. What's gotten into him. He's awfully nice today.*

Back to the letter. Hmm. "From the office of Gilbert J. Tarteki, Corporate Vice President, Marketing. This is to advise you that Chairman Clymer has *written a letter to the Secretary of Defense urgently requesting deferments for named Boeing key personnel . . . Uh-huh, here's the list. Oops! I'm on it.*

"Okay." Jill rushes into Karl's office. "I've got you on United flight 2022 departing at 9:47, returning on United flight 2025 departing San Francisco at 5:10 this afternoon. Your Hertz car will be at the Hertz Number One Club."

"Thanks Jill." Karl leaps from his chair. "I've just got time to park the car and make the flight." He shouts as he rushes through the door.

"Good luck." Jill calls.

*

Later the same day - Palo Alto, California

Karl Swenson and son Harm sit at a luncheon table at The Fish Market on Camino Real in Palo Alto, a couple of miles from Stanford.

"I told you it wouldn't do any good to come up here, Dad." Harm growls.

"But, you know you don't have to get drafted, Harm." Karl is exasperated. "Damn it, son. You can still get in Navy flight training.'

"I don't want to be in ANYTHING, Dad." Harm emphasizes, chewing on a shrimp.

"But you'll ruin your life." Karl says, with a bite of fried oyster.

"No I won't. I'll just be a Canadian." Harm sips his wine.

"You know what this will do to your mom and me."

"Yeah, and I'm sorry." Harm glances up from his plate to meet his dad's eyes. "I'll make a success at something, Dad . . . I promise you'll be proud." Harm curls his lips in a wistful smile. "I love you both, you know." It was very sincere . . . and very final.

A tear glistens on Karl's cheek. *Well, there goes our son, and all our hopes and dreams for his future. All that potential wasted.* "So that's the end of it, eh, son." Karl's voice is hoarse. "Uh . . . waitress?"

"Yes sir."

"The check please."

9
Israel

Mid November - Pacific Palisades, CA.

"Hey, Honey." Marcia Swenson calls from the patio. "Breakfast is ready - and you'll be interested in this article in the L. A. Times."

"Thanks Mush." Karl remarks as he sits down to his melon. "Mmm . . . good melon. Where did you get it?"

"Ralph's . . . as usual." Marcia pushes the newspaper to Karl. "But you've got to read this. It scares me."

"Oh! look at this banner headline: 'SÜLEYMAN III SQUEEZES ISRAEL'. Scary is right."

"Read it."

Munching on a bite of melon Karl begins: "The subhead reads: 'Hezbollah forces storm the Galilee'. That'll get their attention in the Pentagon. It's datelined: 'Associated Press, Izer Goldman in Tel Aviv'. Sounds like a dangerous place for a Jewish American reporter with this Arabic invasion threatening all Israelis."

"He writes: 'Today, Hezbollah, apparently reinforced with conscripted Kurds from Turkey and Iraq and armed with tanks and artillery commandeered in southern Lebanon, stormed into the Galilee with overwhelming close air support from the former Saudi and American aircraft captured last month, joined by aircraft of Russian origin probably from Iran, based in northern Saudi Arabia, no doubt Tabûk Air Base. Israeli Air Force pilots, as well trained and disciplined as they are, were no match for the wave after wave of F-35s, F-22s, F-15s, F-16s, Tornadoes, Mig-29s and SU-24s flown by motivated pilots from across the territory Süleyman III has claimed. We have reports of fifty some Israeli aircraft lost in the air battles over the Galilee while seven Il-Dauli aircraft are reported downed . . ."

Karl takes a sip of coffee and furrows his brow. "We know where they got the American and Saudi airplanes and now apparently Irani aircraft, but I wonder where they got all the ace fighter pilots." He takes another sip. "Could they be mercenaries? But where did they train?"

"How about Irani and Iraqui pilots?" Marcia interjects. "They were well trained."

"That's it, Honey." Karl slaps his forehead. "We know that Irani and Iraqi extremists are part of this 'Il-Dauli'." He eyes Marcia quizzically. "Whatever made you think of THAT, Mush?"

"I read the papers."

"Hmm." Karl Muses. *She's really studying this thing.* "The article continues: 'The Hezbollah force sped south, decimating Israeli army units en-route and capturing the Ramat David fighter base, home to three Israeli Air Force fighter squadrons. Then, joined by the sympathetic and freshly armed Hamas from Palestine, il-Dauli forces moved south to establish a battle line across the narrow neck of Israel north of Tel Aviv. Reports from the field indicate that no air attack has been made on any Israeli air base. It appears that Süleyman III wants to capture as many aircraft in flying condition as possible, to add to his burgeoning air force.'."

"This is scary." Karl groans. "If he keeps this up this Süleyman Three will have the biggest air force in the middle east . . . whoa! Listen to this. 'According to this morning's edition of the Israeli newspaper *Haaretz* a small amphibious force came ashore on the Mediterranean coast near Ashdod under cover of darkness early this morning, and, teaming with a paratroop commando force, captured both Tel Nof and Hatzor Air Bases and their combined complement of about two-hundred fighter aircraft and assault helicopters.'. . . See what I mean?"

10
Orders

Monday Morning - The Boeing office, Los Angeles

"Good morning, Jill." Karl tosses the greeting on the way to his office door. What's happening?"

"Oh!" Jill jumps up as though startled. "Maria, in Mr. Sherman's office called last Friday while you were at the Space Division." She shuffles through the papers on her desk. "Oh yeah the message is in on your desk . . . anyway, she said Mr. Sherman wants to talk to you first thing Monday morning - urgent."

Karl strides into his office. Rrrrinnng. It's the phone. "Mr. Swenson's office" Jill answers. "Oh! Yes Misses Swenson . . . Yes, he just walked in - er - may I have him call you, he has to make an urgent call to Mr. Sherman . . . Oh! It's urgent? Okay, I'll buzz him."

Karl hears the buzz before he sits down and reaches over his desk to tap the intercom button. "What is it, Jill?"

"It's Misses Swenson, she says it's urgent."

"Hi, Mush. What's urgent? . . . Yeah, I told you we might be getting something from the Navy. What does it say? . . . Well, open it . . . Yeah, proceed, report . . . Uh huh, Bremerton. Yeah, I've got it. What's the reporting date? . . . Thirty December, eh? . . . Calm down Honey. That's plenty of time . . . Okay, I'll try to spring early today and we can plan what we have to do . . . It's not that bad, Mush. We've done it before and we can do it again . . . I know, Honey, but there's a war on and they need all the help they can get . . . Okay, Honey, take it easy and think about the plan. I've got to call Sherman . . . Love you too, Honey. See you soon."

Karl steps to his office door. "Hey Jill. You'll be the first to know." He strikes a proud pose. "I just got orders to active duty to recommission USS *Boxer* up at the Puget Sound Naval Station."

"Well, congratulations." Jill shows a querulous look. ". . . I think."

"Thanks." Karl responds while moving back to his desk. He touches the Sherman button . . . "Hi Maria. I understand Mr. Sherman wants to talk to me . . . Thanks, I'll wait . . . Hi, Bill, Karl Swenson here. I understand you want to talk to me - urgently . . . Well, I'm glad my contact report was helpful . . . Thanks . . . In Washington? . . . Yeah, I know where the DIA building is . . . I've got a problem with that, sir. you see, I just got Navy orders to be the executive officer of the recommissioning party for the amphibious assault carrier *Boxer* up in Bremerton . . . Yeah, I know the chairman wrote a letter to SecDef requesting deferments for key personnel, including me . . . Yeah that's right but I think my orders were cut before the letter got there . . . Okay, but I don't think an appeal will do any good . . . Hey, Bill, I really don't think you want me to go, anyway. You'll want continuity in the future and that won't be me. I think you should take Kevin. He knows this end of the business and can provide that continuity . . . Well, taking us both might not be a bad idea. We could introduce Kevin and then he'll be in a better position to continue. When is it? . . . WEDNESDAY? That's day after tomorrow . . . Okay. I guess I'd better go. But my wife'll kill me . . . Well, thanks for that - I think."

Karl buzzes the intercom. "Hey Jill. Is Mr. Davidson here."

The intercom answers: "No sir. He's over at Space Division - be back after lunch."

"Can you reach him. I really have to talk to him right away."

"He's probably over talking to Colonel Barshewski's staff. I'll see what I can do."

Shuffling papers again, Karl hears the buzzer. "Yes, Jill."

"Mr. Davidson is on line three."

"Hey, that was quick. Thanks . . . Hey Kevin. Sherman just called. He's got a big *SparLaunch* briefing in Washington, would you believe - WEDNESDAY - He wants both of us to participate . . . Both program offices and the usual hangers-on from DoD, Navy, and Air Force. Hell. It wouldn't surprise me if the Army showed up . . . Hmm. That doesn't surprise me . . . Colonel 'Bar' and ten of his staff, huh . . . General Klein too. Yeah, I'd expect that - Hey. Jill's making travel arrangements. We'll go out tomorrow afternoon, stay at the Crystal City Marriott and come back Thursday afternoon, late. Does that sound Okay to you? . . . Good. Hey, wait. You should know that I just got Navy orders to active duty to report to Puget Sound Shipyard in Bremerton the end of next month . . . Sorry about that. I pretty much knew they were coming after some of the discussions while I was back in Washington on active duty. I'm going home before noon today - Mush really flipped - I'll see you tomorrow."

*

Monday Noon, Pacific Palisades, CA

"Hi Mush." Karl calls as he comes through the front door. "I'm home - What've you got for lunch"

"Oh! Honey!" Marcia comes running to the front foyer. "What're we gonna do? Do you really have to go? How long will it be?

"Calm down, Honey." Karl takes her in his arms. "All I know is what it says in those orders, and I haven't even seen 'em yet."

"It's is in the office." Marcia speaks as if it is a snake or a mouse or something. "C'mon."

"Let me see." Karl picks up the letter. "Hmm . . . 'Proceed, report to Commanding Officer, Puget Sound Naval Shipyard on or before 30 December 2015h for further assignment to the USS *Boxer* recommissioning party, CAPT Henry McVeigh commanding. Your travel by private automobile . . . blab, blab . . . ' Well, there it is, Honey. Just five weeks to report, but no more detail. Karl sighs. "Well, at least I'll be home for Christmas."

"Well, that's some consolation, anyway." Marcia plunks down on the sofa. "So how long will you be there, anyway?" Marcia is exasperated. "Do we have to move up there?"

Karl scratches his head. "I've been thinking about this for quite a while, Mush. Let's go out on the patio, have a cup of coffee, and talk about it." He gets up and heads for the patio, Marcia close behind.

"But . . . have you had lunch yet?"

"No, but lets just sit down and talk for a bit until you feel more comfortable about this." Karl pours two cups of the leftover morning coffee and slips it in the microwave. "Go on out and sit down. I'll bring the coffee."

"This isn't like the other times is it, Karl?" Marcia calls across the pass-through. "At least then you were ordered to an operating ship and you knew about how long each deployment was. Besides that, the ship was in San Diego, close enough for easy visits back and forth."

"Here's the coffee Mush." Karl sets the tray on the table and sits down. "Yeah, you're right. This looks a lot different . . . honey for your coffee?" He passes the honey while stirring his coffee.

"You say you've been thinking about this." Marcia sips her coffee. "What can we expect?"

"All I can give you is an idea of the times and places involved, and I don't know much about either one." Karl sips his coffee and leans toward Marcia looking into her eyes. "This recommissioning will be on a priority, rush basis so I wouldn't expect it to take longer that six months. All that takes place in Bremerton. I have no idea at this time whether I will stay with the ship when she deploys or do something different. I'll try to find out more, but everything is in such confusion I wouldn't expect much useful advice."

"So I should just stay here when you go up there in a couple of weeks?"

"No, Honey." Karl leans back in his chair. "There's nothing holding you here. We could just drive up there a week early, stay in quarters, and look for an apartment . . . or just stay in quarters if they're satisfactory."

"What would we do with the house?" Marcia shows her anxiety.

"Same thing we do when we go on a trip for a month." Karl assures, in matter-of-fact manner. "I should know within a week what to expect."

"But it sounds like it will be longer than a month."

"Well, I think it best for you to go with me to Bremerton and we can play it by ear. Okay?"

"I'll think about it." Marcia stands and picks up the tray. "How about some of the chicken soup I just made this morning."

"Ahhh . . . Jewish Penicillin." Karl smiles broadly. *Well, we got over the first challenge.* "I'd love it, honey, even if I don't have a cold. Hey, where's the paper. I didn't see much of it at breakfast."

"It's on the tea wagon . . . This'll be ready in about ten minutes."

"Hmm. Listen to this." Karl shouts in from the patio. "They put this on page two - TYPICAL - says *Süleyman III* has been rousing the rabble in Northern Iraq and in Bulgaria. Makes you wonder what he's going to do next - capture Turkey?"

"Here's the soup, Honey." Marcia calls as she comes through the door to the patio.

"Thanks, Mush. That smells terrific." Karl says cheerily. *NOW. How the hell will I break the news of this Washington trip Wednesday . . . Hell, I'll have to leave Tuesday. She'll flip.*

"Well, what's going on at the office today." Marcia starts. "Gee, I would think Boeing would do something to keep you from going."

"Yeah, The chairman wrote a letter to the Secretary of Defense requesting a waiver for identified key personnel, me included." Karl squirms a little. "I think my orders were cut before the letter got to the Navy."

"YOU HOPE!" Marcia fumes. "This'll fulfill your lifetime ambition - command at sea. Jeez, Karl, you may even get to command a carrier - You'll love it!"

"Take it easy, Honey." Karl tries to smooth it over. "We have both agreed that I should stay in the Reserve because of the benefits at retirement and in spite of the sacrifices - and here's the biggest one. Apparently they need guys like me . . . er . . . and I have a duty to respond."

"Okay, Patriot." Marcia spits out the word "Patriot". " I know you'll do it, and I respect you for it, but I'm the one left holding the bag."

"Gee Mush." Karl touches her hand. "You know I've got to do it, so let's make the best of it."

"Okay, Karl, I'll try." Marcia gets up from the table. "I'll get the soup."

"Hey, Mush." Karl shouts through the patio door. "It says: 'The UN Security Council has met in emergency session at the request of the Turkish ambassador who denounced the invasion of Israel by il-Dauli and proposes a resolution condemning the action and requesting an international force under UN authority to stop Süleyman III before he carries out more of the threats he made at Tabriz'. Now, here's the kicker: 'The bitter but polite discussion showed the sharp divisions that exist in the Council and the vote that followed confirmed them by defeating the Turkish initiative.'"

"Here's your lunch Honey." Marcia sets the tray before Karl. "Sounds pretty bad if they can't get agreement in the Security Council to do something about this 'Jihad' . . . hey, what does 'Jihad' mean, anyway?

"Holy War, I understand." Karl takes a sip of the soup. "Delicious Jewish penicillin, Mush . . . Oh, there are Jihads everywhere in the Middle East, all working for the overthrow of their own governments and the expulsion of the USA for the advancement of their own extreme brand of Islamic fundamentalism. Uniting all these extremist groups is a threat to the whole world, as we have seen." Another slurp of soup. "Mmm! This is REALLY good."

"Thanks." Marcia replies taking a spoonful of soup.

Now's not a very good time, but here goes. "There's something else, Mush." Karl catches Marcia's eye with a sheepish look.

"Oh oh! Here it comes." Marcia drops her spoon. "What else could happen in one day?"

"Er . . . well, uh . . . Sherman's got a big *SparLaunch* briefing in Washington on Wednesday."

"I know - YOU'RE GOING."

"'Fraid so." Karl cringes. "Sherman wants to be sure we establish continuity from me to Kevin on the Washington scene. Kevin's going too. I'll have to leave tomorrow afternoon and I'll be back Wednesday night."

"For God's sake, Karl." Marcia fumes. "Why'd you let 'em do that to us. Right in the middle of this active duty stuff."

"Well." Karl frowns. "I can't just drop Sherman on his head. I need to retain a good rapport."

*

Wednesday Evening, Pacific Palisades, CA

"Hey Mush, I'm Home." Karl calls as he slams the front door behind him. "Where are you?"

"Here, Honey." Marcia coos as she embraces Karl and he drops his overnight bag. "I'm glad you're back. It seems each of our meetings is becoming more precious."

After the kiss, Karl agrees: "You're right, darling, I'm having the same feeling. *Hmm. Sounds like she is beginning to cope with the situation.*

Marcia steps away and puts hands on hips. "Well, 'Admiral'. What happened in Washington that I need to know."

"Strange you should ask." Karl laughs, taking her arm. "Let's get a couple of snifters of Grand Marnier and we can talk about it."

Two snifters in hand, Karl eases into the family room. "Well, I had a chance to slip over to CNO Surface Warfare Division to get a little better feel for our situation." He raises his glass. "Click?"

"What are we toasting?" Marcia takes a sip. "Mmm, that's bracing. So what'd you find out?"

"More or less confirmed what I thought, that I won't know anything firm until I report."

"What's new about that?" Marcia frowns and takes another sip of Grand Marnier.

"Well. It made me think that the best thing to do may be for me to fly up to Bremerton next week and meet with Captain McVeigh to understand what I might expect." Karl takes another sip and eyes Marcia hopefully.

"Hey." Marcia raises her glass with an air of triumph. "Why don't you just call Captain McVeigh on the phone. Who knows? He might have it all planned out."

Karl raises his glass to clink with Marcia's glass. "I knew there was a reason I married you. You're SCHMART! I'll do it tomorrow."

11
Boxer

Monday: Puget Sound Naval Station

Captain Swenson, after a greeting by the Officer of the Day, strides to the door with a textured glass panel inscribed: "COMMANDER USS BOXER RECOMMISSIONING PARTY". Below that a smaller caption announces: "CAPT HENRY C. McVEIGH".

"Come on in Captain." Came the greeting from within, revealing that Karl had been announced.

As the door opens Karl sees Captain McVeigh rising from his tall leather upholstered executive chair and stepping around the large mahogany desk to greet his executive officer. He is silhouetted against the large window overlooking the few active ships still in their home port and the group of mothballed carriers and other inactive ships. Captain McVeigh is a tall bulky man of about six-foot-two and about two hundred, forty pounds. His graying hair has receded enough to permit a glint from the overhead lights and his piercing hazel eyes frame a strong Scottish nose.

"Captain Swenson reporting, sir."

"Welcome aboard, Captain." McVeigh gives the standard Navy welcome with a firm handshake as a smile of satisfaction spreads across his rugged face. "I'm delighted to have you aboard." Emphasis on "delighted", a little beyond the standard. "Have a seat on the couch." He offers with a wave of the hand to the Navy issue brown leather overstuffed couch. "Coffee?"

"Glad to be aboard, sir." Karl responds with unconcealed enthusiasm as he takes his seat. "Yes sir. I would like a cup, thank you."

"How do you like yours?"

"Black with sugar, please."

Mobilize!

McVeigh reaches over his desk to press the intercom button. "Roberts."

"**SIR**." Came the yeoman's response.

"Two coffees please. "A glance back to Karl. "Captain Swenson will have his with sugar only."

"Aye, aye, sir. Right away."

"Most of my shipmates call me 'Mac'." McVeigh invites as he sits down next to Karl. "Actually, I find that you are senior to me by date of rank, as most reserve captains are." He says, factually and without deference.

"Well, that's interesting." Karl muses. "Don't worry, 'Mac', I don't want your job. Hell, I couldn't handle it. I think I know quite a bit about *Boxer*, having been aboard *Belleau Wood,* another amphib assault ship, as a *Harrier* pilot and as flight deck officer and as skipper of a *Harrier* detachment aboard *Boxer*. But I know very little about hull and ship's systems." Karl stops. "But you probably know all that, and I know you've already put two ships in commission."

"Right, 'Karlo'." McVeigh stabs his finger with a knowing grin, demonstrating his research. "Or shall I call you 'Swede'."

"Either one is fine." Karl answers. "'Karlo was my squadron nickname and I was known as 'Swede' during my deployments in ship's company." He scratches his head. "Probably 'Swede' is more appropriate for this job." Then. "I understand you commanded a couple of cruisers before you went to BuShips and then to this commissioning business . . . I gather you were an engineering major at the Academy."

"Coffee Sir." The yeoman enters and places the tray on the coffee table.

"Thank you Roberts." McVeigh lifts his cup as the yeoman leaves. "To USS *Boxer*."

"I'll drink to that." Clink. Then a sip of coffee for both.

"You've done your homework, I see." McVeigh smiles approvingly. "By the way, did you bring your wife?" McVeigh inquires. "You mentioned your dilemma in our phone call last week." "No, Mrs. Swenson didn't come up." Karl crosses his right leg over his left. "You said on the phone that you want me to handle the aviation side so I don't think I'll spend much time up here. Am I wrong?"

"No, Swede, you're right." McVeigh smiles approvingly. "Shall we get into that right now or do you need to arrange quarters?"

"No problem, Mac, I checked into the BOQ last night . . . got a sumptuous suite fit for a ship captain." Karl uncrosses his legs and turns to face McVeigh. "Let's Go."

McVeigh laughs. "Nothing but the best for visiting four stripers, Swede." Then. "First: We've just got 'til next May up here. Then we move to San Diego for final fitting out and systems integration before commissioning."

McVeigh continues: "I'm sure you know what comprises the aviation part of this job but we need to review all the related tasks in detail." McVeigh picks two sheets of paper off his desk and hands one to Karl. "Here's the list of aviation tasks as I see them. Let's have a thorough discussion of each one to develop a complete understanding." McVeigh touches the paper with his right index finger. "First: Assemble the air assets we need. With the crazy mix of aircraft *Boxer* will carry the sources are quite spread out and hard to pin down. I've already talked to the marines and AirPac about most of our needs. They have experienced the same reductions as the rest of the Navy and so have no spare air detachments available, so you'll have to start from scratch for both aircraft and personnel."

"Now there's a tall order." Karl squirms a bit. "But I think I know where to start on both."

"Now, the second is more difficult." McVeigh eyes Swenson. "You'll have to develop a basing plan for all stages of training."

Karl scratches his head. "Off hand I presume most of our training would be conducted out of Miramar and North Island, or perhaps Camp Pendleton, and NAS Yuma for the *Harriers* so I'll have to pursue that."

"Ri-i-ight!" McVeigh lifts his cup as for another toast, ostensibly to Karl's brilliance. "Miramar would be very convenient since we'll take *Boxer* down to San Diego for final fitting out, systems installation, and commissioning."

"Yeah." Karl sighs. "I'll work on getting us established at Miramar . . . Oh. You haven't said anything about the ship's air department. Do you have an air officer?

McVeigh furrows his brow. "I don't know anyone who's available but AirPac said they might be able to assign a senior commander from the staff."

"I think I should start at AirPac headquarters anyway so I'll see if they have an acceptable candidate." Karl sighs. "My problem is, I don't understand the amphib community at all so I've got a lot to learn. So I'll go over to ComSurfPac and get acquainted."

Mobilize!

"Then when I go to Air Reserve Training Command in New Orleans to fill the squadron billets I'll see what they might have to offer."

"Good idea Swede." McVeigh's eyes light up. "You might rather have a reserve for air officer anyway."

This comment confuses Karl. "Are you hinting that I might go to sea with you Mac?"

"Not with me, Swede." McVeigh shakes his head. "I'll be going on to recommission another ship . . . but you'll probably go with *Boxer*."

"Sounds like you know more than I do." Karl digs.

"Just guessing." McVeigh smiles.

"Well, I think I'd better bail out of here as soon as possible, Mac. There's a hell of a lot do and damn little time." Karl turns to face McVeigh. "I'll use the next couple of days to develop a plan with your staff so it fits with your time line for recommissioning." Karl snaps his fingers. Then I'll whomp up a travel itinerary with related objectives So we can both track it." Karl stands. "And I'll update you daily . . . wherever I am."

"Good idea, Swede." McVeigh rises. "Come on, I'll introduce you to the staff."

*

Tuesday - Breakfast at Bremerton Officers' Quarters.

"Two eggs over easy with bacon, please." Karl orders from the Steward.

"Coffee?"

"Oh yes. Coffee with my eggs . . . Oh! I'll have orange juice to start." Karl looks around the room. "Do you have a morning paper?"

"Yes sir. Seattle Post-Intelligencer, I think." The steward turns. "I'll get it for you."

Karl sips his orange juice while he scans the headlines. *Whoa! Look at this:* CANADIAN PARLIAMENT DEBATES DRAFT. Dateline Associated Press, Ottawa. "The Tory Parliamentarian from Windsor, Cedric Hardacre, has proposed that Canada reinstitute conscription to permit Canada to join other western nations in NATO to blunt the advance of *il-Dauli* in the Middle East. This resolution has sparked an uproar in the Parliament not seen since conscription was proposed during the Viet Nam war. Raw nerves are frayed on both sides of the issue. Hardacre is accused of pandering to the United States and members take the podium in turn to denounce the resolution in humanitarian, economic, and nationalistic grounds. Hardacre has some supporters but it seems likely that this bill will go down to defeat. It is known that Hardacre has allies in the Parliament but the opposition is strong. A vote is scheduled for next Tuesday." *It seem a long shot but it worries me. I'd hate to see Harm end up a grunt in the Canadian Army.*

"Here's your bacon and eggs, sir. Coffee now?"

*

12
Istanbul

January 2016 - Pacific Palisades, CA

"It's great having you back, Karl." Marcia emotes as she sits down to share breakfast. "How long does this last?"

"Not very long, Honey." Karl takes a bite of grapefruit. "I've got to go down to AirPac and PhibPac today and that might take a couple of days . . . then off to CNAResTra . . . Er - Naval Air Reserve Training headquarters in New Orleans." Another bite of grapefruit. "Hey What do you hear from Harm?"

"You wouldn't believe it." Marcia throws her arms up in the air. "He says Canada is considering a draft . . . talk about irony." She shakes her head in disbelief then takes a bite of grapefruit.

"Yeah, I read about it in the Seattle paper. Fortunately, the opposition seems to be strong enough to sink it."

"Well, Let's hope so . . . Excuse me." Marcia takes the plates and slips through the door to the kitchen.

"Hey, Honey, where's the L.A. Times?"

"On the kitchen table, I'll bring it in when I come."

"That's Okay." Karl stands. "I'll get it."

Karl sits back down and takes a look at the L.A. Times. "Whoa! Listen to this: 'ISTANBUL FALLS'." He turns to shout into the kitchen. "That's the banner headline, and then it says: 'By Rashid Mohammed, Associated Press. Dateline: Istanbul.' The subhead reads: 'Ancient Ottoman Capital Lost to Advancing il-Dauli forces.'" Karl folds the paper purposefully. "Hey, Listen to this!"

"Hold it." Marcia calls as she brings in the bacon and eggs. "Here's your breakfast."

"This is HOT, Mush. 'Yesterday, hordes of Süleyman III followers stormed through large gaps in Istanbul's ancient west wall blasted by il-Dauli fighter bombers and advanced toward the city center under cover of strafing attacks. Their assault followed the route of many invaders, down Vatan Cadisi toward the city center, laying waste to buildings along the way and dispatching those who would offer resistance.

'This morning, two amphibious landings brought more invaders ashore near Kumkapi on the Sea of Marmara and at the Sirkeci train station at the mouth of the Golden Horn to establish a three pronged pincers against any defending force. However, it appears that the defense of Istanbul has been reduced to a small garrison of police due to the massive uprising of Kurds on Turkey's eastern border drawing Turkish armed forces to that area.

'It is reported that this assault was planned and led by Abdul Wahid al-Ali, assassin of Saudi King Faisal and architect of the capture of U.S. assets at Prince Sultan Air Base south of Riyadh in February, timed to coincide with the devastating attack on USS *Stennis* in the Gulf.

'*Il-Dauli* soldiers I have interviewed profess their faith and devotion to Süleyman III. They know that they are capturing Istanbul as his personal headquarters and seat of il-Dauli administration, purging all Turkish institutions and American influence. These soldiers have already shot dead, at point blank, two American journalists just because they appeared American. I feel fortunate to be Arabic and to speak a language they can understand."

Karl takes a bite of egg. "Whoa! Here's another one: 'NATO MEETS. Resolves to Organize Against *il-Dauli*." He slaps the paper to the table. "Well! It's about time. They hardly stirred when Israel was sacked."

"How do you know." Marcia sips her coffee. "They might have had secret meetings."

"Yeah, RIGHT." Karl picks up the paper again. "Now it says: 'Today, acting on staff recommendations flowing from the invasion of Israel, NATO unanimously passed a resolution to organize forces and forward support on an urgent basis to stop any further advance into NATO jurisdiction by *il-Dauli*. The participation of U.S. President Wyatt and prime ministers of Britain, France, and the Chancellor of Germany gave this conference unprecedented political clout with all pledging their countries' full support.'." Karl scans the paper for more as he sips his coffee. "Oh! Listen to this: 'After the formal meeting, Director General Santana held a press conference to explain the actions of the conference. The first question, posed by a Turkish reporter was; 'Sir, where was NATO's Mediterranean fleet when Istanbul was overrun by Süleyman's il-Dauli yesterday?' Slightly flustered, Santana replied that the *Eisenhower* Battle Group was in Naples Harbor for replenishment but secured that operation to deploy as soon as possible. 'She is now underway and headed for the eastern Mediterranean.'."

Karl slaps the paper down again. "God DAMN! Nobody knew what was coming down until it happened. Just as President Wyatt said - We have no 'HUMINT' so we're blind to il-Dauli plans." He gulps some more coffee. "I'll bet Süleyman knew exactly what our fleet was doing . . . And he arranged the Kurdish diversion from the east to draw forces from Istanbul. Clever!"

"Well, what happened to the CIA." Marcia asks, innocently.

"Like I said, Honey." Karl pokes the paper with his index finger. "'HUMINT'! That means 'Human Intelligence', you know, spies on the ground. It's a nasty business but you have to have it or get surprised like the whole world was when Süleyman took Istanbul . . . No warning." He chews the last of his toast. "They've become completely dependent on their so-called 'technical means' . . . er . . . satellites, listening stations, and the like, so when their budgets got cut back over the last ten years they used what money they had to operate the 'technical means', leaving no money for 'HUMINT' . . . which is very expensive . . . in more ways than just money."

*

Friday Morning - NAS North Island Officers' Quarters.

Hmm. I'll call Mac and report on the results of my meetings at AirPac. I'm dialing. "Hello Roberts, This is Captain Swenson. Is Captain McVeigh there, please . . . Good . . . Oh, Hi Mac, Swede here . . . Yeah, I had a nice morning at home, thank you. Got down here about noon yesterday and met with the PhibPac *(Amphibious Force Pacific)* staff all afternoon . . . ComPhibPac? . . . Well, I guess Admiral London is a believer in MBWA, er, that's 'Management by Walking Around'. Hell! He's off reviewing all his Expeditionary Strike Groups, ships and shore stations across the Pacific so I missed him this time . . . ComAirPac? Yeah, the staff tried to be helpful but the result is about as expected - good news and bad news . . . Yeah, bad news first: I confirmed that they don't have any pilots, crew, or aircraft for us and the guy they offered for our air officer is a senior commander who's spent practically his whole career in Training Command . . . Oh no, Mac, I didn't refuse - just put him on hold 'til I talk to Admiral Reston at CNAResTra *(Naval Air Reserve Training)*. I've got an appointment with him next Monday. Hell, they're still on a five day week down there . . . I don't know, Mac, I guess they have so little resources that there's no call for overtime . . . Oh yeah, there's some good news. I found an old friend from our *Belleau Wood* days in the aircraft assignment office . . . No sir, he couldn't help on aircraft for *Boxer* but he was able to arrange an old beat up two seat A-4 Skyhawk for my transportation . . . Yeah, she's a pretty old bird, left over from adversary duty. Hell, she's still painted in adversary camoflage but only has twenty-three hours since her last major overhaul. I'll be taking her down to New Orleans Monday . . . Well, my appointment with Admiral Reston is at 0830 . After that I'll come back to San Diego for a meeting with Admiral London at PhibPac to see what kind of help he can offer and see if I can find some more friends for future reference. Oh! I forgot to mention, I got an office assigned to me over at PhibPac so I have someplace to hang my hat - whenever I happen to be here . . . Yeah, they also gave me a yeoman - third class - but I think he'll be some help . . . Yeah, I'll drive back home tomorrow afternoon. Looks like that'll be the last for a while with my schedule . . . I'll call you tomorrow before I leave here. Y'never know. I might find a gold mine - Hah . . . Okay, Bye.

13
What Reserves?

Monday Morning - The office of the Commander, Naval Air Reserve Training

"Welcome to New Orleans, Swenson." Admiral Reston is expansive as he joins Karl on his Navy issue brown leather couch.. "Did you have a good time in the 'Quarter' last night." The admiral is a small man of about five foot nine and a hundred, sixty pounds with a full head of reddish brown hair, mischievous hazel eyes, and a small, straight nose. He has a youthful look, thanks to his handsome face and very good physical condition.

"No sir. I got in sort of late last night and just checked in to the VOQ."

Reston gives Karl a suspicious glance as though he doesn't really believe that. "Well, What can I do for you."

As I told your aide when I made the appointment sir, I am the Executive Officer of the USS *Boxer* recommissioning party . . . er, do you know Henry McVeigh, an old cruiser captain? He's running the recommissioning."

"No. I don't know McVeigh, but how the hell did you get tapped for the commissioning party." Reston scratches his head. "My aide tells me you're a reserve officer with squadron command experience and a couple of active duty deployments in emergencies."

"Well, I was on my annual training duty in Air Systems Command when all this Süleyman business hit the fan." Karl shifts to look out the window. "I met Admiral Massey, the CNO, and he said they would be needing people who know something about the assault ships, suggesting that I might be needed. Three weeks later I had orders." Karl shifts to face Reston. "Captain McVeigh delegated all aviation matters to me. "Did you get the message I sent from NAS North Island Saturday?"

"Yeah, I've got it right here." Reston picks up a sheet of paper off his desk. "You're asking for a lot, especially under these circumstances when practically all our personnel and aircraft have been drafted into the war effort. Not only that but I just got orders to rebuild the Naval Air Reserve to 2000 levels so it looks like you and I will be competing for fresh talent . . . But I'll try to help."

"Thanks Admiral, I need all the help I can get." Karl squirms in his chair. "I hope you won't lock me out of your air stations as I press my search."

"All I can say is: Good luck." Reston offers. "I won't do anything to hinder your search. As a matter of fact, you can have this directory and you can review the files of any individuals you may be interested in.

"That'll help a lot sir, thanks. I'll see if I can find a willing volunteer to help me put together the air assets we need." Karl leans toward Admiral Reston. "I'll need a Marine you know."

"Well, I've got one eager jarhead, a Light Colonel who has commanded reserve fighter and attack squadrons until he ran out of his command eligibility at three different air stations. He worked *Harriers* and *Ospreys* at Pax River and he's had a couple of deployments in *Harriers*, same as you have - volunteered both times."

"Sounds good." Karl comments. "What's his name?"

The admiral turns pages in the directory. "Well. Let's see." He runs his finger down the page. "Ah, here he is. Lieutenant Colonel Horace H. Cavallo, a marine, currently in at WEPTU Norfolk (WeaponsTraining Unit at NAS Norfolk)."

Yeah!" Karl claps his hands. "I knew 'Horse' Cavallo. He was in the reserve at St. Louis when I was there. An eager beaver as I recall. Set an excellent record with his squadron." A little glint comes to Karl's eye. "Uh . . . Sir . . . Is it okay if I talk to him?"

"Oh, sure." The admiral offers - with enthusiasm. "Those guys in the tech training units have used up their maximum time in command and are really out of my hands - good luck . . . oh! And you need an air officer." The admiral reaches for another file on his desk. "We found a couple of very senior commanders who were active in reserve squadrons until their eligibility ran out. Now they're out of the reserve and working in industry."

"Sounds good to me." Karl slides over closer to look at the file. "Let's see."

"Here's Commander Ozmond Z. Johnson." He points to the top of a short paragraph of career highlights. "Looks like he spent most of his time in the VS community . . . Finished up as a VS skipper." The admiral points to the last part of the paragraph. "See? He had a pretty full civilian career in the combat trainer business with Spheriqe Corporation in San Diego . . . in between two active duty periods, one aboard *Eisenhower* during the Afghanistan and Iraq action as assistant air officer." Handing the file to Swenson he says: "Johnson could be your man."

"Thanks." Karl peruses the file. "How do you like this. His squadron nickname was 'Oz'. I see he was in Real Estate in San Diego." Karl turns to the admiral. "How current would this address be?"

"Within the last year, along with our Annual Qualification Questionnaires."

"Thanks, admiral. You've been a big help. " Karl stands. "If I may take the directory I'll jump up to Norfolk and see if 'Horse' will join us." The directory changes hands and the two men shake hands. "Don't be surprised if you see Cavallo back here searching files in a week or two. That'll be his first assignment." Karl steps to the door, turns to salute, opens the door, and leaves, closing the door.

"Er . . . Captain, sir?" The admiral's yeoman calls.

Swenson turns. "Yes?"

The yeoman stands to attention. "Er . . . Sir, I'm Yeoman First Beizholtz. I understand you are trying to organize the air detachments for your ship."

"Stand at ease!" Karl relieves the yeoman. "That's true, er . . . Beizholz you said?"

"That's right, sir." The yeoman assumes the formal "at ease" posture. "I've been wanting to get back to sea, sir. Back where the action is. Do you think you could take me?"

"We'll need people like you." Karl looks down at the yeoman's name plate. "Huh, Billy Beizholtz, is it?"

"Yes sir. I can go any time sir." Beizholtz stands to attention again. No family y' know.

"Good." Karl has to be careful. "But I can't request you. You'll have to request transfer through Admiral Reston."

*

Friday Morning, 10 January 2014 - PhibPac, Naval Station, San Diego

"Hi, Mac, Swede here." Karl is on the phone to Captain McVeigh. "Yeah, I'm here in my office at PhibPac . . . Actually, the week went pretty well. I think I got pretty good cooperation out of Admiral Reston at Air Reserve Training . . . Yeah, he gave me good candidates for both air detachment commander and air officer . . . Well, I hopped directly from New Orleans to Norfolk to offer a Lieutenant Colonel Horace, 'Horse', Cavallo the Air Det job. Hell, he could hardly wait . . . Oh! You signed his orders yesterday? That's great 'cause I've got an appointment at AMARC Monday and I want him with me . . . Oh! AMARC is the Aerospace Maintenance and Regeneration Center on Davis-Monthan Air Force Base in Tucson. If 'Horse' has his orders by Monday he can fly out Military Airlift, no sweat . . . Yeah, that'll be good. Cut his orders for AMARC and I'll take him from there in my trusty, uh, rusty, A-4 . . . Oh, The air boss candidate. I talked to him yesterday afternoon here in the office . . . Well, he's been out of the reserve for about four years and pretty comfortable in the real estate business so he wasn't quite as gung-ho as Horse but he liked the idea of being the air officer . . . Osmond Johnson, 'Oz' to you . . . I'll give all the facts to Roberts and he can cut the orders . . . Well, I'd think you'd want him in Bremerton to get acquainted with the ship - and you . . . You keep saying that, Mac . . . We got pretty well acquainted yesterday . . . Really, he's quite a character - big impressive black guy . . . Yeah, he's about six-four, two hundred, thirty pounds, round face, gray streaks in his black hair, and piercing black eyes that'll get - and hold - your attention. He has a commanding presence that'll serve him - and us - well. . . Yeah, I'm sending you a written report by secure FAX . . . Okay then, I'll call you after we finish our shopping at AMARC . . . Okay, Bye.

14
Eisenhower Sacked

Saturday Evening - Pacific Palisades, CA
"Hey Honey, I'm back." Karl shouts into the house as he steps through the front door.

"Darling! You're home." Marcia runs to Karl and wraps her arms around his neck, delivering multiple kisses while raising her right foot off the floor in an expression of exuberance.

"Mmmm!" Karl is smothered. Then: "Is the bar open yet?"

Mush gives him one more long kiss. "Let's have Martinis to celebrate your weekend home."

"Good idea, Mush." Karl muses. "These shore leaves are getting fewer and farther between . . . Uh, what do you hear from the kids?"

Ice clinks into the cocktail mixer. "You'll love this." Marcia pours the gin and Vermouth. "Your daughter called last night." She stirs and pours Martinis into chilled cocktail glasses wiped with lemon twist and hands one to Karl. "Here."

"**MY** daughter?" Karl gives her a suspicious glance. "So what'd she say?"

"She has orders to Navy flight training in Pensacola."

"Great!" Karl raises his glass. "I'll drink to that." Clink. "Er, when's she going?" Karl wraps his arm around Marcia's waist to guide her to the patio.

"She's detached Monday with a weeks travel allowance." Marcia takes a sip of her Martini. "Hahh! That's good. But the bad news is that the Canadian Parliament just passed a law establishing military conscription and the president is expected to sign it.'

"Oooh." Karl sets his drink on the patio table and sinks into a chair. "That puts Harm at risk . . . In harm's way, may I say."

"Oooh! That's **BAD**." Marcia scowls. "Anyway, I talked to Harm last night." Marcia announces. "He's near panic. He's really between a rock and a hard place."

Karl takes a big gulp of his Martini. "Damn! I told him to just volunteer for flight training or OCS and become an officer in the U.S. forces. He's fully qualified for either, but . . . No sale. Now he'll probably end up in the Canadian army. Did he say anything about any notice from the draft board?"

"No. From what he knows it'll take them a few months to organize the draft system. That'll give him a little breathing room anyway."

Karl fidgets with his Martini. "I'll call him . . . see if he can get back to the States."

*

Sunday morning - Karl and Marcia return from church discussing what to have for breakfast.

Marcia hugs Karl and gives him a kiss.

Karl flushes a little. "Thank you, Mush . . . er . . . what was **THAT** for?

"A wonderful night last night, honey." Marcia shows a coquettish smile. "Hey, Why don't we have some of your famous Mexican omelets. We've got all the goodies."

"Work, work, work . . . Okay, you get the stuff out and I'll put on the apron."

*

At the patio table Karl takes a bite of his grapefruit and peruses the L.A. Times headlines. "Whoa! Listen to this." He rustles the paper. "'*EISENHOWER* BATTLE GROUP REPULSED IN ATTACK ON ISTANBUL' and 'USS *Eisenhower* and two destroyers severely damaged by coordinated *Silkworm* cruise missiles, air attack, and submarine launched torpedoes while attempting to recapture Istanbul from il-Dauli forces'." Another bite of grapefruit. "Mmm, good grapefruit . . . Then it says: 'The *Eisenhower* battle group steamed from Naples yesterday with the intention of liberating Istanbul from il-Dauli forces. Instead, the well equipped and motivated forces of *Süleyman III* blunted the American attack with a coordinated Silkworm cruise missile attack supported by swarming air strikes and submarine launched torpedoes. *Eisenhower* herself sustained severe damage from at least one Silkworm, a torpedo, and multiple bomb strikes from the air attack rendering her unable to operate aircraft. The destroyer *Briscoe* was dead in the water and being taken under tow by the USS *Cole*, a guided missile destroyer. The battle group is now retiring to its base in Naples while surviving strike aircraft are recovering at Athens. Casualties in the force and aircraft losses have not yet been reported. The Battle Group reports the sinking of one il-Dauli submarine and the downing of numerous enemy aircraft. The Navy cannot replace *Eisenhower* at this time as the next Atlantic Fleet carrier to be recommissioned is the *Harry Truman* now in the Norfolk Navy Yard and not slated for recommissioning for another six months."

Marcia gulps a bite of omelet. "This *Süleyman* seems to be building an empire."

"Yeah. With him as the emperor. Hell. He signaled that when he named his 'gang' *il-Dauli*, meaning 'The Empire'." Karl grouses. "This is going to put even more pressure on getting these recommissioned ships out to sea as soon as possible." Karl takes a bite of his omelet. "What they really needed was an Expeditionary Strike Group built around an Amphibious Assault Ship like *Boxer*."

15
Ottoman Revisited

Tuesday Morning: Davis-Monthan Air Force Base, Arizona:

"Good morning, skipper." "Horse" Cavallo calls to CAPT Swenson as they both emerge from the Visiting Officers' Quarters. "'J sleep well, sir?"

The two join and head toward the mess building for breakfast. "I notice they don't have 'Officers' Mess' in the Air Force any more." Karl comments.

"Been like that for quite a while now." Horse frowns. "Even Breezy Point at NAS Norfolk welcomes chiefs and petty officers of any stripe."

"Hmm." Karl muses. "Progress . . . I guess. "Ah. Here's the newspaper machine . . . Well, all they have is the Arizona Daily Star."

"That'll work." Horse squints into the rising sun. "It'll have the main news, anyway."

Click - clank. Karl picks a paper from the stack in the machine. "Whoa! Look at this headline: 'SÜLEYMAN III CLAIMS TOPKAPI PALACE'. Hey, let's get our breakfast and peruse this article. Sounds like this Süleyman is trying to take over the world."

"Yeah, and we'll be fight'n' 'im . . . somewhere, and soon."

The two men rush in to get in the short breakfast line and check the menu on the wall behind the smoking grill. "What's the 'Desert Special'?" Karl asks.

Jus' Huevos Rancheros." The messman replies. "A lot o' these Air Force Gringos don't speak Spanish so we jus' call 'em 'Desert Special'." He wipes his hands on the towel hanging out of his hip pocket. "It's pretty good, 'f I do say so m'sef."

"Sounds good. I'll have one." Karl opts. "And orange juice."

"Juice's in d' machine, dere." Go ahead an' sit down Cap'n. I'll bring de orders . . . An' what would you like Colonel?"

"Desert Special's too rich for me, er . . . y' got any oatmeal for a healthy heart?"

"Yes suh, we got dat. An' you want or'nge juice too?"

"Yeah, thank you."

Karl and Horse go to a free table near a window with their orange juice.

Karl lays out the paper. "Well, Süleyman was able to hold on to Istanbul over the weekend and in the process he gave the Med Fleet a black eye." A wry grin. "And some other wounds too, I guess." Karl takes a gulp of orange juice. "Well. Süleyman Three in Topkapi Palace. That's scary."

"So what's Topkapi Palace that this Süleyman would start a war to get it?" Horse muses.

"Well, I understand the palace was built by the original Süleyman's father . . . er, or grandfather, I forget, but it was sometime in the fifteenth or sixteenth century. Then Süleyman the Magnificent embellished it as he brought the Ottoman Empire to the pinnacle of its power in the sixteenth century, ruling from Topkapi." Karl rustles the paper.

"Wow." Horse exclaims. "This Süleyman guy is going to a lot of trouble to emulate THE Magnificent." Horse spoons some oatmeal into his mouth. "He seems obsessed."

"Y' got that right, Horse." Karl rustles the paper again. "Says here: 'By Rashid Mohammed, dateline Istanbul' . . . Huh, that's appropriate. An Arab reporting for the Associated Press from Arab land."

"Yeah? What does he say." Horse is impatient. "The sub-head says: il-Dauli now Headquartered in Ancient Ottoman Compound'. Then: 'This morning, following the ancient tradition of conquerors entering Constantinople, Süleyman III rode through the Golden Gate at the fortress Yedi Kuléh on a magnificent red plumed white Arab stallion wearing a gold brocaded dark red kaftan and a huge white turban reminiscent of Süleyman the Magnificent, conquering Sultan of the Ottoman Empire. His gold studded saddle rested on a large red and gold tapestry which covered the horse from withers to croup and flowed down below the stirrups in opulent splendor. A cavalry escort riding handsome chestnut mounts, each decorated with a red plume on its head followed a few paces behind, holding aloft on two meter poles the severed heads of the former governors of Istanbul, by now a familiar trademark of this Süleyman's ruthlessness.'"

"Wow!" Horse interrupts. "Ruthlessness is right , , , uh, and arrogance, and er, ego. Yeah, a giant EGO. A throwback to 'The Magnificent'? . . . Oh, go ahead."

"Okay er, here, 'Suddenly a horseman in flowing white robes and matching turban of modest dimensions rode up to welcome Süleyman III to his new seat of government. The man, Abdul Wahid al-Ali, assassin of the Saudi king, dismounted and prostrated himself before his sovereign. With a signal from the sultan al-Ali mounted his horse with a flourish and joined his master to guide the column to and along Koka Mustafa Pasa Cadisi, thence to Ordu Cadisi and Divan Yolu, streets lined with cheering soldiers standing shoulder to shoulder firing their weapons skyward in celebration. The procession continued through the unpretentious gate into the First Court of Topkapi Palace where they found a kneeling multitude muttering a continuous prayer to Allah and repeated exclamation of their fealty to Süleyman III. Waving to his supplicants, Sülyman III led the column through the massive gate into the Second Court where he and Abdul al-Ali dismounted and proceeded to the Third Court as a stable groom led their two horses to the stables as the cavalrymen stabled their horses. It is interesting to see Topkapi restored nearly to its original splendor from its recent service as a Museum of Ancient Art and Science.' Oh . . . 'See page eleven - TOPKAPI'." Karl shakes the paper to fold it to page 11.

"Boy, this guy really has an ego." Horse exclaims.

"Yeah. That's how he gets all his minions to worship him." Karl frowns. "He makes himself a godlike figure to the Muslim masses." Karl turns back to the paper. "The report continues: 'I have a report that Süleyman III will rule from the Throne Room restored to its original royal opulence under the direction of Abdul Wahid al-Ali. Thus Süleyman III has used this symbolism to announce to the world his intention to build an empire from Gibraltar to the Philippines in his continued attempt to emulate Süleyman the Magnificent who led the Ottoman Empire to the pinnacle of its power in the sixteenth century.'" Karl puts the paper down and takes a sip of orange juice.

"Here's yer breakfast gentlemen." The messman sets the trays on the table and leaves."

"Thanks." Karl doesn't look up.

"Is that all?" Horse queries.

Karl takes a bite of his "Desert Special". "Nope, now it says: 'Moments after Süleyman III and Wahid al-Ali disappeared through the Gate of Felicity into the third courtyard a man in the uniform worn by the escorting cavalry announced at the parapet atop the great gate that Süleyman III would come there to address the multitude within the hour and, true to the announcement, Süleyman III appeared at the same parapet about forty minutes later to a chorus of adulation in the First Court. He was accompanied by a man, a woman, and the same cavalryman, seemingly Süleyman's Aide de Camp. Here is the transcript of his proclamation, translated to English: "I, Süleyman the Modern Magnificent, hereby declare TOPKAPI my palace and the seat of the *il-Dauli* Jihadist government." At that the throng in the court went absolutely wild, waving banners and firing weapons into the sky.'."

"Boy, this rag head sure has these people snowed." Horse comments.

"He's got the charisma." Karl notes. "There's more: 'I have, today, elevated my faithful servant Abdul Wahid al-Ali to the position of Grand Vizier, to be my executive in all operations mounted by il-Dauli and my principal advisor in matters of State. You will recall that Wahid al-Ali conceived and executed the plan to assassinate Saudi King Faisal, capture the American air base at Al Karj, and commandeer all their aircraft. You may not know that he organized and led the forces that captured Israel and Istanbul. Lastly, I have taken a wife to bear my heir and to preside over my Harem. She shall be known as Sultana Aleksandra of Crimea.' Another wild celebration in the court."

"Hey!" Horse's eyes light up. "I saw something last week about one of Süleyman's emissaries paying a Crimean family a handsome sum to allow their daughter to marry Süleyman and become his queen . . . er empress?"

"Sultana." Karl smiles. "I think the emissary was Abdul Wahid al-Ali but I didn't really know who he was at the time."

"Oooh!" Horse drops his spoon. "Looks like this al-Ali is sittin' in the cat bird seat."

Karl finishes his coffee. "Well. We'd better get over to AMARC. Our appointment is at oh-eight-thirty."

16
AMARC

Tuesday Morning: Davis-Monthan Air Force Base, Arizona
As Karl and Horse approach the gate they are impressed by the adobe brick entrance marker:

Horse, driving, stops at the gate. "Can you direct us to Mister Swearingen's office, er, it's the Navy office"

"Oh, you must be Captain Swenson." Mister Swearin . . ."

"No. I'm Lieutenant Colonel Cavallo." Horse offers. "This is Captain Swenson." Tapping Karl on the left hand.

"Yessir. Mr. Swearingen wants you to come directly to the AMARC command center in building 42 and ask for Colonel Robison." He points down the road from the gate house. "Take this road down three blocks, turn right and go to the dead end. Building 42 is on the southwest corner. The command center is at the end of the main corridor. You'll see 'Visitor Parking' at the end of the concrete walk to the building."

"This is quite a facility, Horse." Karl starts as Horse pulls away from the gate. "They've got over five thousand aircraft in storage on this plot of something close to three thousand acres."

"Yeah, but why here?" Horse queries.

"The low humidity here in Tucson lets them store aircraft indefinitely after they are properly preserved." Karl continues. "And they have an expert crew here that can, and does, take aircraft out of storage, refurbish them, and return them to service."

"I guess this is the AMARC building." Horse comments as he parks the car in the visitor parking. "No sign that I can see."

"Yeah, this is it. I've been here before." Karl assures Horse. "These folks aren't much for show."

Entering the spartan office complex Karl announces to the receptionist: "Captain Swenson and Lieutenant Colonel Cavallo to see the commanding officer."

"Yes sir. I'll buzz." The buzzer could be heard in the waiting room.

Then, a tall black man in camouflaged working uniform emerges from the end office with a portly white man in civilian clothes in hot pursuit. The eagles on the big man's uniform and the name tag on his right breast identify him as Col D. Robison. His straight nose, light brown eyes, and thin lips along with his medium brown skin suggest a heritage other than pure African. At six-foot-three the colonel's muscular frame is not concealed by the baggy camoflage uniform.

With an infectious grin the colonel extends his strong hand. "Welcome to AMARC, Captain Swenson. I'm Colonel Robison, the commander here."

Karl is prepared with his "Big Man" handshake, grasping the hand aggressively and squeezing hard. "Thank you, Colonel. Let me introduce my Air Detachment Commander, Lieutenant Colonel Cavallo, U.S. Marine Corps."

Horse steps forward to shake the colonel's hand. "Good to know you, Colonel . . . er, call me 'Horse'."

"I love your Navy nicknames . . . oh, this is Earl Swearingen, the manager of our Navy contingent here. He and his staff will see to your needs."

"Glad to see you again, Captain." Swearingen extends his hand with a respectful smile, then greets Horse. "I got your letter and the staff has already started to work your request. We'll get into that later." Swearingen has a physique typical of an executive type - love handles and a slight paunch. His florid face, logoed golf shirt and slacks betray his penchant for golf.

"Play a lot of golf, Earl? Horse inquires the obvious.

"Yeah, on weekends." A sidelong glance at the colonel. "Actually, I run the tournaments for civilian employees on the base."

"Come on into my office." Col Robison offers. "We'll get things started."

In the colonel's office Karl and Horse are seated opposite Robison's executive chair and Swearingen takes a chair at the end of the desk, at the colonel's right hand.

"Do they still call you 'Stretch', Colonel?" Karl inquires with a wry grin.

"Where the hell did you get that." Robison probes.

"Well." Karl smiles. "I remember you as the corner back on the Air Force football team that gave Navy such a headache on offense back around twenty aught five . . . DeRon Robison, right?"

"You got it Cap'n. And yes, folks still call me 'Stretch', and you may do the same." He eyes Karl with a sly grin. "And what shall we call you?"

"Just 'Swede' will work fine, thanks."

"Okay . . . Let's see." Robison picks up a letter from a small stack. "I've got this letter from General Sinclair, at Air Materiel Command, my boss." He looks up over his reading glasses. "You were smart to get a priority at the top." He smiles at Swearingen. "It'll make it easier to service your needs."

"Yes sir." Swearingen draws a sheet from a file folder. "I've got your list here, fairly typical amphibious assault ship air complement. Hmm. . . six Harriers, eight SH-60 *Sea* Hawks, at least four 'F' models, twelve MV-22 *Ospreys,* and nine CH-53 *Sea Stallions* . . . but do you really need ALL of them. Don't you have any other sources?"

"AirPac and the Naval Air Reserve are the only sources we have access to. The Marines at Miramar and Pendleton need all the aircraft they have for their active squadrons." Karl leans forward to fix the colonel's eyes with a purposeful gaze. "AirPac had nothing but the old two-seat A-4 I'm using for transportation and the reserve has orders to build up, so no airplanes or pilots are available from them either." He turns to Swearingen. "And we're supposed to deploy in September. Horse is scrounging for pilots and you're our last source for aircraft . . . and YES! We need all of them."

"Well. We can upgrade your transportation at least." Swearingen offers with a sly grin. "Aggressor squadrons are still clamoring for A-4s of any age. We'll trade you an old two seat F/A-18B for it."

"Well, thanks." Karl offers cautiously. "But when do I have to give it back?"

"Just whenever you go to sea." Swearingen offers with a self satisfied smile. "Or when you don't need it any more."

"Mighty generous of you." Karl remarks with a glance at the colonel.

"Well." Karl gives Swearingen a wry smile. "If you need A4s that badly you could give us two F/A-18Bs. Horse and I need to travel to different places you know."

"We can do that . . . er, eh Colonel?" Swearingen eyes Col Robison. "These are left over from that last Spanish Air Force order . . . uh, and we don't get much call for B model *Hornets* these days anyway."

"Okay." the colonel cringes. "I'm outnumbered."

"Well, thank you, Gentlemen." Karl bows just a little. "I'll have to check with my AirPac contact before I make a trade. I'll let you know after noon."

Swearingen again: "Anyway, I can tell you that we can handle most of your requests with some variations." He gives Karl a sidelong glance. "We can give you eight *Harriers* easily but some may not have had all the upgrades for night operation. We have plenty of SH-60Bs but very few 'Fs'. You'll have to take 'A' model *Ospreys* . . . and we may not have twelve of those. All the later model birds are spoken for. We can give you four CH-53s but they'll be "D" models. Okay?"

"Sounds like you're pretty close." Karl frowns. "But we only need six *Harriers*. Perhaps you could find just **six** night *Harriers*? Notice that we didn't even ask for any F-35s."

"Good thing. We don't have any . . . Yeah, we can try on the *Harriers* . . . but don't count on much."

"Beggars can't be choosers, eh Skipper." Cavallo slaps Karl on the back. "They ARE aircraft after all."

"What can I say?" Karl slouches a bit.

Swearingen rises from his chair. "If you'll excuse us, Colonel, we'll . . ."

Karl raises his right hand. "Wait! How soon can we expect delivery of these birds?"

Swearingen sits down again. "Well, we're running about ninety days for the helicopters and *Ospreys*. A little less for the *Harriers*."

"We'll probably have some pilots within sixty days." Karl eyes Horse. "It would help us if we could have delivery of just some of the birds in sixty or seventy days.

"Sixty is a no go." Swearingen replies. "We might be able to get a few to you in seventy-five days. That's really the best we can do and you shouldn't use that for any planning."

Swearingen rises again. "Now we'll go and look at some hardware."

"Good idea, Earl." Robison stands. "Drop in and see me before you leave, Swede."

"Okay, Stretch." Karl grins. "I'll do it."

Swearingen takes the driver's seat in a Navy car as Karl takes the passenger seat and Horse jumps in the back. "First we'll whip over to where our helicopters are." Swearingen announces.

"A bit of advice." Swearingen starts as he picks his way along a dirt track among some big airplanes - trash haulers, bombers, and patrol aircraft. "We'll make up a list of aircraft that could fill your needs, along with Bureau Numbers." He holds up a list. "Like this. I'll call you when we have the list completed and you should send some of your pilots down to check the log books and kick the tires so they can make some specific selections. Oh! Here are the SeaHawks."

"Hey, thanks for the suggestion, Earl." Horse comments. "We'll do it that way."

*

Back in quarters at Davis-Monthan AFB Karl calls Captain McVeigh to report progress. "Hey Mac, We're makin' progress here . . . yeah, we'll get enough aircraft for our air detachments even though some will be slight variants from what we requested . . . Well, the most important is the substitution of the old MV-22A *Ospreys* for the Cs we asked for and the *Harriers* we get may not all be the night version but we can work that problem. . . Yeah, we'll have some minor shortages here and there but we'll work on those later . . . I'll send Horse up to Bremerton to make a complete report. He needs to meet you anyway . . . Orders?" Karl gasps. "What kind of orders? . . . You're right, this is not a secure phone . . . Good. I was planning to go right back to my PhibPac office so I'll see 'em when I get there. Oh, by the way, I've got my first enlisted recruit . . . Well, Admiral Reston's yeoman wanted to volunteer for *Boxer* duty. I told him he would have to request transfer through the admiral . . . Just tell Roberts to be on the lookout for the request and cut the orders right away . . . Well, I'd like to have him in my PhibPac office but I guess I'll have to find out what these orders are all about. I'll let Robers know . . . Hey. I think you'll enjoy Horse. He's a character - real gung ho . . . Okay. I'll call you when I see my orders."

*

Karl and Horse meet at the officers' club for dinner. "Hey skipper." Horse greets Karl. "Did you see the paper this evening?"

"No. I didn't think they had an evening edition."

"Oh, this was the on-line edition." Horse explains. "It reports on another aggressive move farther east by Süleyman's *il-Dauli*. The news is that his right hand man, Abdul has been in China, wooing *Falun Gong* leaders, recently and paving the way for Süleyman to preach to *Falun Gong* members the glory that could come to them if they associated with *il-Dauli*."

"I've heard a little about *Falun Gong*." Karl muses. "I got the impression that it was just a shadowy cult which gives the ChiComs a bad time with its massive protests and bazaar tactics, such as self immolation."

"Yeah but *Falun Gong* has enough members, er, practitioners they call 'em, to be a serious threat to the PRC government." Horse emotes. "Hell, the report says *Falun Gong* has more than eighty million members in China alone, I said **million**. Enough to give the communist government fits. The report says that if Falun Gong teams with *il-Dauli* they could really give the government a run for their money."

17
Sea Duty

Saturday noon - Pacific Palisades:

"Hi Honey, I'm home." Karl calls as the screen door slams behind him.

"Well! The lost is found." Marcia giggles as she runs to embrace Karl in the foyer. "Where have you been."

"Come on." Karl invites as he draws Marcia toward the couch in the living room. "Let's sit down and I'll confess." He says with mock guilt.

"I'm all ears." Marcia gives Karl an admiring glance.

"Well, first; the Tucson trip. That's where I met 'Horse' Cavallo - you know, our new air detachment commander - at Davis-Monthan Air Force Base to scrounge for the airplanes and helicopters we need from the aircraft bone yard there. Then I spent the day yesterday at PhibPac." Karl looks down. "Er . . . I got some orders."

"Orders?" Marcia exclaims. "For what?"

Karl draws a manila envelope out of his shirt and pulls out a sheaf of papers. "It says here: 'Proceed, report, USS *Rainer,* wherever she may be, for temporary duty involving flying as commanding officer . . . etc. . . . etc.' Hah. 'Duty involving flying.' That's funny."

'Oh, oh." Marcia frowns. "Sounds like sea duty to me, but . . . since when are you qualified for command at sea?"

"First I've heard of it." Karl gives a self satisfied smile. "But I guess this will do it."

"I never heard of *Rainer* . . . uh, except as a mountain in Washington." Marcia muses. "What kind of carrier is it."

"Not a carrier, Mush." Karl chuckles. "That's what's so funny about that 'duty involving flying'. She's a fleet oiler . . . er, actually a fast combat support ship, a versatile ship that cruises with carrier battle groups and expeditionary strike groups, supplying all needs: Fuel oil, aviation fuel, ammunition, and general supplies."

Marcia gives Karl a wry smile. "Since when do they put aviators in command of supply ships."

Karl smiles back, with a wink. "You notice the orders said 'temporary duty'. Well, Mac has been hinting that I would take *Boxer* to sea. I suppose this oiler command is my baptism of fire . . . how I will qualify for command at sea on a large awkward boat like an amphibious assault ship."

"But Karl! What in the world do you know about a fleet oiler." Marcia pins Karl with a look of disdain.

"Nothing Mush., absolutely nothing, " Karl shakes his head. "That's the hard part. I'll have to depend entirely on the exec who is probably in line for command before I come along. He'll resent me moving in and I'll have to gain his confidence and support . . . something I've never had to do before in my life. But I guess every candidate carrier or LHD skipper has faced the same situation so these senior oiler officers come to expect some airdale to come in and take over the ship to earn his seamanship merit badge.

"Then that means you will command *Boxer* when she deploys." Marcia confronts the inevitable.

"Only if I don't flunk the tanker exam." Karl's eyes show anxiety. "And I'll have to depend on my exec for the training and then for a good fitness report."

"No. Your exec wouldn't write your fitness report . . . would he?" Marcia's puzzled.

"Oh, the admiral will sign it. But my exec will either write it or have major input."

So where is *Rainer* now." Marcia eyes Karl suspiciously.

"Damned if I know." Karl shakes his head. "I'll have to find out, I guess."

"Well, '**CAPTAIN**'." Says Marcia with a touch of derision. "How long will you be gone?"

"I'm told that these tanker tours run about six months." "Well." Marcia stands to attention and salutes. "The CAPTAIN finally got his wish . . . but it took a war to make it happen." Then, as her lip curls and her eyes tear she slumps into the couch, elbows on her knees, her face in her hands, and begins to sob. "Oh, Karl, I was afraid this would happen . . . sob . . . and now I've lost you."

Karl wraps his arm around Marcia's shoulders. "No, no, Honey. This is wonderful. "We'll have fun along the way . . . You can follow me part of the way . . ."

"Yeah, sob . . . like a camp follower." Marcia puts her face in her hands again and resumes sobbing.

"No, Honey." Karl pleads. "I'll be gone for a few months on *Rainer* but you can get a place in Pearl where we can get together when I'm in port." Karl is pleased with his patter. "Then back to San Francisco for fun on the town."

"Sob, sob."

"Honeee!" Karl is clearly exasperated. "You must have known this would happen sooner or later after I got the first set of orders . . . huh?"

"Sob." Marcia raises her head to face Karl, wiping the tears from her face. "Yeah, later I could hope. Now there's no more hope." Her lip curls again and she begins to cry again.

"Come on, Mush." Karl stands and puts out his hand to Marcia. "Lets go down and have a nice lunch at the beach, just the two of us. Like old times - Chart House?"

Marcia looks up at Karl. "Oh, Karl, I'm such a mess. I can't go like this."

"I'll give you just ten minutes to return to your beautiful self." Karl taunts. "Come on!"

"I've got some bad news for you too, Karl." Marcia blurts out, spitefully.

"Good . . . or bad . . . whatever." Karl takes Marcia's hand and pulls her to him. "We can talk about it over lunch."

"Okay." Marcia wipes away another tear. "I'll be ready in fifteen minutes."

*

The Chart House on Pacific Coast Highway

"Will this be okay?" The hostess points the menus at a window booth.

"Perfect! Just late enough to get a nice window table." Karl gloats as he slides into the window booth across from Marcia. "Look at that blue Pacific with the sun glinting off the crashing surf."

"Are you training to be a poet?" Marcia taunts.

"So what's this 'bad news' you're advertising." Karl squirms a little.

"The letter came . . ."

The waitress arrives. "Would you care for a menu?

"Yes, please." Karl shifts in the booth bench. "And we'll need something to drink." He turns to Marcia. "What would you like, Mush?"

"Uhh . . . Margarita?

"Good." Karl elates. "Two Margaritas - rocks - salt. Okay, Honey?"

"Love it!"

The waitress heads for the bar.

"Anyway." Marcia starts again. "A letter came yesterday from Harm."

Karl's head snaps up from the menu. "That's great! What's he say."

"It's from Shilo." Marcia's lip curls into a pout. "He got drafted onto the Canadian Army. He's in basic training at the Canadian Forces Base at Shilo."

"Oh oh! Boot camp." Karl frowns. "So where the Hell is this Shilo, for Christ's sake."

"Harm says it's in Manitoba, way out in the boonies."

"Well." Karl looks out at the ocean. "This is what we were worried about."

The waitress comes with the Margaritas and places them on the table. "Are you ready to order?"

Karl glances at Marcia who is looking out at the ocean with a tear on her cheek. "Uh . . . give us about five minutes, will you?"

"Sure. I'll be back."

18
The Admiral

Monday, NAVPHIBPAC, San Diego.

As Karl steps into his office Yeoman First Beizholtz stands to attention. "Good morning Captain."

The Yeoman stands about six-foot-two in his freshly ironed white uniform. His lean, angular build topped by a long face and short-cropped red hair make him look taller than he is. His steel-blue eyes exude a deep calm.

Karl eyes Beizholtz incredulously. "Er, at ease . . . God! You sure got here in a hurry. I thought Admiral Reston would hold you up for a relief."

"Yes sir." The yeoman steps into the "at ease" posture. "Actually the admiral encouraged the transfer and let me go right away. Gosh, he even complimented me for transferring into a combat command. He said you need me more than he does."

"Well, that's terrific." Karl moves toward his office door. "Come on in, Beizholtz. I'd like to review our situation here."

"Yes SIR! I'll be right there."

"As Karl sits at his desk he notices some mail and a couple of messages arranged on his desk. *Hmm, looks like Beizholtz is working the problem.*

The yeoman enters, carrying a small note pad, and closes the door behind himself. "At your service, sir."

"Sit down, Beizholtz." Karl leans forward to engage the yeoman in conversation. "First: How are the PhibPac people treating you? Are you getting the cooperation you need?"

"Yes sir." Beizholtz shows his pride. "The facilities and communications people turned to immediately to get me the furniture I need and, best of all, they've got us all set up with a secure telephone, FAX, and Internet."

"And personally." Karl leans forward and eyes the yeoman. "Are you getting settled in . . . er, and your family, and . . ."

"Don't have a family, sir." Beizholtz lowers his head. "Not no more, anyway."

Karl's eyebrows go up. "Er . . . Not any more? Uhh, what does that mean? If I may ask."

"Oh that's okay sir." Beizholtz gazes out the window, wistfully. "I had a wife . . . Betty." Beizholtz looks down at the back of his hands. "We got married in her home town of Spartanburg, South Carolina in two thousand-eight. Then on my third deployment, this time on *Eisenhower,* our cruise got extended because of Afghanistan and that was the end of it for Betty. She took the kids and went back to Spartanburg to live with her folks."

"Oh! I'm so sorry." Karl empathizes. "So you're divorced?"

"That's okay sir." Beizholtz smiles. "No, we're not divorced. Betty just likes being with her folks, her folks love having her, and the kids are being brought up in a fine environment . . . better'n Norfolk, that's for sure." Beizholtz straightens his back as if standing at attention. "And I really like being in the Navy . . . especially sea duty."

"And where are you from, sailor?" Karl inquires, hoping to lighten up the conversation.

"Schulenburg, Texas, sir, between Houston and San Anton', goin' west." Beizholtz swells with pride. "In the big cattle ranch country."

"Do you ever think of going back to Texas?"

"Yes sir." Beizholtz fidgets in his chair. "Maybe after another hitch or two. My dad still runs the ranch but by then he might need help."

"Well, Beizholtz, I'm glad to have you aboard."

"Glad to be aboard, sir." Beizholtz shifts in his chair. "What do we need to do first . . . oh, I almost forgot. The admiral wanted to see you as soon as you got in."

*

The admiral's yeoman stands to attention as Karl enters, offering a smart salute. "Good morning Captain Swenson."

Karl returns the salute. "At ease Sailor. Beizholtz tells me the admiral wants to see me."

"Yes sir. I'll buzz."

"Yeah, Branch, what's up?" Came the admiral's voice.

"Captain Swenson is here sir."

"Okay. Send him in."

"Go on in, sir."

"Thanks." Karl tosses over his shoulder as he steps to the admirals office door and knocks.

"Come on in, Swenson." The voice booms from behind the door.

The Commander, Amphibious Force, Pacific looks up from the papers he is working on. "I'm glad we can meet after all this time." He says, without enthusiasm.

Vice Admiral John H. London. His full head of graying blond hair crowns a square forehead, a round face, and a small, straight nose. "Sit down, Swenson."

Admiral London sits beneath a beautifully framed oil painting of a four star admiral resplendent in his blue uniform exhibiting ribbons from his left breast pocket up to a point where there is little room left below the shoulder seam for his Surface Combat Badge. There is a resemblance. Plaques of all sizes, shapes and colors cover the walls and a beautiful model of a cruiser lies in a glass case to the admiral's right.

"I see you've been busy since you've been down here." The admiral picks up a paper.

"Yes sir, Admiral. There's a hell of a lot to do settin' up an air detatchment and everything that goes with it." Karl looks up at the imposing admiral in the painting. "But you know how that goes."

"Well." Admiral London leans toward Karl. "I don't recall having to scrounge aircraft and personnel. Things are tougher now." The admiral permits himself the hint of a smile. "But, I must admit you've done a good job, both scrounging aircraft and finding volunteers to fill flight and air department positions." The admiral looks down at his desk, shuffles a few papers, then looks curiously at Karl. "You know, Swenson, I can't figure out how you got orders to the *Boxer* recommissioning party."

"Well sir." Karl squirms a little. "I met Admiral Massey at the JCS emergency meeting when *Stennis* was attacked and Saudi Arabia was taken over by the so-called *il-Dauli*. I got orders to the *Boxer* recommissioning party just two weeks later. Perhaps my engineering background, three cruises on *Belleau Wood* and *Boxer,* and command experience in the reserve had some effect."

"Yeah, but now you have orders to command *Rainer* at sea, a common prerequisite to commanding a carrier. We don't usually do it that way with aviators in the amphibious business. We usually put a potential aviator CO in as exec of an amphib assault ship for a year or so and then fleet him up to CO. Since your ship is in the yard we decided to use the carrier model and send you to *Rainer*." The admiral squirms a little. "I hope you understand that I might be a little uncomfortable with a reserve officer with no command experience at sea and not even any sea duty as ship's officer."

"Maybe it will ease your concerns a bit when I tell you that, during my deployment on *Belleau Wood* as flight deck officer I stood a lot of deck watches, even while refueling, entering port, and docking."

'Well, that helps." London smiles. "But you were an aviator and didn't have to stand deck watches."

Oh! He's studied my Bio. "Nobody seemed to mind about that, sir. In fact the watch list was delighted"

"Yeah, I'll bet." London leans forward a freezes Karl with his eyes. "But now you'll have the full responsibility, Captain, and I'll be watching . . . very closely."

Karl squirms. "Er . . . Yes sir. I expect that . . . uh, and I hope I can perform."

19
Command

Aboard USS *Rainer,* Western Pacific:

After a long trip via military airlift to Yokosuka Air Station and the short flight to USS *Lincoln* via C-2 Greyhound, CAPT Swenson hops from the side hatch of the SH-60 ASW helicopter onto the helo pad on the fantail of USS *Rainer* (AOE-7) to be greeted by a female commander and a small group of officers and men as he salutes toward the bridge structure where he noticed the stars and stripes flying. The commander steps forward to salute Karl and offer her hand but Karl salutes her and gives the standard request:

"Request permission to come aboard, sir."

"Permission granted, Captain." The commander salutes and again offers her hand for a firm handshake. "And welcome aboard *Rainer*. I'm Commander Steyern, Sylvia Steyern, the executive officer. The captain is on the bridge."

No dead fish handshake for this female commander. More like my big man handshake.

Sylvia Steyern is about five foot nine with strong shoulders and a slim waist and hips but her service dress blue uniform nearly conceals any other attributes she may have. Her Germanic features, high cheek bones, small straight nose, thin lips, and prominent chin are crowned by ash blonde hair in a short shag, mostly concealed by her barracks cap.

"The quartermaster of the watch will show you to captain's quarters, sir." The commander announces after the clatter of the SH-60 fades as the pilot sets his course to USS *Lincoln*. "Captain Carbo is using the sea cabin until he is relieved."

A sailor arrives with Karl's gear.

"I'll ring you in about half hour so we can get together with Captain

Carbo to discuss the relief ceremony." The commander allows herself a wry grin. "And perhaps he can give you a heads-up on some of the pitfalls in the learning process. He's an airdale too, off to command *Vinson,* soon to be recommissioned . . . er, we'll be in the Executive Office. I'll send the yeoman in thirty minutes . . . give you time to freshen up."

"Follow me, Captain." The sailor leads forward to the ship's superstructure.

Karl follows. "Thanks, Commander. I'll see you then."

*

Captain Carbo stands with Commander Steyern to greet Karl as he steps through the hatch. Carbo is a barrel of a man about five foot nine with a barely restrained paunch probably weighing in at about a hundred, ninety-five pounds. His bald pate sports a few strands of black hair slicked straight back, his black eyes protrude noticeably, and he shows the beginnings of a double chin.

"Welcome to the support fleet, Swenson." Carbo booms, offering his hand in greeting.

Karl responds with his firm handshake noting that the firmness was not returned. "Thanks Captain, er, Carbo isn't it?"

"Yeah. Tony Carbo. Gee, I don't think we've met before. What class were you in?"

"Oh. I'm a reserve ranking with but behind Academy class of '95." Karl offers. "My active duty included an F/A-18 squadron on *Truman,* Service Test at Pax River, and two deployments flying AV-8B *Harriers* off *Belleau Wood* and *Boxer.* I've held a mobilization billet in Naval Air Systems Command since I ran out of squadron command time in the selected air reserve."

"And you have orders to command a carrier at sea?" Carbo exclaims in amazement. "How the hell did that happen"

"Not a carrier." Karl begins. *"Boxer,* one of the amphibious assault ships. You know, the little carriers with Harrier STOVL fighters, all different kinds of helicopters, boats, and a division of Marines. "Harrier Carriers" they're dubbed by some. I'm actually the exec. of the recommissioning party with temporary orders to *Rainer* in preparation for taking *Boxer* to sea. I guess they just ran out of bodies with all the ships being dragged out of mothballs. I got orders to the recommissioning party shortly after my last reserve active duty period which coincided with the sneak attack on *Stennis."*

"Well." Carbo shakes his head. "I sure as hell wouldn't believe it if I hadn't seen it with my own eyes . . . Hey, have a seat. we have some things to talk over. Carbo takes his seat in the brown overstuffed chair while Commander Steyern and Karl take the couch.

Carbo continues: "I'll be taking *Vinson* to sea in September. She just came out of Bremerton shipyard and I've got to get back for the commissioning and to supervise the systems integration." I'll get back to *Lincoln* tomorrow and leave you in the capable hands of Commander Steyern, here." He nods to the commander. "And capable hands they are. She protected me from my own mistakes and gave me a continuous lesson in seamanship from the bridge . . . a crash course in command at sea."

Commander Steyern flushes. "That's too much Captain . . . er, why don't we go over the plans for the change of command ceremony tomorrow."

*

USS *Rainer* at sea, Western Pacific

On the bridge *of Rainer* Karl calls: "Quartermaster!"

Aye! SIR.

"Find Commander Steyern and tell her I'd like her to meet me in my office in fifteen minutes."

"Aye, Aye, Sir." The Quartermaster departs through the nearest hatch.

Karl calls to the officer of the deck: "You have the con Mister Hatch." And he departs.

"I have the con sir."

*

"You wanted to see me sir?" Commander Styern enters the captain's office.

"Yeah, Commander." Karl greets his exec. "Sit down. I'd like to review the security measures we've taken to prepare for this underway replenishment."

"Sir, we have established a combined defensive screen deployment with 'Dunbar', the replenishment group commander, using all of our 'cans', we'll place all of our Zodiac boats on alert for launch in case of a surface bogey, and one of our ASW helos will patrol ahead of the force."

"Sounds complete." Karl muses. "Uh . . . when was the last time you inspected the crew for contraband, er, weapons, explosives, and the like."

The exec hesitates a moment as Karl eyes her carefully. "Er, that's not a requirement, sir."

"Well, it is now!" Karl states positively eyeing the commander.

"But sir." Steyern begins to plead. "We're scheduled to rendezvous with the *Vinson* battle group tomorrow."

"That means we'll do the inspection . . . TODAY!

"Or . . . perhaps we can postpone the rendezvous?" The exec ventured hopefully.

"We rendezvous tomorrow, as scheduled." Karl states flatly. "The inspection is today. I want your inspection plan in an hour and a report by twenty hundred tonight. Be sure to include the method to be used to assure that all hands are covered, how you will handle contractor personnel on board, and how you will detect unauthorized personnel." Karl fixes the commander with a stern stare. "Remember, weapons and explosives."

"Aye, Aye, sir." Commander Steyern vanishes through the hatch.

*

2000, same day.

Commander Steyern enters the captain's office followed by a chief petty officer. "Good evening, Captain." She motions the chief to step forward. "This is Master Chief Zymantz, the master-at-arms. He will give you our report."

"We've met." Karl nods to the chief. "Proceed."

"Sir, we interviewed each man and woman on ship's roster, officer and enlisted, all clean. On the other hand, we found two contractor personnel whose names didn't match any names on the manifest from the contractor. They're both in the brig while we search their quarters."

"Good work, Chief." Karl commends the Master at Arms. "What contractor are we talking about?"

"Sea Services, Incorporated, sir." The chief responds. "They provide a variety of non-technical support to the fleet - such as food service and cleaning."

"Commander." Karl addresses his exec. "I want a complete report on this incident after you complete your investigation. CinCPac needs to know the details of this threat, if we find that it is one. Also, I want a daily update on your investigation."

20
The Bosnia Trigger

Aboard USS *Rainer,* Western Pacific:

Captain Swenson brings up the San Diego Union Tribune web page. The headline reads: "IL-DAULI CAPTURES SARAJEVO - PALE SACKED". The text: "Islamic Jihad members brought to predominantly Muslim Bosnia-Hertzegovina twenty years ago to fight Serbian aggression and genocide are now loyal to Süleyman III. As Bosnia-Hertzegovina has stabilized over the last decade, these Jihad cells have set up Madrasses, the radical Islamic schools, and terrorist training camps, both of which have served as recruiting centers for *il-Dauli*. The result has been a formidable force. Yesterday, *il-Dauli* forces captured the capital city, Sarajevo, killing most of the presidential staff and capturing others. It is reported that Bosnian president Stephan Kotromanic survived the assault and was smuggled out to Vienna. Kotromanic has demanded NATO assistance to repel the il-Dauli forces from Bosnia. Also yesterday, *il-Dauli* irregulars overwhelmed Pale, the headquarters of Republika Srpska, traditional home of Bosnian Serbs. The fate of Bosnian Serb president Milan Cvetkovic is currently unknown. European Capitals are astir with assertions about what to do about the new *il-Dauli* expansion. In Washington, President Webster calls for an emergency meeting of NATO and calls on the United Nations to condemn the incursion."

Phew! Karl muses. *I wonder how this will affect Harm . . . Hmm, I'd better call Mush, see what she knows.*

*

Zagreb, Croatia

Pfc. Harm Swenson of the Canadian Army Commandos finds himself in Zagreb, Croatia, training with Canadian and Russian Special Forces as part of NATO Peace Stabilization Force (SFOR). The days are filled alternately with all day forced marches and weapons training on the complete arsenal of weapons assigned to this unit. After a week of this energy sapping schedule Harm is ready for some diversion.

Harm watches a news report on Armed Forces TV. "Hey Wiz." Harm calls. "Accord'n' to this, *il-Dauli* forces have consolidated their gains in Bosnia-Hertzegovina and are bringing in more insurgents." He sighs.

Corporal Eddy Wizniewski is a soldier of unremarkable appearance. Six feet tall, about a hundred, ninety pounds, dishwater blond hair in an army cut, and blue-grey eyes which seem to be apologizing for something. His accent speaks of a Chicago upbringing. "Yeah, Süleyman is trying to expand his empire into the Balkans by occupying Bosnia."

"Scares Me." Harm offers. "Hey, I see where NATO just voted to send us some reinforcements." Harm shakes his head. "D'ya think we'll get involved."

"Hell yes! Ski exclaims. "I figgered that's what we're here for to start with but with reinforcements comin', that seals it."

A commercial comes on the TV. "Hey Wiz, what does a troop do for amusement around here?"

"Hah!" Wiz huffs. "I'm told there's a few spots in town where they have music and sometimes some girls come in from around the countryside. Why? You lookin' for some excitement tonight?"

"I don't know about 'excitement'." Harm muses. "I've got a pass so might as well get off the base for a few hours and see some of this country we're in."

"Not much to see." Wiz offers. "But these Croatian girls are generally pretty cute." Wiz scans a chart taped to the wall. "There's a bus going to town every hour on the hour and returning every hour on the half-hour until midnight - Y' wanna go?"

"Yeah." Harm shows some enthusiasm. "D' you want to go?"

"Sounds like fun to me." Wiz grins. "I can use you for bait . . . heh."

*

"THE SHOWBOAT" screams from the gaudy neon lit sign in the shape of a paddle wheel steamer on the front of what looks like a warehouse from the outside.

"Now there's an American touch." Harm comments. "How do the Russians like it."

"They go to the Russian clubs. Actually, this is a pretty good spot, Harm." Wiz moves toward the red door.

A little boy approaches Wiz and Harm. "Sleep with my sister, fifty dolla' 'merican?"

"Get outta here kid!" Ski takes a swipe at the boy. "Go home to your mama."

Inside SHOWBOAT, a portly woman in her forties sits at a table blocking further entrance. Her dyed blond hair is swept up into a pony tail resembling an out-of-control fountain and her rouge and mascara combine to invoke a comic image. "Admission, ten dollah American."

Wiz digs for money. "Sounds kinda' heavy to me. What're we payin' for?"

"We have nice group of girls from Vrapce, farm town west of here . . . **Very** nice. Is church youth group."

"Sounds okay to me, Harm . . . Okay with you?" Wiz plunks down a ten.

"Yeah, er . . . Okay." Harm donates his ten.

"You can take table or stand." Blondie offers. "What you like."

Inside, two couples are dancing to a poor imitation of an old American tune from the 1990s and three pairs of girls are dancing together. All the tables are taken, mostly by two girls each but a few couples. Harm offers: "There's a nice pair, over there. Whaddya think."

"I'll take the little brunette." Wiz claims. "The tall blonde is more your size."

"Hello ladies." Harm bows just a bit. "May we join you?"

The girls huddle and whisper back and forth. Then the brunette replies politely: "As you please."

Harm takes a seat next to the blonde. "Thank you, I'm Harm, er, Harm Swenson." He nods to the blonde. Then, to both girls. "And this is Eddy Wizniewski, heh, otherwise known as Wiz."

The blonde responds: "Pleased to know you. I'm Katja and this is Nikki."

Wiz leans forward. "Would you ladies like some refreshment?"

The response is a timid chorus: "Champagne please?"

"Okay, two Champagne. Uh, do they serve at the tables here?" He eyes Nikki.

"No. But bar is there." Nikki points to a small alcove at the back of the room.

"I'll get this round." Wiz offers. "Beer for you Harm?"

"Yeah, thanks." Harm begins to stand. "Can I help?"

"Siddown, Harm. I can handle it." Wiz heads for the bar.

Katja probes: "Swenson sound Swedish."

"My grandparents were born in Sweden and immigrated to the United States around nineteen-sixty to settle in a little Swedish community on the plains of Kansas . . . Lindsborg."

"So you are American?" Katja turns to Nikki. "Boys are from America."

Nikki eyes Harm suspiciously. "That right, Harm?"

"Not quite." Harm responds. "Wiz is from Canada . . . er . . . We're both in the Canadian army."

Nikki is curious. "How did a 'Wizniewski' get to Canada?"

"Same way, I guess." Harm assumes. "Hey, I understand you ladies are from a little town west of here." Harm scans both faces. "Is it 'RAP-CHEE'?"

"Is 'VR-AP-CHAY'. Start with 'Vee' sound." Katja giggles. "But close for American." .

"Ha! Here comes Wiz with the drinks." Harm stands to help unload the tray. "Thanks Wiz"

Wiz raises his stein of beer. "Croatia." He toasts.

"And to Vrapce." Glasses clink while Harm looks into Katja's liquid blue eyes.

"Vrapce? . . . Uh." Wiz stammers. "Oh yeah! That's where these young ladies are from."

"Duh." Harm laughs, the girls giggle, and the band starts playing.

"Hey." Harm stands. "I think they're playing 'The Girl from Ipanema', an old Brazilian favorite." He holds his hand out to Katja. "Dance."

Katja stands. "I'd like that." She steps toward the dance floor.

Harm watches as Katja walks ahead of him with a poised stride, emphasizing her athletic figure. At the dance floor she turns to face harm, raising her arms in an inviting gesture, and revealing the full beauty of her lithe figure. Her honey blond hair frames her fine features, falling to her shoulders, a small straight nose, full lips, and a firm chin. Harm reaches around her slim waist to take her in his arms. The aroma is not of perfume or eau de Cologne but of some strange soap or face cream. Very nice, though..

Out on the dance floor, Harm comments: "Your English is very good, Katja."

"Schools teach English from fifth year."

"Have you traveled much?" Harm leads Katja over to a corner of the dance floor.

"Two years ago my parents take me to Switzerland for skiing." Katja stumbles a little. "Sorry."

"Where in Switzerland?"

"Zermatt, under Matterhorn." Katja twirls. "They speak funny German there."

"You speak German too?"

"A little. Oops."

"May I cut in?" A young soldier asks.

Harm looks at Katja for an answer. She just shrugs. "Okay, I guess."

Katja dances away with the other soldier and Harm wanders back to the table.

At the intermission Katja seems to linger on the floor with the other soldier so Harm walks out to reclaim her.

Extending his hand to the soldier Harm says: "I'm Harm Swenson, second battalion, fourth division." And reaches for Katja's hand.

The soldier accepts the greeting and shakes hands. "Sergeant O'Brien here, Seventeenth. Hey, rookie, she doesn't belong to you!"

"I'm workin' on it." Harm begins walking off with Katja.

"Not good enough." O'Brien steps in front of them.

Harm glances at the two Military Police standing near the entrance. "What do you plan to do, Sergeant, pull rank?" Harm starts to walk around O'Brien, Katja on his arm."

Wiz comes up to see what's happening. "Hey Swede. What's goin' on.?

"Well, Sergeant O'Brien, here, wants to kidnap Katja."

Wiz faces the sergeant, standing between him and Harm. "I wouldn't do that, Sarge. No rank here, you know."

O'Brien wanders off quietly and Wiz, Harm, and Katja return to their table.

"What was happen there." Nikki queries.

"Nothin'." Harm grunts. "Just an 'Ugly Canadian'."

*

After a few more dances: "We should go." Nikki ventures. "Our bus leaving soon."

"Okay." Wiz stands. "We'll walk you out to the bus."

The two couples walk separately out of the SHOWBOAT. Harm draws Katja close and whispers: "I'd like to see you again, Katja. May I call you?"

"I like call, Harm. You have paper?"

"Yeah." Harm reaches in his hip pocket for his little notebook. "What's your number?"

"I give you my cell number: 4319/8609." She shows the phone to Harm.

"And write down your last name, if you would."

"Oh! Ja." Katja writes, then hands the notebook back to Harm. "Last name, Vrbovec." She gives a coquettish smile.

"Thanks, I'll call you next week when I know when I'll have a pass."

*

Zagreb, Croatia

On a day off, Harm and Wiz take in a little Armed Forces TV.

"How'd you do last night, Harm." Wiz inquires.

"Oh." Harm reacts. "That Katja is such a charmer. She took me to a Croatian club. The music was all European, probably Balkan . . . Er, or maybe Slavic. We had a lot of fun, but Katja had to translate throughout the whole evening."

"What was the name of the club?" Wiz wondered.

"I probably can't pronounce it." Harm hesitates. "Something like -er - 'Ykaterinburg Dacha'. Sounds Russian to me."

"Yeah." Wiz grinned knowingly. "Catering to our Russian friends."

"Hey, wait a minute." Harm points at the TV.

"Breaking news from Sarajevo: il-Dauli forces have captured Sarajevo and, in a simultaneous strike, sacked Pala. Islamic Jihad remaining from Bosnian-Serb war now loyal to Süleyman III and reinforced by local Muslim recruits show formidable force - Bosnian president was smuggled out last night - demands NATO help. More later. Now back to our regular programming."

"Well, they're not picking sides between Muslims and Serbs." Wiz opines. "Pala is the Serb headquarters in Bosnia and the Bosnian president is a Muslim."

"But it probably makes sense to Süleyman and his *il-Dauli*." Harm interjects. "He just wants to take over the world - or at least this part of it. Yeah. I remember my dad raving about bringing in the Jihadists from Araby to help Bosnia during the war back in the 1990s." Harm remembers. "He said these Islamic extremists would cause trouble sometime. Now, here it is."

"Yep. Here it is." Wiz groans. "And you know we'll be involved in this thing before too long. Maybe NATO knew what they were talkin' about when they voted reinforcements for us."

"And speakin' of takin' over the world, did you hear about *il-Dauli* movin' on the *Falun Gong* in China?"

"Now there's a switch." Wiz reacts. "What's that about?"

"Well, I read on-line the other day that Süleyman had been in China wooing *Falun Gong* leaders to achieve an *il-Dauli* proxy to spread his influence in Asia. *Falun Gong* seems to be a pseudo-religious movement numbering as many as a hundred million members . . . uh, they call 'em 'practitioners' . . . globally which really bothers the ChiComs to the extent that *Falun* members have been the subject of persecution including imprisonment, torture, and even harvesting of organs from live *Falun Gong* practitioners.

"Wow!" Wiz exclaims. "They're surroundin' us."

"Yeah. Anyway, after a few dances, Katja took me out to her house to meet her folks." Harm shakes his head. "What the hell does that mean."

"She likes you." Wiz is curious. "Then what happened?"

"You won't believe it."

"Try me."

"Well." Harm continues with some embarrassment. "They put me in the barn office . . . nice cot. Then I woke up with Katja standing at the foot of the cot in her filmy white night gown."

"Wow! Then what happened?"

"Let me just say: we got well acquainted."

"Do you think the Vrbovec folks are just trying to get their daughter married off to an American." Wiz winks.

21
Terror at Sea

USS *Rainer* (AOE-7) at sea in the Northern Pacific
On the bridge *of Rainer* preparing for underway replenishment.
"Dunbar Bearing Zero-four-seven, four-four miles, course one-niner-three degrees, speed ten knots, Sir." Reports the quartermaster of the watch. Dunbar is the radio call for the resupply group consisting of fleet oiler, ammunition ship, combat stores ship, and escorts.
"Dunbar position aye." Lieutenant Barnes, the officer of the deck, responds. Barnes is a stout man at about five foot nine tall and a hundred and seventy pounds, appearing much older than he is with his generous, befreckled face and forehead, sparse reddish hair, a pinkish complexion, and watery sky blue eyes.
"Mister Agnello." Captain Swenson calls to the navigator. "Establish course to intercept Dunbar at twenty knots.
"Aye, sir." comes Lieutenant Agnello, the navigator. "Give me two minutes, sir."
Karl looks to Commander Steyern in the aft starboard corner of the bridge to see her nod approvingly.
"Intercept to Dunbar at two-zero knots is six-four degrees." Reports Agnello."Expect sighting in one hour, fifteen minutes."
"Mister Barnes, stand by to execute heading six-four degrees, speed twenty,." Karl calls.
Aye aye, sir." Responds Lieutenant Barnes.
Then the quartermaster calls: "Signals, hoist 'COURSE SIX FOUR, SPEED: TWENTY' at the dip." Signifying 'stand by to execute' the command Calls the quartermaster..
Foster and *Sides* acknowledge by hoisting the same signal. USS*Paul F. Foster* is the destroyer stationed at two thousand yards on *Rainer's* port

bow and USS *Sides* is the Guided Missile Frigate cruising at two thousand yards on her starboard bow.

"EXECUTE!" Calls Lieutenant Barnes. "LEFT STANDARD RUDDER, COME TO ZERO- SIX-FOUR DEGREES AND MAKE YOUR SPEED TWENTY KNOTS."

The flag signal is noisily two blocked as the "EXECUTE" command to *Foster* and *Sides* and the engine room telegraph clangs as *Rainer* gently heels to starboard as she turns port to the commanded course.

Karl scans the horizon to see *Foster* in a sharp turn to port to maintain station while *Sides* is belching black smoke and kicking up a wake as she accelerates to maintain her position.

"Commander Steyern." Karl calls. "Meet me in Command Plot." Then: "Steady as she goes, Mister Barnes. Call us if you have a sighting. You have the con."

"Aye aye sir. I have the con"

*

Karl and Commander Steyern take seats at the rear of Command Plot, facing the maneuver display and swivel their chairs to face each other.

"Well Commander." Karl begins. "My first encounter with a double UNREP. Give me a little primer."

Commander Steyern begins: "UNREP is the acronym for "UNderway REPlenishment. Double signifies that we will have an oiler on one side and an Ammo ship on the other. Incidentally, at the same time we will receive various stores and provisions from a combat stores ship via CH-60 *Sea Hawk* helicopter - That's called VertRep."

"What does this operation entail?" Karl inquires.

The commander reports: "We will be taking on about a million gallons of diesel fuel and a little less than two million gallons of aviation jet fuel from the fleet oiler *Willamette* on our port side, sixteen hundred tons of ordnance from the Ammo ship *Shasta* on the starboard side, and about seventy tons of miscellaneous provisions and . . . MAIL from the Combat Stores Ship *Saturn*. That should top us off so we can high-tail it back to Lincoln."

"Those numbers are startling." Karl muses. "For a reserve airdale on his first taste of fleet duty after ten years out of it. But remind me of our defensive posture?"

"Dunbar has a couple of cans." Steyern begins. "So our combined four will take positions in a forward screen guarding against subsurface, surface, and air threats of all kinds."

Karl frowns. "Does that mean we don't need our small boats patrolling forward as we would coming into port?"

"As I said, sir, our boats will be in emergency stand-by since they couldn't keep up as we need to maintain a speed fast enough for easy station keeping and slow enough for optimum operation of the destroyers' SONAR - fifteen knots is about right."

"I think we should be at General Quarters." Karl ventures.

"We usually just put the gunnery department at their battle stations." Steyern replies. "The replenishment crew needs to be at their UNREP stations."

"Yeah. That makes sense."

*

"All high lines to *Willamette* set to port and transfer hoses connected, sir." The officer of the deck reports. "High lines to *Shasta* to starboard are secure and transfer has begun, and we are now receiving the first CH-60 load from *Saturn*."

"What was THAT?" Karl reacts to the sound of an explosion to port.

The port lookout runs in from the port bridge wing. "Explosion on *Willamette*. Appears to be at one of the pump stations." He takes a breath. "The fire is spreading and the west wind is blowing the flames over our port side."

"Disconnect all hoses and high lines on the port side and break our lines to *Shasta*. On the double." Karl orders. "Report when all connections are broken."

Moments later: "All connections broken, sir."

"All engines ahead full!" Karl commands.

"All ahead full, aye!" The officer of the deck affirms as the engine room telegraph rings.

Seconds later Karl orders: "Execute a tight circle to port to arrive alongside *Willamette* as soon as possible to fight their fire."

"Aye aye, sir." Then: "Left full rudder. All engines ahead full. Stand by for rapid changes." And: "Boatswain's mate! Order our fire detail to stand by to fight the fire on *Willamette to starboard*."

"NOW HEAR THIS: FIRE DETAIL MAN STARBOARD FIRE STATIONS. STAND BY TO FIGHT FIRE ON WILLAMETTE CLOSE ABOARD STARBOARD SIDE . . . NOW HEAR THIS: FIRE . . . . ."

"Gimme the bull horn mike, Bosun." Karl commands. "AHOY

WILLAMETTE. THIS IS RAINER CAPTAIN SWENSON. HOLD COURSE AND SPEED. WE'RE MANEUVERING TO COME ALONGSIDE ON YOUR PORT TO ASSIST IN FIGHTING YOUR FIRE. ACKNOWLEDGE."

Willamette responds: "WILLAMETTE CAPTAIN VAN VOLK HERE. I ACKNOWLEDGE 'HOLD COURSE AND SPEED' WE STAND BY FOR YOUR FIRE ASSISTANCE."

"Er . . . Captain?" Commander Steyern calls. "May I have a word?"

Karl steps to the aft bulkhead of the bridge to join Commander Steyern. "Yes?"

"Sir, do you think it wise to put *Rainer* at risk to fight *Willamette's* fire. If there is an explosion we could sustain severe damage." Steyern warns.

"I acknowledge your caution, Commander." Karl spits. "But we **will** assist a U.S. Navy ship in distress. Wise or not, it is Navy tradition and I'm not breaking it. And, tradition or not, we need to save that oil and aviation fuels so we can fill up and get back to the *Lincoln* battle group on schedule. **Now,** I expect you to direct the fire fighting effort. Understand?"

"Aye, Aye, SIR!"

*

30 minutes later on the bridge of *Rainer*.

"Quartermaster!" Karl calls.

"Aye, sir."

"Find Commander Steyern and tell her I wish to see her on the bridge."

"Aye, Aye, sir." The quartermaster departs.

Ten minutes later: "You wish to see me sir?" CDR Steyern enters the bridge.

"What is the status of the fire on *Willamette* and her capability to transfer oil and aviation fuel?"

"Sir, the fire is under control and will be completely extinguished within the half-hour." Steyern reports. "Two stream stations were unaffected by the fire and another will be operational, probably in an hour. You should know, sir, that six of our fire fighters, led by Chief Button, transferred to *Willamette* via high line to help, and they may have made the difference."

"That's great." Karl acknowledges. "Resume fuel transfer from the surviving stream stations, er . . . Well done Commander."

22
Sarajevo Sortée

Zagreb, Croatia

Canadian Major General Ian MacKenzie, commander of the NATO Peace Stabilization Force (SFOR) stands in the center of the base gymnasium stage backed by a large map of Croatia and Bosnia-Hertzegovena, a large scale map of the Sarajevo area, photographs of buildings, and a few plan views of selected buildings and the airport. He addresses a selected group of commandos made up primarily of troops representing Canada and Russia.

"Gentlemen." The general begins. "Er . . . and ladies. Although we are still the NATO Peace Stabilization Force, our next mission is quite more aggressive, that is: to oust Süleyman's occupying forces from their Bosnian strongholds in Sarajevo and Pale to eliminate the *il-Dauli* threat to the whole region. Tonight, we liberate Sarajevo, and your job will be to prepare the objective for the insertion of a company of SFOR troops. Major Monaghan will brief you on the details of your mission."

"Thank you, General." Major Dan Monaghan, Commando company commander, with a salute to the general, mounts the gymnasium stage. Members of the selected commando platoons are seated in folding chairs facing the stage.

Cpl. Harm Swenson sidles closer to Sgt. Wizniewski. "What're we in for, Ski?"

"Big operation tonight, I hear. We lead!" Wiz whispers. "Shh! Major Monaghan is gonna tell us."

"Ladies and Gentlemen!" The major shouts into the microphone.

The troops stand to attention and shout "YES SIR!" In unison.

"As you were." The major begins and the troops resume their seats: "As you know, *il Dauli* forces now occupy Sarajevo after a bloody incursion which killed most of the presidential staff while the three presidents escaped to unknown locations via small military transport." He moves to the selection of maps and photos and picks up the pointer, then begins:

"Tonight, we will conduct reconnaissance in force to secure the airport ahead of the C Company strike aimed at destroying the enemy and occupying Sarajevo for NATO. You have each volunteered for this mission. We appreciate your willingness to participate."

"We have six squads for this operation, designated Detachment one and Detachment two - Det 1 and Det 2." He looks to the lieutenant seated in one of the front seats. I will command Det 1 and Lieutenant Brownlow here will command Det 2, understand?"

"Yes **SIR!**" Lt. Brownlow responds.

"Our transport tonight will be two Air Force CV-22 *Ospreys*." Major Monaghan points to the seats behind the commando platoon. "Meet your pilots, seated behind you, Captains Patrice and Iarrobino, and Lieutenants Price and Kirchner." Then: "Lieutenant Brownlow, you and I and our first sergeants will meet with the air force pilots right after this brief to firm up procedures."

"With weather and trees masking our approach, our *Osprey* pilots will be able to deliver us within range of the airport tower and operations building, our targets." He looks to the four Air Force pilots. "Does that sound right to you Captain Patrice."

"Yes suh, Major." Patrice's drawl signals agreement. "By the look of the dispersed hard points around the airport we should be able to put your troops in fairly close to the objective with some cover."

Major Monaghan peruses the wall map and then captures Captain Patrice in his gaze. "Uhh . . . Cap'n, do you think you and Captain Iarrobino could put the troops in simultaneously on either side of the objective so they can attack in a pincer movement?"

"No sweat, Major." Patrice turns to Iarrobino. "What do you think, Jim?"

"You said it boss." Iarrobino confirms. "The photos we got from SOCom er, Special Operations Command, show a few designated landing spots for Ospreys or helicopters around the airport - mostly with pretty good cover. They're all labeled so we can coordinate our selections for best tactical effect."

"Yeah." Patrice summarizes. "We'll just pick a couple o' good ones when we get there - with input from the detachment leaders aboard each aircraft."

"Sounds good to me." Major Monaghan looks to Lt. Brownlow. What do you think, Lieutenant?"

"Sound okay to you, Sergeant?" Brownlow addresses his First Sergeant.

"Yes sir." Msgt. Maruyama agrees. "And we can discuss details after we get together with the pilots and . . ."

"Okay, Lieutenant, and this is for the two *Osprey* crews too." Monaghan interrupts. "The two *Ospreys* will take off tomorrow morning at 0230 hours and land as stealthily as possible at 0400 hours to deploy commandos. We'll have a short time line as Capt Freitag plans to bring C Company into the airport aboard a C-130 thirty minutes after our insertion - 0430 hours, depending upon our success in securing the airport. Keep in touch with me by radio to let me know when the airport is secure so I can advise Capt. Freitag when it is safe for him to land and deploy his company. The commando detachments will take up positions to assure that the enemy force does not compromise airport security during and immediately after C Company lands."

"Commandos!" Major Monaghan calls.

All the commandos again stand to attention. "Yes **SIR**."

"As you were." Monaghan begins. "You have black uniforms and black ski masks. Wear them. Your weapons will be: One Uzzi machine pistol with silencer and ammo; your commando knife; and a garrote . . . to be used in the reverse order." The major displays each as he speaks. "Use the garrote on sentries and guards as much as possible to maintain your stealth. If you must use the knife be sure to cover the subject's mouth to stifle a scream. Use the Uzzi only if you need to subdue a group of the enemy or when your mission is threatened directly by an armed group. Of course that may blow our cover and bring reinforcements, and we don't want that.

*

0330 Hours, Over the Bosna River

Cpl. Harm Swenson and his squad leader, Sgt. Wiz Wizniewski sit at the aft end and on opposite sides of the CV-22 *Osprey* cabin in silence. Major Monaghan is seated just aft of Swenson. They have been briefed by the major on their exit order and on their planned deployment thereafter. Sgt. Wisniewski's squad will be first out of the aircraft following the major.

Harm views each of the six members of his squad seated across from him: Sgt. Wizniewski seems in deep thought, head bowed as if examining the deck of the cabin; Pfc. Phil Buck, a lean man with a sallow complexion, sits straight backed, eyes straight ahead, as though at attention, his thoughts a mystery; Pvt. Ian Strayhorn, a heavy set man with a round face and black tousled hair . . . Is sound asleep; Pvt. Etienne Moreau, a tall lean man with a curved French nose and neatly combed black hair is reading a book; Pvt. Antoinette Martin, another French Canuk, peers straigh ahead, unseeing, as though reviewing her role in this operation; and Pvt. Rico Cruz, the Panamanian, shows some fear in his eyes.

The troops feel the reduced power as Capt Patrice begins his descent to the Sarajevo airport environs.

"Beginning our descent now." Capt Patrice intones over the cabin speaker. "Insertion in five minutes."*

"Hey Wiz." Harm half whispers. "I think we're landin'."

"Stand by for landing." Comes Capt Patrice's voice from the cabin speaker. "Your objective is one hundred yards, bearing one five zero."

After the jolt of the touchdown Major Monaghan stands at the rear of the cabin. "We disembark, spread out, use cover when available, and move quietly to the tower building, weapons on semiautomatic. Shoot to kill. And watch for the rotating beacon. Sergeant Wiz, keep your squad with me. Sergeant Fritz, keep your squad to our right and Sergeant Liebau, stay left. Thirty minutes to take our objective, the control tower."

"Squad." Wiz calls, quietly. "Weapons on semi, we stay with the major, thirty minutes to secure tower. Got it troops?

"Yes **sir**." Comes the whispered chorus,   "We got it."

The rear cabin door opens and sets on the ground providing an exit ramp. "**Go!**" Major Monaghan orders as he leads the way down the ramp and out into the night.

Harm is advancing toward the tower. *Hmm, plenty of trees out here where those air force weenies let us off. Oops, here comes the beacon - stay behind a tree. Okay, now move. dodgin' the beacon will slow us down quite a bit. Keep it movin' Swede. Oh oh, the major is hunkered down at the edge of the airport clearing with a clump of bushes as cover, only about fifty yards from the tower. He's wavin' for us to join 'im. Oh oh, here comes the beacon again - get flat on the ground.*

Major Monaghan whispers: "We'll move in one at a time. Head for the back door to the tower as we discussed. The group here will provide cover. Watch the roof of the ops building. I lead. Wiznewski, follow me with your squad at my signal, Fritz and Liebau follow in order with your squads." He waits for the darkest moment between searchlight swings and moves off silently, picking his way carefully to avoid leaves and twigs. At the tower door he turns to wave Wizniewski on. A look at his watch tells him he has just seventeen more minutes to secure the tower.

With Wizniewski, Swenson, Strayhorn, and Moreau with him, Major Monaghan opens the door, outward, and Wiz, Swede, Stray, and Frenchy enter with weapons at the ready and spread out across the room, the major joining them. There's noone in the lower lobby of the control tower building but they can see a guard standing outside the glass front door, facing outward. The major points to Wiz and Swede and then to the guard and draws his forefinger across his throat.

Wiz and Swede ease out of the back door, almost running into Trok, just arriving. Then around the building quietly until they can see the guard, calmly smoking a cigarette on the steps of the building. Unable to get on both sides of the man they crawl slowly toward him with the decorative hedge as cover. When they are close enough, Wiz throws a stone into the bushes on the opposite side of the guard and in the same motion jumps over the hedge and throws the garrote over the guard's head to his throat and draws hard with both hands. There is only a soft whimper from the man as he sinks to the concrete, eyes bugging out. Wiz and Swede drag the body into the bushes along the front of the building taking one more check to be sure he is dead before entering the building to join Det 1 gathering in the tower lobby.

Major Monaghan whispers: "I'll take Wiz and some of his squad up to the control tower with me; Fritz, take your squad to the front of the building and take cover; Liebau, do the same at the rear of the building. Repel any incursion."

Sgt. Liebau complains in a whisper: "Not much cover at the back, Sir."

"Use the ground." The major spits. "Just lie still . . . **Do it!**

"Yes sir."

Major Monaghan moves to the foot of the spiral staircase, points to Wizniewski, Swenson, Strayhorn, and Buck, and waves to them to join him. To the others he whispers: "Take positions here in the lobby to repel any incursion that gets by the squads outside. Then: "Who's got the radio?"

"Corporal Kuhn here, sir. I have one."

The Major points to Kuhn. "You're communicator for the lobby here."

"Seven minutes to go." Monaghan whispers. "C'mon." He mounts the stairs and moves quickly but quietly, avoiding any vibration of the staircase.

At the top the major sees two doors, both marked in the Bosnian language. He looks to his men, spreading his arms and shrugging his shoulders signaling a request for someone to read them.

Strayhorn steps forward and points to the door on the right.

The major sees that the door opens outward and grasps the door handle carefully. He turns the handle and pulls gently. **LOCKED!** *God damn! We'll have to blow it.* He aims his Uzzi carefully at the lock and in one motion fires one shot and yanks the door open.

The four commandos stream into the room firing selectively to bring down all seven of the enemy present. As the major moves to the communication console to figure out the system a short burst of gun fire comes from under one of the desks and Harm goes down, clutching his chest. Buck fires two shots to eliminate that threat and Strayhorn makes sure the rest will be no threat.

"Srayhorn!" Wiz calls. "Check Swenson's wounds and report."

Major Monaghan is on the radio to call Lt. Brownlow with Det 2: "Hello Brownie, Irish here, what's your state?"

"Ops building secure, sir." Lt. Brownlow responds. "We did not use Uzzis."

"Well done, Brownie."

"Hey Wiz." Strayhorn calls. "Swede's got a shoulder wound, bleed'n pretty bad, and a nasty bruise on his chest from a bullet to his flack vest. He can walk okay but that wound will need attention to stop the bleeding."

"Our medic is in the lobby." Wiz whispers. "Take him down there. I think we'll be okay here."

"The Major selects a channel and begins a transmission: "Hello TGIF" Captain Freitag's radio call. "This is Irish. Over."

"Hello Irish, this is TGIF, what's your status."

"Irish here, tower and ops building secure, and airport clear of any obstacles." Monaghan reports. "What is your position?"

"TGIF is on a long final approach to runway one-two-zero, about five kilometers out."

"Irish here." Monaghan replies. "Suggest you land on this approach. We may have company soon and we'll need reinforcements."

"Roger that, Irish. We'll be on the ground in two minutes."

"Hey Brownie." the major calls on the radio. "TGIF will be on the ground in less than two minutes. I see all clear out of the tower. What's your status over there at Ops?"

"Clear, so far, Irish."

*

Same day: The Army Hospital at Camp Zagreb

"Oh! My dear Katja. Thank you so much for coming." Harm lies in an hospital bed, his left shoulder wrapped in an out-sized bandage, his left forearm strapped firmly to his waist, and an intravenous tube stuck into his right wrist.

Katja advances to plant a gentle kiss on Harm's forehead then a more serious one on his lips.

"Mmmm . . . " Harm reacts to the long kiss. "And flowers too. Hey, I'm not dead yet . . . but thanks. That was very thoughtful of you."

"How you feel, Harm?" Katja strokes Harm's hair.

"Well, they've been giving me pain killers and antibiotics ever since I got here so I may be a little out of it." Harm shifts in the bed. "Oww! That smarts."

"What happen to shoulder, honey."

"A bullet went in there and rearranged the bones." Harm tries for a little humor. "The nurse tells me that the doc did his first surgery on it this morning. Sounds like the surgery is a little like a rotator cuff surgery usually reserved for baseball pitchers."

"You say 'first surgery'. Is more?" Katja probes.

"The nurse says I'll be in here for two or three weeks for one or two more bouts with the surgeon." Harm groans. "Then I'll be in rehab for about a month before I can go back to duty."

"What 'rehab'?" Katja frowns.

"Oh, 'rehab' is rehabilitation. Exercise and stretching to make the shoulder work the way it's supposed to." Karl cringes. "Hurts too, I understand from those who have been through it."

"What happen in Sarajevo." Katja sits in the bedside chair.

"Aha! Now the good news." Harm brightens up. "We went in, just fifty of us, and secured . . . er, defeated the Jihadist defenders and took control of the air field . . . er, that's when I got shot."

Katja frowns. "Anyone else shot?"

Harm looks down at his hands. "Well, we lost two of our commandos before the main Army force arrived by air and eliminated the *il-Dauli* defenders."

"Miss. You have to leave now." The nurse announces.

Katja stands and gives Harm another kiss. "I'll be back tomorrow."

"I look forward to it." Harm smiles. "When I get out of here we'll go out and do something important."

23
Commissioning

June 2016 - La Jolla

"Hi, Honey." Karl calls as he steps into the compact little apartment near Bird Rock in La Jolla.

"Hi Darlin'." Marcia emerges from a collection of boxes, most of which are opened. "What's happening with the Navy, **Captain**?"

Karl draws her into his arms with a hug and a kiss. "Hmmm. That's nice." The two of them stroll, arm in arm, into the smallish living room in the one bedroom apartment Marcia had rented to be near Karl during *Boxer's* work-up preparatory to deployment, expected to take about sixty days. "Let's have a drink on the balcony and enjoy the fabulous view of the ocean at sunset, complete with sea birds and surfers . . . scotch?"

"Martini?" Marcia suggests. "A real gin Martini, up, with a twist?" She rolls her eyes.

"You actually have the ingredients, Mush?" Karl is incredulous. "Hell, you're not even unpacked yet."

"Only the best for our naval hero: Bombay Saphire, Cinzano dry vermouth, a lemon twist, and plastic Martini glasses." Marcia wraps her arms around Karl's neck. "we're celebrating!" Then a long kiss.

"Oooh!" Karl emotes. "Starting now, you mean?"

Marcia breaks free with laugh and heads for the little kitchenette. "Are you mixing, or am I."

"Do it, Mush." Karl snickers. "You've come this far. . . but very light on the vermouth."

"I know, I know." The ice clatters as Marcia stirs the mixture.

On the balcony their plastic glasses click, they look into one another's eyes and take the first sip. Karl ventures: "Mush, you made such a wonderful selection. This place is the perfect size for us, and the view is magnificent." A sip of Martini.

"Glad you like it." Marcia eyes Karl curiously. "So what **is** going on with the Navy."

"Well, er, I'm getting used to the ship . . . **and** the crew." Karl exudes pride. "Looks like we've got a good one." Karl looks to the ocean view. "I've got an appointment with the admiral tomorrow morning."

"Is that the same admiral who gave you such a bad time last January?" Marcia touches a nerve.

"'Fraid so." Karl cringes. "Perhaps after my cruise on *Rainer* he might be a little more accepting . . . we'll see."

Marcia gives a sly smile. "Maybe he'll cancel your orders."

"No comment."

*

NEXT MORNING:

Karl slips into the little kitchenette with a hug for Marcia. "What's for breakfast, Honey?'

"Bacon and eggs and rye toast. "And I've got some marmalade." Marcia brags. "But you have to cook the eggs."

"Work, work, work." Karl feigns displeasure. "The life of a sous chef."

"You know you love it, Honey."

At the table on the balcony Marcia and Karl click their orange juice glasses with enthusiasm befitting a toast with screwdrivers.

Marcia gives Karl an coquettish look. "Here's to a long work-up." Both sip their orange juice.

The front page of the San Diego Union Tribune lying on the table screams: "TAIWAN INDEPENDENCE DECLARED BY NEWLY ELECTED PRESIDENT. Analysis."

After reading the headline aloud, Karl invites: "Listen to this, Mush. 'Newly elected Taiwan President Chiang Shui-chan, in a speech to the nation before the presidential palace yesterday, declared the Republic of Taiwan a sovereign state to thundering applause from the hand picked audience. Further, he announced the mobilization of Taiwan armed forces and a request for United States assistance. Until now, Taiwan presidents of the Kuomintang party have followed the path of least resistance, a tenuous peace with the PRC, but Chiang's Democratic Progressive Party (DPP) has exploited the growing nationalist movement in the countryside to get Chiang elected. See *Analysis* page 7."

Karl pages noisily to page seven, then reads further. "In the past, the reluctance to declare independence from the Peoples' Republic of China was understandably due to the power of the PRC economy and military thanks to the huge trade surplus China enjoyed with the rest of the world, until recently. A series of events have changed things. Just last January, after years of increasing pressure from the World Bank and the United Nations the PRC agreed to peg the yuan higher and the result has been a severe blow to the PRC economy. Add to that the sharp reduction of the PRC population over the past twenty years due to birth limitations. Of course, there is the direct reduction of young citizens and beyond that the severe gender gap caused by the enforced preference of male over female births. The British Medical Journal study reported last month that, in China, young men outnumber young women by a startling fifty million individuals. The PRC has experienced a mass exodus of young men to southern Asian countries where women are more plentiful and increased crime by the men left in China has surged. Another effect is the severe tension between the burgeoning coastal area of China and the backward and economically disadvantaged western provinces. The combined effects have caused broad disruption of government functions and severe personnel shortages in the armed forces and even a reduction in weapon systems and support procurement. It is clear that Taipei judged that this is the opportune time to challenge the PRC.'."

Karl noisily turns the page to the continuation. "Oh. Here it is. 'Not only that but the *Falun* Gong, the dissident group in China's Western province of Zingjiang, in a recent association with Süleyman Third's il-Dauli and with spreading influence and enhanced power, has recently organized massive demonstrations in the three major financial centers of China, Shanghai, Beijing, and Xianggang. It appears that President Chiang chose this time of Chinese turmoil, both financial and social, when the PRC armed forces are in chaos, to do what the Taiwan people have wanted since her separation from China in 1949.'." Karl puts the paper down and: "What do you think of that, Mush?"

"I thought we knew this would happen when a Taiwan nationalist like Chiang became president." Mush muses. "But always before the president softened his stance after being elected because of the fearsome Chinese strength. Not this time! Chiang probably thinks the PRC is preoccupied with all the social an economic upheaval."

"Speaking of social upheaval." Karl begins. "Now we have Tibet protesting its subjugation by China with strong support from India and Pakistan."

Marcia gives Karl a sidelong glance. "D'you think this will effect us?"

Karl takes a bite of fried egg. Then a deep breath. "The answer to that question is: 'Probably'."

"Why do you say that, honey?"

"Well." Karl sips his coffee. "Right now, we have no carrier battle group in WestPac, **nor** do we have an Amphibious Strike Group there . . . Nothing. A few years ago the Navy sent *George Washington* to be forward deployed at Yokosuka to replace the retiring *Kitty Hawk* but they sent her back to the Atlantic fleet after the fleet-wide draw down. The only U.S. force in the region now is the cruiser *Shiloh* and guided missile destroyer *Mustin*, both forward based at Yokosuka. They recently transited the Taiwan Strait as a caution to China, but that small force can't do much if the PRC gets serious . . . with whatever force they can muster." Now a bite of rye toast smothered in orange marmalade.

"So, what does the Navy do?" Marcia is getting impatient.

"Well, Honey." Karl begins calmly. "The next big deck ship ready for deployment is . . . guess what: **Boxer** . . . and her Amphibious Strike Group."

"Whoa!" Marcia reacts. "Does that mean you might deploy early?"

"Probably." Karl takes a bite of toast and sips his coffee. "Oh, by the way. What have you heard from the kids?"

"Last I heard from Harm he had gotten out of the hospital." Marcia heads for the kitchenette for coffee so she shouts over her shoulder. "He says he doesn't have any pain anymore but his shoulder is in a cast so he's kind of a one-armed bandit . . . er, soldier."

"Does he think he'll get back to duty?" Karl's concerned."

Marcia pours the coffee. "Thirty days, he thinks. Oh! And you remember that your daughter gets her Navy wings of gold pinned on this Saturday."

"Wow." Karl puts down his coffee and spills some in the process. "With all this other stuff going on, that slipped up on me . . . uh, have you made any plans?"

"Not yet. I didn't know how we should plan it or whether you can even go."

Karl thinks a moment. "I know I can't spend any time over there . . . but I definitely want to go." He eyes Marcia. "Why don't you make reservation to get there Friday evening and stay as long as makes sense. I'll steal a *Harrier* and meet you there Friday evening but I'll have to get back Saturday soon after the ceremony. I can't be away any longer than that."

*

Same morning - Naval Station, San Diego

"The admiral will see you now, Captain." The yeoman announces.

"Thank you, Branch." Karl moves to the admiral's office door and knocks.

"Come on in, Swenson." Comes the admiral's booming voice.

As Karl enters the admiral steps around his desk and extends his hand to greet Karl. "Welcome to the 'Gator' fleet, Swenson." Vice Admiral John H. London. stands about five foot ten with an athletic build, like a tennis player, and probably weighs in at about a hundred and sixty pounds. His ruddy face shows his active nature and years at sea.

Shaking hands, Karl responds: "Glad to be aboard sir."

"Have a seat . . . er, may I call you 'Swede'? The admiral eyes Karl.

"Please do, sir." *Whew. This a lot warmer greeting than our last meeting. A good start.*

Admiral London returns to his desk chair. "I must tell you that I was very pleased with what I heard about your cruise on *Rainer*."

"I'm glad to hear that, sir." Karl responds cautiously.

"Commander Steyern was quite impressed . . . shall I say 'shocked' by your aggressive command style." The admiral smiles approvingly.

"Shocked?" Karl reacts. "That doesn't sound like fitness report language, sir."

"Yeah, probably not. But I didn't read it. I just spoke to Commander Styern directly." A smug smile. "I wanted her first hand comments. She reports that you took over in an emergency situation after an explosion on the oiler you were receiving fuel from and turned a potential disaster into a minor glitch."

"Oh." Karl smiles. "Yes sir. An explosion started a fire on *Willamette,* our tanker, and the wind was blowing the fire onto our port side so I just ordered the OOD to put our starboard side alongside *Willamette's* port side and stand by to fight the fire. Lieutenant Barnes, the OOD pulled a clever maneuver he called an 'Anderson Turn' and our fire detail and water made the difference."

The admiral leans forward and eyes Karl. "With Commander Steyern objecting, I understand."

"She told you **THAT**." Karl is flabbergasted.

"Yeah!" The admiral smiles broadly. "She said that was one of the instances of your 'shocking' command style."

"Well, sir." Karl diverts his eyes. "I commanded fighter squadrons and events never leave much time for decisions . . . and they'd better be right."

"I like that, Swede." The admiral smiles. "I also understand that you demanded a security inspection that may have saved *Rainer* from the same kind of sabotage."

"Well, sir." Karl squirms in his chair. "When you take over a command, you've gotta be sure it's secure. Like when you accept a rifle from someone. You check the chamber and the magazine."

"You're damned right, Swede, I like that too."

Karl averts his eyes to ignore the accolade. "Admiral, I was really impressed with Lieutenant Barnes and his seamanship so I suggested he request transfer to *Boxer* . . . he did . . . and I forwarded his request recommending approval before I left. Er . . . do you think that was cheating?"

London bursts into laughter. "Ha! Probably so, but since he will be coming to amphibs, I'll support it."

Karl eyes Admiral London. "Perhaps you could pull a few strings, sir."

With a sidelong glance the admiral says: "I'll see what I can do . . . Hmm, I'll have to hurry. You'll be deploying in thirty days."

"Thirty days?" Karl jumps in his chair. "I thought it was sixty days, sir." *Yeah, I figured this would happen with the Taiwan thing hittin' the fan.*

"You've probably heard that the new president of Taiwan has declared independence from the PRC and requested U.S. assistance."

"Yes sir. I read the morning paper."

"Now, both AirPac and Surfpac - me - have recieved orders to provide support ASAP." The admiral sighs. "And, right now, we have just one cruiser and a guided missile destroyer at Yokosuka and AirPac has nothing . . . **NOTHING!** And with the Chinese threatening action against Taiwan we need an amphib strike group over there . . . **NOW!** Thirty days, Captain**,** can you do it?"

Karl squirms a little in his chair. "Thank you for your confidence, sir. But it will be tight, a real surge deployment."

"That's what it is, Captain, **SURGE**." Admiral London leans forward to capture Karl's eyes. "**Can you do it**?

"Yes sir Admiral." Karl sits forward. "***Boxer* will do it**!"

"Good. I have confidence you and *Boxer* can and will." End of conversation." The admiral is unequivocal. "If there's any way I can help, let me know."

"Thank you, sir . . . er, there is something you need to know."

With a quizzical look Admiral London asks: "Yeah, what."

Karl starts cautiously. "Uh . . . my daughter will receive her wings at Pensacola this next Saturday and I intend to pin them on. Do you have a problem with that, sir?"

"Hell no, Swede." The admiral exults. "I commend you for having an offspring in the Navy - and an aviator at that. By all means go. And give your daughter my congratulations. I'd like to meet her whenever she gets to San Diego."

"There's one more thing, sir."

"What's that?" The admiral leans forward in his chair.

"Well sir, I thought this lull before the surge would be an opportunity to run up to Point Mugu to check the status of any new self defense weapons the NAVY may have in the labs up there." He eyes London for a reaction.

"So what's your connection with Point Mugu?"

"Back when I was a commander drilling with the WEPTU . . . Uh, Weapons Training Unit, at El Segundo I served one active duty period as Shops Officer at Point Mugu when I got acquainted with a Doctor David Eisenberg, the leader of a way-out innovative group that was developing a stealthy attack missile using advanced active electronic spoofing measures. So, I've made an appointment with Dr. Eisenberg next Monday morning. The combination of trips means I'll take one of our *Harriers* to Pensacola to meet Marcia for Karen's winging and get back here on Sunday. Then I'll fly up to Mugu on Monday. I'll be back here Monday evening. My exec, Commander Flintley will be organizing the surge during my short absence."

"That's a great idea, Swede. Do it!" Admiral London sits back in his chair, a satisfied look on his face. "I'll look forward to your report on any of Eisenberg's magic we can use.

The admiral snaps his fingers as though he has forgotten something. "Oh, how's your wife holding up under all this sea duty?"

"Pretty well, thank you, sir." Karl shifts in his chair. "She came down here and rented a small apartment up in La Jolla for the duration. She'll move back to the Palisades when I go to sea."

"We'd like to have you and, er . . . what's your wife's name?"

Hmm, gett'n more friendly. Karl thinks. "Marcia, sir."

"Perhaps you and Marcia could come over for dinner sometime this week. Let me check with Misses London." Admiral London punches buttons on his phone. "Hey Mike. When would be a good night this week to have Captain Swenson and his wife over for dinner . . . Wednesday?" He looks to Karl for a response.

Like I have a choice. Karl muses. "Perfect, sir . . . uh, what time?"

"How about eighteen hundred?" The admiral suggests.

"Fine, but how do we find your quarters, sir?"

"Over on North Island. Just ask the Marine guard at the gate for directions."

24
Surge

Aboard *Boxer* at Naval Station, San Diego

Karl arrives at his office. "Good morning, Biezholtz."

Biezholtz stands to attention. "Sir."

"As you were." Karl eyes Beizholtz. "I want all hands on deck at oh nine hundred. I have something to announce to the crew."

"Aye, sir." Biezholtz responds. "I'll advise Mister Flintly immediately . . . anything else, sir?"

"Yes. set up a meeting in my office at ten hundred. I need Commander Flintly, Commander Johnson, and Colonel Cavallo and tell commander Johnson to bring his flight deck officer. Find Colonel Cavallo first - he may not be on the ship.

"Aye, aye, sir.

*

Tooeee too. The boatswain's pipe calls for attention to the announcement. *"BOXER*! ATTENTION!" The boatswain's mate hands the microphone to Captain Swenson while the division officers bring their divisions to attention.

"Greetings, *Boxer*. Stand at ease." Karl shuffles his notes. "Some of you are aware that *Boxer* has been ordered to a **surge** deployment. The orders call for us to deploy on 23 July, just thirty days from today, instead of deploying in mid August. We have a long way to go: Radars aren't yet calibrated, sick bay is not fully equipped, communications installation is incomplete, and I know that's not all. As a matter of fact our air detachments are not fully equipped and manned, an issue the exec, the air boss, and I will address this afternoon with a visit to MCAS Yuma.

"Some of you also know that the reason for our surge deployment is the real threat of Chinese military action against Taiwan in the wake of her declaration of independence from the Peoples Republic of China and the fact that we have no carrier battle group nor amphibious strike group in WestPac at this time. Currently, US interests there are being protected by the cruiser *Shiloh* and guided missile destroyer *Mustin*, both forward based at Yokosuka. *Boxer's* Amphibious Strike Group Five is the closest force to being deployable at this time. The *Vinson* carrier battle group will be ready for deployment in sixty to ninety days, so we will be alone out there for at least a month. And what will the Chinese do . . . no one knows."

Karl takes a breath and a sip of water. "The surge deployment has robbed us of a shakedown so our shakedown starts today and extends into our deployment or until Commander Flintly and I decide *Boxer* is in fighting shape - ready for combat. All hands will be under unusual scrutiny for their performance and conduct during this period. Those of you who have been through a shakedown know the drill. We all must have patience through this trying time as it will turn us into a fighting **UNIT**, capable of bringing the fight to the enemy . . . whoever an wherever he is. Remember. The shakedown ends when *Boxer* is ready to **FIGHT!**

"Admiral London has told me he has confidence in *Boxer* and expects us to succeed. Let's not disappoint him.

"Thank you for your attention." Karl hands the mike back to the boatswain's mate.

"*Boxer* dismissed." The sound of every division officer releasing his division is heard.

*

"Thank you for coming, gentlemen, especially on such short notice." Karl greets the senior officers of his command. "Please be seated . . . oh, Oz, whom did you bring?"

"Skipper." Oz reaches to push the young Lieutenant Commander forward. "This is your flight deck officer, Lieutenant Commander Dom Matsuoka."

Matsuoka is a short man, about five foot seven, but with a barrel chest typical of Japanese men. His short, shiny, jet black hair falls straight down all around making it look like a typical bowl haircut. His round face is accented by nearly invisible black eyes, a small nose, and a strong chin. Naval Aviator wings are pinned over his left breast pocket.

Karl offers his hand. "Glad to have you aboard, er, Mat-su-o'-ka. Is that correct?"

Matsuoka smiles. "No sir. It's Mat-suo'-ka. The 'u' is almost silent . . . er, as in Yokosuka."

Mobilize!

"Thank you." Karl eyes the man quizzically. "So what do we call you to make it easy?"

"Just 'Mats', sir."

"Thanks Mats. That does make it easier. Oh, have a seat." Karl seats himself at his desk. "Okay, Mats. what qualifies you to be flight deck officer on *Boxer*?"

"During my last active duty, sir." Matsuoka sits straight in his chair. "I was the wing LSO on *Vinson*, attached to VFA-146, working closely with the flight deck officer. Since then I have commanded a reserve F/A-18 squadron at LeMoor."

"What do you think of *Boxer* as an aircraft operating base." Karl inquires.

"It's different, sir." Mats responds. "No arresting gear and spotting aircraft is a major challenge. Our aircraft come in all shapes and sizes."

"Right." Karl starts. "We'll all get a better idea of operating our aircraft at sea this afternoon. we're going over to Yuma to meet some of our pilots and kick a few tires. Is that all set, Horse?"

"Yes sir." Horse responds, with enthusiasm. "We have an *Osprey* on deck. We board everyone at twelve thirty, ETA Yuma thirteen hundred. The air detachments are ready to brief us on their status and give us a little air show . . . uh, they'll just fly some of their aircraft and show us some precision landings and ground handling."

"Good." Karl stands. "We'd better grab an early lunch and get going."

*

Same day - MCAS Yuma

Horse Cavallo steps to the stage in the PhibDet52 ready room. "How're we doin' guys . . . er, and gals?"

"GREAT!" Comes the enthusiastic greeting from the air detachments.

Horse smiles with satisfaction. "Let me introduce *Boxer's* senior officers: Some of you have met Captain Karl Swenson, our skipper, just returned from his successful qualifying cruise aboard USS *Rainer*, a Fast Combat Support Ship; Then there's Commander Spark Flintly, our Exec; The air officer, Commander Oz Johnson; and our flight deck officer, Lieutenant Commander Dom Matsuoka - we call him 'Mats'. Lieutenant Colonel George Parnoussis is our lading officer but he's out at MCB Hawaii checking readiness of our Marine Expeditionary Unit over at Makapuu which we'll pick up when we get to Pearl.

"There are three reason for this visit: A greeting from Captain Swenson; A status briefing from each detachment commander; And a tour around our flight line to familiarize all of us with your aircraft and their ground handling characteristics . . . hell, we might even fly some aircraft." Horse turns to Karl. "Captain?"

"Thanks Horse." Karl mounts the stage as Horse steps to the rear. Does your invitation apply to me?" Karl gives 'Horse' a sly smile. "I need a *Harrier* flight to stay current."

"You got it, skipper."

Karl turns serious. "One reason I wanted to come over here is to meet each of you individually and to thank you for signing up for our important and challenging mission. And we thank you for entertaining us this afternoon. I know this cuts into your training but I assure you that your status briefings will contribute to our overall preparation for deployment. Also, I want to assure you that 'Horse' and I will move on your shortages promptly and, we believe, effectively.

"Speaking of deployment, I now have orders for surge deployment. That means we are scheduled to deploy on 23 July, just thirty days from today."

A murmur runs through the air detachments.

Karl raises both hands, asking for quiet. "As I said to the crew, Admiral London has confidence that *Boxer* can do it and surely we don't want to disappoint him . . . do we?"

"Hell no!" Is the near unanimous response.

Karl smiles with satisfaction. "Now I'll give it back to 'Horse'." He steps down to take his seat in the front row.

"Thanks skipper." Horse steps forward. "We'll hear first from Captain Tony Cribaldi, heading up the CH-60 Seahawk detachment, Tony?"

Cribaldi steps up on the stage. "Thanks Colonel. I'll be brief. We're in pretty good shape with just a few discrepancies. First: We have our eight birds but they vary in configuration from one to another, problems for maintenance and operation. But our supply sergeant tells me he can kumshaw the needed parts - guns, radios, etc. - says he'll have 'em all ready for deployment . . . er, it may be pushing it to get all that stuff in thirty days but he's workin' it. I'll show you some of the variations when we go out to kick the tires. Second: Our maintenance crew is short four rates so we're training up some airmen to fill in, but we'll still need more bodies. Third: We've just got fifteen pilots so far but I understand more are promised. We'll need 'em. That's all I have, Colonel."

"I'll call my contact up at Pendleton - see if he can help on the bodies." Horse offers. "Now, Captain Brown has the *Sea Dragon* story, Jim?"

"Sir, we are in good shape hardware wise with our nine CH-53s - all 'D' models. But they are all good aircraft and our pilot complement is complete. We join the rest in being short of qualified maintenance personnel. That's all."

"So. More work for my friend at Pendleton." "Horse" looks around for his next speaker. So now we will hear from Major Harold Sapperstein on the situation with the *Harrier* detachment. Hal?"

"Yes sir." Major Sapperstein steps up on the stage. "We actually got six *Harriers* but we have two different configurations. Only four of them are night mods. The good news is, they are all very good birds, operationally. On the personnel side, we're about the same as the others - enough bodies but too few technical rates. We all need help on that score."

"Okay, more work for my Pendleton contact . . . I'll work it."

"Now I'll review the readiness of the *Osprey* group." 'Horse' pulls an envelope out of the shoulder pocket of his flight suit and eyes it. "We've got Good news and bad news: All the MV twenty twos we got are the same configuration, that's good; But we've only got ten so far - short two. Swearingen at AMARC tells me we should get the other two in thirty days. That's too tight. Personnel wise, we are in about the same shape as the rest, we need maintenance rates."

"So, skipper, I've got quite a few personnel items for my friend up at Pendleton." Horse acknowledges. "And it looks like the skipper and I will have to put the arm on AMARC to get those other *Ospreys* before we deploy."

"Thank you all for those concise reports." Horse closes the session. "Now, all four of you give us your problem sheets for both personnel and aircraft before we go back to the ship and we'll see what we can accomplish." Horse turns to Karl. "Let's go out and look at the aircraft, Skipper. C'mon Mats. You've done some deck spotting exercises and some precision landing trials. Show us some of that."

"yes sir." Mats responds. "We've had our flight deck aircraft directors out here for most of the time and our landing directors have been able to work with all the pilots on precision recoveries."

*

Karl is driving to San Diego Airport with Marcia. "Hey Mush." Karl begins cautiously. "There's been a little change in plans."

Marcia whirls in her seat. "What change? Here I am on my way to Pensacola and you have a change of plans. What now?"

Karl glances at Marcia to find her eyes blazing. "Nothing that changes our trip to Pensacola. I just have to go to Point Mugu for a meeting on Monday." Another glance at Marcia. "I'll be back in La Jolla Monday night."

"What does the admiral think of that?"

"He thinks it's a good idea." Karl sighs. "Oops! Here comes the North Terminal."

"Marcia is worrying. "D'you think we're early enough?"

"Oh yeah." Karl turns in to the parking lot. "It's just six thirty and your flight doesn't board until eight thirty. No perspiration."

"Look at the bright side, Mush." Karl smiles. "This means I'll be with you in Pensacola Saturday night."

At the check-in counter Karl pops Marcia's rolling suitcase up on the scale and the agent completes the check-in. "One passenger to Pensacola, one stop Dallas/Fort Worth, American flight 1398, boarding at seven-fifty, gate 16. Your baggage is checked through to Pensacola. Here is your ticket packet."

"Thank you." Marcia starts for the security check line.

Karl walks with Marcia toward the departure gate. "My flight in a *Harrier* will only take about three hours. I'll get a Navy car and pick you up at the airport. You should arrive about four-thirty."

"Thanks Karl. I can make it from here okay."

"Gimme a kiss, Mush."

25
Wings

NAS Pensacola

Karl and Marcia are seated in the distinguished visitors' section in front of the National Museum of Naval Aviation awaiting the start of the "winging" ceremony during which Karen will receive her Navy wings of gold. Karl is resplendent in his white uniform - with medals. Marcia is her most charming in her colorful summer frock.

"That's quite an assortment of graduates, Mush." Karl remarks. "Navy, Marines, Air Force, and some from other nations, including two female graduates."

"Yeah." Marcia whimpers. "And one of them is our daughter, Karen."

"Be Proud, Mush." Karl cajoles, peering through his binoculars at the graduates. "One of the foreigners is from Taiwan. I can tell by the uniform."

"ATTENTION TO ORDERS!" Comes the order to the assemblage arrayed before the Museum. "Graduating class six, cee, fourteen, Training Squadron Eighty-six - Attayn-hut!" Candidates for designation as Naval Aviators shuffle to attention as the station band begins the National Anthem. "Right hand salute!" The sixteen candidates salute toward the stars and stripes flying from the air museum flag staff and the male parents and guests in the reviewing stand come to attention and sing the words - most with gusto. Karl and Marcia are overcome by the moment as are others and kerchiefs come out to blot the tears.

Captain Bruton Bright, Commodore of Training Air Wing Six stands at the podium at center stage. "Distinguished guests, parents, graduates. Welcome to the June designation of newly graduated Naval Aviators. And here to do the honors is Captain Dan Willard, the commander of advanced training squadron Eighty-six." He turns to greet Captain Willard.

Captain Willard steps to the podium. "Graduates!" He nods to the assembled flight class, all in their white uniforms, Navy ensigns with their one stripe shoulder boards, Marine second lieutenants with their gold bars, Air Force candidates, and two foreign students. "I congratulate each of you for completing the rigorous training which brings you to this rewarding point in your lives." The captain turns his head to cough. "Within the month I know that most of you will scatter to advanced training stations and fleet units, world wide. I wish you all fulfilling careers in Naval Aviation. And I know some of you will stay right here to help train more Naval Aviators. Welcome back. Be assured that your service as instructors will be an important contribution to the vitality of the Naval Aviation establishment." He turns to Commodore Bright. "Commodore?"

Commodore Bright turns to view a group in civilian clothes seated at the end of the stage to his left. "Our keynote speaker today is an Naval officer of great achievement in building Naval Aviation to the modern and effective force it is . This outstanding officer rode the fighter desk at Naval Systems Command back in the mid two thousands and was instrumental in the modernization of fighters and their weapons, sensors, and communications, an initiative interrupted only by the severe cuts in Defense budgets in two thousand, nine. Please welcome Retired Rear Admiral Bernard 'Birdie' Benson. Admiral." The commodore steps aside and offers Admiral Benson the dais.

"Thanks 'Brute'." Benson opens with a little snicker. "See, I know something about you too: "Brute" Bright, commanding the last F-14 *Tomcat* squadron. But that 'Birdie' drags me back to VF-24 when we upgraded to "E" model *Hornets*. Where'd you find it?"

"Oh, we have sources, Admiral." Bright suggests with a wry smile.

"Yeah, I can tell." Admiral Benson sips from the glass of water provided to the podium and clears his throat as Captain Bright takes his seat to the left of the podium.

"Parents, guests, graduates." Admiral Benson begins. "The commodore mentioned the new and upgraded weapon systems brought along during the last decade. The Air Force graduates will soon find themselves flying the F-35 Lightning while the Navy and Marine Corps graduates will enter squadrons equipped with the next generation F/A-18G and H *Hornet* and some F35s.

"And we all know how timely these modern weapons are in the face of new threats brought by Muslim extremists reorganized as *il-Dauli* - 'The Empire', and the potential of conflict between China and Taiwan over Taiwan's recent declaration of independence. The United States and her world partners are already engaged with *il-Dauli* and we can expect to be drawn into any China-Taiwan fray." Another drink of water.

"We have allies who support the war against *il-Dauli* - some more reliable than others. For that reason the United States must be prepared, in every way, to meet any threats that arise from any quarter - ALONE. An example is our Muslim partners who have joined us because they recognize that *il-Dauli* is a threat to their own sovereignty but demure when it comes to operations in some regions in Southeast Asia, such as the Ferghana Valley of Uzbekistan where the Huzb-ut-Tarir stirs new threats to stability in the region. On the other end of the spectrum is Australia, our staunchest ally on the Pacific rim. You probably have already perceived that you may find yourself fighting in any part of the world.

"And we can't forget natural disasters such as Hurricane Georgia which flattened our own gulf coast just last fall. The Navy, Marines, and Coast Guard were first responders, rescuing stranded survivors and providing food, shelter, and transportation to thousands, er, hundreds of thousands of victims. That event was in the United States but we have responded to similar emergencies throughout the world. You may be called upon to assist in such cases.

"You are our front line of the future, the tip of the spear, as we say. Make the most of your advanced training at one of the Weapons Training Units, both Navy and Air Force. You'll need all the skills and savvy you can absorb from those rigorous training venues. And for those of you selected to stay as instructors, keep in mind the solemn duty you bear to your nation and to those aviators you train. Make them effective instruments of America's strength for the projection of power, liberty, and peace in the world . . . and the preservation of their own lives."

The admiral turns to Captain Bright. "You have the wings Commodore?"

"Yes sir, Admiral, here." He hands the package to Admiral Benson. "Shall we proceed?"

"Okay. You lead."

Captain Bright and Admiral Benson leave the dais and proceed to the lower stage in front of the guest seating area where they are joined by the squadron commanders of the primary and Intermediate squadrons.

The wing training officer, Commander Bell begins: "Ensign Karl A. Mitscher!"

The young ensign steps out of the line of candidates and marches smartly to the lower stage, executes a smart left face to face the Admiral and comes to attention and salutes. "Ensign Mitscher reporting, sir."

"I see no sponsor is present so I guess it's my duty." Admiral Benson takes one set of wings out of the package and begins to pin them on.

Commander Bell recites: "Ensign Mitscher was born and raised in Coronado, California, where many of the Mitscher clan resided. You may have sensed by the name that he is related to Admiral Marc Mitscher who commanded Task Force 58 in the defeat of the Japanese fleet in the greatest sea-air battle in history. Ensign Mitscher is his great, great, grandson." A nod to Ensign Mitscher - no reaction. "He was appointed to the Naval Academy right out of high school and excelled there, finishing third in his class, then came here to finish first in his class." Commander Bell claps formally, inciting applause among the guests. "Ensign Mitscher will carry his squadron call sign, "Dutch" to the Air Force Fighter Weapons school at Nellis Air Force Base, where his orders direct him."

"Good genes eh, 'Brute'." Admiral Benson comments to the commodore as he finishes pinning on Mitscher's wings above the single row of ribbons. "Ensign Mitscher, I hereby designate you a Naval Aviator." . "Congratulations . . . and Good Hunting." He reaches out to shake Mitscher's hand.

Ensign Mitscher salutes smartly, executes an about face and returns to his place in the formation.

Candidates are called in succession and wings are pinned on white uniforms as anxiety builds in Karl and Marcia, waiting for Karen to be called. Finally:

"Ensign Karen A. Swenson." Commander Bell calls.

Karen marches smartly to the lower stage as Karl and Marcia make their way to the same location. Karen faces Admiral Benson with a sharp salute. "Ensign Swenson reporting, **sir!**"

"Ah." Admiral Benson exclaims. "We have parents. Welcome Captain Swenson." He reaches out to shake Karl's hand. "Delighted to have you aboard for this important event in your daughter's life."

Shaking hands, Karl announces: "And this is Misses Swenson, sir. Er . . . Marcia."

"Delighted to meet you Misses Swenson." Admiral Frost bows slightly. "You must be very proud."

"I am proud of Karen's achievements." A tear comes to Marcia's eye. "But I'm afraid of what comes next." Marcia chokes a little as she continues. "Carrier aviation is truly dangerous business."

"Mo-om." Karen scolds.

"It's okay Ms Swenson." The admiral soothes. "Moms are like that - especially with girls. She's proud of what you have achieved and she will be proud of your performance in the fleet."

Marcia tries to comment but is caught up on the emotion of the moment.

"We'll have time to talk after the ceremony." The admiral placed his hand softly on Marcia's shoulder, then reaches in the package for a set of wings and hands them to Karl. "You do the honors, Captain."

"Thanks Admiral." Karl reaches in the left breast pocket of his white uniform. "I brought my own."

"Very traditional, Captain, then proceed."

Karl stands at attention before Karen and salutes while Marcia reaches out to take her hand with a tear on her cheek.

Commander Bell begins: "Ensign Swenson was born in Patuxent River, Maryland where her dad, the captain here, flew carrier suitability evaluations, and was raised in Saint Louis and Pacific Palisades, California. Ensign Swenson came to us from Iowa Preflight and was selected for fighter-attack training. She was dubbed 'Kay-Kay' by her squadron mates and she uses that as her call sign." The commander checks his notes. "Ensign Swenson will now continue her training at FAWTUPac . . . er, Fleet Air Weapons Training Unit, Pacific Fleet. We wish her success in the Pacific fleet."

"I dub you Naval Aviator, Ensign Swenson." Karl pins his own golden wings just above the single row of ribbons and takes Karen into his arms. "You know you have made me so proud. I know you will carry out your duties faithfully and with excellent effect." Then to the admiral: "Sorry Admiral, my pride got carried away."

"Understood, Captain. We're proud of your family . . . and your service."

Marcia cries openly and embraces the new Naval Aviator.

*

06 July 2014 - La Jolla, CA

"Another relaxing Sunday morning at home, Mush." Karl exudes. *There won't be many more.* He thinks. "What's for breakfast?"

"I thought I would make bacon and some French toast." Marcia offers. "Sound good?"

"yum." Karl licks his lips. "And I'll fry a couple of eggs to go with it."

"Anything new in the paper today, Mush?" Karl rustles the eggs.

"I don't know. It's on the table."

Karl takes his seat at the breakfast table and scans the Union Tribune. "Hey Mush, listen to this." Karl rustles the paper. "'WYATT PRESSES CHINA FOR CALM'. I think they're talking about the Taiwan situation. Let's see what they say." Karl digs out a wedge of grapefruit and continues: "'Recognizing the anxiety in China over the declaration of independence floated by Taiwan's President Chiang President Wyatt has dispatched a contingent of diplomats led by former ambassador to China Harley George to meet with President Chiang to try to persuade him to soften his claim of independence and the mission already has a planned extension for talks with China's president Wang, pressing for calm . . .'" Karl puts the paper down. "Well, that's a good idea but it sounded like Chiang pretty much had his mind made up."

"Hmm." Marcia muses. "So you've got to go out there and straighten the whole mess out. Well, good luck."

26
Point Mugu

Naval Air Weapons Station Point Mugu

Karl eases his *Harrier* down to a soft landing on the parking ramp in front of the operations building and kills the engine as the ramp crew chocks the wheels. Karl hops down to the tarmac and greets the crew chief: "Thanks, chief. I won't need any service. I'll just be flying back to San Diego this afternoon and I have plenty of fuel."

With a return of salute Karl heads for the ops building to close his flight plan and advise the duty officer of his intentions. Concluding that formality he strides off in the direction of the "shops" offices.

In the office Karl introduces himself to the duty yeoman. "Captain Swenson here. I have and appointment with Doctor Eisenberg."

"Yes sir, Captain. He's expecting you. His office is at the end of this passageway." The yeoman points down the passageway to his left.

The frosted glass door at the end of the passageway announces: "Dr. David Eisenberg, Technical Director." Before Karl can knock, the door swings open and the hand of Doctor Eisenberg is thrust forward for a welcoming hand shake - and a friendly embrace. "Come on in Karl. There's someone I want you to meet."

Eisenberg leads into another office to a small conference table where a young man stands. "'Am', meet Captain Karl Swenson. Karl, this is Doctor Amadeus Fogg." Eisenberg puts his arm around Am's shoulders in a fatherly gesture. "We call him 'Am". He has a physics degree from Cal Tech and his doctorate thesis was entitled 'Radio Frequency Wave Shaping'. Just what we're working on here."

Doctor Fogg is a frail appearing young man about five foot eight and one hundred twenty-five pounds; a rumpled shock of black hair frames a square forehead and lean features. He reaches forward to shake Karl's hand. "Happy to know you, Captain. Dr. Eisenberg has talked a lot about you."

"What's your schedule, Karl." Eisenberg inquires.

"I plan to go back to the ship this afternoon." Karl replies. "I just got orders from Admiral London to deploy in thirty days - a surge. So I don't have any time to waste. I came up today to see all I can see about the promise of a defense against the Chinese *Silkworm* or *Sea Eagle* anti-ship cruise missile you told me about." He turns to Dr. Eisenberg. "I think we could encounter *Silkworms* in any potential engagement with il-Dauli forces or, in the case of the Taiwan flap which is heating up, China. You know the attack on *Stennis* in the Persian Gulf involved both Silkworms and *Skud* ballistic missiles so we need to be prepared for both. But I'm very interested in the concept you hinted at on the phone, David. Can you cover it in the time we have today?

"Definitely, Karl. Am will brief you on the concept and some of our results, we'll show you the bench prototype in the lab, and you'll see a demonstration of the prototype this afternoon." Eisenberg remembers a warning: "But please, anything you hear today doesn't go beyond this discussion. This program has been classified TOP SECRET due to it's potential for neutralizing our own *Harpoon* cruise missiles." Eisenberg continues.

Karl ponders the situation. "Do you have support from either ONR (Office of Naval Research) nor DARPA (Defense Advanced Research Programs Agency)?"

Eisenberg responds: "Both are aware of this program but say that they have too much on their plates to tackle a small program with no operational support." Now a wry smile. "We'd like to interest you to the extent that you and your admiral could support us."

Karl is enthusiastic. "If your concept shows promise I guarantee I will push for support, both organizational and financial."

"I hoped that you might." Eisenberg smiles. Then he waves his hand toward Fogg. "Introduce the captain to the concept, Am."

"Well, sir." Fogg shows some awkwardness as he begins his presentation at a chart board showing the elements of the potential mission - US capital ship, *Silkworm* missile, and decoy. "We start with the radar response electronics in one of our air-to-air target aircraft such as the BQM-34 *Firebee* by Northrop Grumman. The production version of this electronics suite has the capability to simulate the radar return of most, if not all known military aircraft. With our advanced radio frequency wave forming we have been able to enhance the *Firebee* electronics to simulate objects as large as a surface ship." Also, some versions of the *Silkworm* are known to have infra red terminal guidance so we have also incorporated enhanced infra red response."

"How large a surface ship?" Karl queries.

"A carrier." Fogg intones.

Karl's eyebrows go up. "Have you demonstrated this capability." Karl inquires.

"Yes sir." Fogg proceeds. "Let's go over to the lab now and you'll see the performance of the bench hardware. Then, this afternoon we'll go aboard USS *Vinson* to see a tactical demonstration with our prototype mounted on a *Zodiac* inflatable boat and an F-18 as a stand-in for the cruise missile. The test F-18 is fitted with standard *Harpoon* electronics and uses Harpoon approach tactics."

"Great." Karl's enthusiasm shows. "Lets go."

*

Over lunch at the club the three discuss various aspects of the demonstration. Eisenberg begins. "You probably wonder how we are able to use USS *Vinson* for our little demonstration." A wry smile. "She was out qualifying her air group and agreed to support some carrier suitability tests on some of our new weapons and we snuck in the decoy as an adjunct to those tests." Eisenberg eyes Karl slyly. "Just for you."

"Well, I appreciate that David." Karl takes a sip of his clam chowder. And by the way, I have met *Vinson's* skipper, Tony Carbo." A sheepish smile. "Under less than ideal conditions."

"How so?" David inquires.

"I relieved Carbo of command of *Rainer,* you know, one of those Fast Combat Support ships, for my obligatory oiler cruise prior to taking command of *Boxer."* Karl smiles to himself. "He thought someone had made a serious mistake assigning a reserve officer - me - to command a big deck."

David had a little laugh at that. "You're in luck Karl. You'll have an opportunity this afternoon to renew an old friendship - heh."

"We'll see."

*

Aboard USS *Vinson* off the Channel Islands

"As the small party disembarks from the HS-60 *Seahawk* a seaman comes forward and salutes. "Captain Swenson?"

"Yes."

"Captain Carbo would like to see you on the bridge, sir. Follow me."

"May I bring my associates?"

"The captain just asked to see you, sir."

"Just a minute." Karl turns to Eisenberg. "I guess I better go, David. I'll have to invite Carbo to see the demo. D'you think that'll be okay?"

"Yeah! That'd be great." David gives it a sly grin. "Perhaps we can get his support too. We'll wait at the base of the island."

On the bridge Captain Carbo slides out of his captain's chair to greet Karl with a surprisingly warm handshake. "Welcome aboard *Vinson*, Karl. I know you got *Boxer*. How's it going."

"Quickly is the word." Karl smiles. "Admiral London just ordered *Boxer* to a surge deployment - thirty days - probably the Taiwan flap."

"Whew!" Carbo reacts. "You'll be in WestPac before we will . . . by about a month . . . Anyway, what are you doing out here?"

"The weapons lab at Point Mugu has a promising concept for a decoy to counter the *Silkworm* cruise missile and they're demonstrating it for me today, with your approval, I assume."

"I signed on to some carrier suitability tests and they tacked on some small boat demo but no one was very willing to talk about it . . . TOP SECRET I'm told.

"I'm sure you'll be very interested in the concept and, of course, the results of this demonstration." Karl takes a peek over the bridge combing to find Eisenberg. "Come on with me for the briefing and demo."

"I guess I'd better see what's happening on my own ship. Mister Simonic, you have the con." Carbo tosses over his shoulder to his deck officer.

"Hell, You might even want one." Karl snickers. "Remember what happened to *Stennis* in the Persian Gulf."

Down on the flight deck Karl introduces Carbo to Eisenberg and Fogg and they proceed to a position on deck where they can view the F-18 simulating a cruise missile and the decoy when it is launched from the hangar deck. "Hey David. Give Captain Carbo a quick rundown on what we are going to see while we walk over to our viewing position in the forward, starboard catwalk."

"What you are going to see first, Captain, is an approaching F-18 which has been fitted with the *Harpoon* missile terminal homing radar. The pilot of this F-18 is following a guidance display fed by the homing radar. As the F-18 approaches ten thousand yard range the test decoy will be launched and your ship will turn sharply to port in an Anderson turn.

If the transponder works as advertised the F-18 will home in on the decoy . . . OH!"

"TARGET BEARING ZERO-SEVEN-FIVE, RANGE TEN THOUSAND YARDS." Blares the bull horn. "LAUNCH ZODIAC." Comes the order from the bridge.

"There goes the Zodiac." Shouts Eisenberg as he peers over the starboard catwalk. "Now, watch the F-18."

The lurch to port and list to starboard signal the start of the Anderson turn.

"He may still be below the horizon." Carbo comments.

"We'll see him when he executes his pop-up maneuver." Karl assures. "Oh! There he is now."

The F-18 pushes over from its pop-up and dives directly toward the Zodiac, missing *Vinson* by over two hundred yards.

The Point Mugu crew cheers as the F-18 disappears over the horizon to the west.

All eyes look to Captain Carbo.

"Hey, that was pretty good, Doctor." Carbo turns to Karl. "What do you think, Swenson?"

"I think I need one of these Tony." Karl starts. "But David needs support, both organizational and financial. I'm going to see what kind of support I can get through Admiral London. And you?"

"I'll work it, Karl. Perhaps we can make something happen."

"Thank you gentlemen." Dr. Eisenberg bows, ever so slightly. "I need all the help I can get."

*

Back at Eisenberg's office Karl is closing out his visit. "That was impressive, David. But I was just thinking; If you can make a little boat look like a carrier, maybe you can make radar targets disappear with your wave shaping."

"We've demonstrated that but that's as far as we've been able to go." Eisenberg responds.

"No interest."

"Are you telling me that what you have is as good as 'stealth'?."

"Yeah." Eisenberg breaks a smug smile. "And without special materials and paints. Just a black box - electronics."

"That's something to think about." Karl rubs his chin. "Can you get these packages manufactured in small quantities for fleet evaluation?"

"Yeah, Karl. We have a small shop that makes things like that for us." Eisenberg encourages. "Would you like me to get a price for those?"

"Yeah. Let's go for quantity thirty . . . Both boxes."

ELEMENTS OF AMPHIBIOUS STRIKE FORCE FIVE
PHIBRON5

USS *BOXER*, LHD-4 CRUISER

USS *COWPENS*, CG-63

USS PEARL HARBOR, LSD-52

USS RUSSELL, DDG-59

USS GREEN BAY, LPD-20

USS CROMELLIN, FFG-37

AMPHIBIOUS STRIKE FORCE FIVE
AIR ASSETS

MV-22 *OSPREY* LANDING

MV-22 *OSPREY*

SH-60 *SEAHAWK* HELICOPTER

CH-53 *SEA DRAGON*

AV-8B *HARRIERS* CRUISE

AV-8B *HARRIER* ON DECK

27
Deploy

USS *Boxer* off Point Loma
 Underway!
 Captain Swenson stands to starboard of the enclosed bridge scanning the tip of Point Loma with the high powered binoculars to find Marcia waving from the Cabrillo National Monument view point. He waves back, using a signal flag to make his wave visible - he hopes. *Well, here we are, separating again.* Karl muses. *And all with the turmoil around Taiwan and Indonesia, who can tell how long this cruise will last.* Karl smiles. *At least we had a nice month together in that little beach front apartment, enjoying the view, each other, and the charming little town of La Jolla. Hmm, gotta talk to the crew.*
 "Hello *Boxer*. This is the captain speaking. Hello *Boxer*. This is the captain speaking!" Karl speaks over the ship's address system. "*Boxer*, Stand at ease! I Congratulate all hands. You have brought *Boxer's* systems up to operational status and have worked through the pier-side shakedown. Now we'll finish the shakedown with aircraft aboard and operating. Again, a hearty WELL DONE!"
 Karl takes a drink of water. "Now on to our mission - at least the first leg of it: To Hawai'i to pick up our Marine Expeditionary Unit. Looking around us you can see that we have with us the cruiser *Cowpens*, the Amphibious Transport Dock *Green Bay*, and the Dock Landing Ship *Pearl Harbor*. We'll pick up the Guided Missile Destroyer *Russell*, and Guided Missile Frigate *Crommelin* at Pearl and we'll meet Attack Submarine *Omaha* somewhere en route . . . yes, SOMEWHERE. And our assigned *Poseidon* patrol aircraft will join us in WestPac and you'll find our two SeaEagle surveillance SUVs hanging from the overhead in the hangar deck.

"This afternoon, we'll receive all of our air assets, flying in from MCAS Yuma - *Osprey* short takeoff, vertical landing transport aircraft, two kinds of helicopters, and finally, *Harrier* fighter jump jets. For many of the pilots it will be their first time landing aboard a ship. Then, at Hawai'i we'll cruise around to the north side of Oahu near Makapuu Point to receive our Marine Expeditionary Unit using their ACLC . . . er, Air Cushion Landing Craft, and with the help of our embarked aircraft. And last, but certainly not least we will embark our Flag, Marine Brigadier General Aaron Foote, probably with the Marines from the Makapuu Bay Marine training base. He will fly his flag in *Boxer*." Karl takes a sip of water. "Now, I'll warn you once: Don't expect this, or any other, Marine general to tolerate sloppy or inappropriate dress or any conduct other than a strictly military bearing so we all have to shape up.

"We will receive fresh orders at Pearl and I expect them to send us to WestPac . . . we'll see.

"Thank you again for your excellent response to our surge deployment."

"TOOO-EEE. Now hear this. AIR DEPARTMENT MAN YOUR FLIGHT QUARTERS STATIONS FOR RECOVERY OF AIRCRAFT . . . NOW HEAR THIS . . ."

The air officer, Commander "Oz" Johnson, steps over to the bridge from PriFly. "Captain."

"Yeah." Karl turns in his chair. "What's up Oz?"

"Sir. we are expecting the first flight from Yuma in about twenty minutes. That'll be all twelve MV-22 *Ospreys* led by Colonel Cavallo." He looks over the bridge combing to see Lieutenant Commander Matsuoka and his crew huddled up. "Mats is ready for them."

"Sounds Good." Karl peers out the bridge windshield searching for the incoming aircraft. "How about the rest?"

"The next flight will be all the helicopters - eight SH-60 *SeaHawks* and nine MH-53E *Sea* Dragons." Oz pulls a piece of paper from his pocket. "They'll be here about an hour later. We're givin' Mats plenty of time to strike the *Ospreys* below." Oz shrugs. "We cut 'em a little slack the first time. Then we get our six *Harriers* a half hour later." Oz smiles. "It should be quite a show."

"Thanks for the status, Oz, but when do we get all squadron personnel aboard?" Karl slides out of his chair.

"Oh, yes sir." Oz steps back a little. "The air detachments will bring all their personnel, equipment, and spare parts on their aircraft, except for the *Harrier* detachment, of course. Their crew and equipment will come out on some of the helicopters or *Ospreys*."

"Oh yeah. That makes sense." Karl remarks. Then: "Mister Barnes. You have the con."

"Aye, aye, sir. I have the con." Lieutenant Barnes salutes smartly as Karl steps out onto the port bridge catwalk with Commander Johnson.

"This ought to be quite a show, skipper." Oz remarks proudly.

"I'll be here . . . watching with great interest."

"Oh! Here comes Horse's flight of *Ospreys*." Oz points off the port bow.

"Mister Barnes." Karl calls. "What wind do we have?"

"Five knots, variable, from West North West, sir."

"Sounds easy." Karl smiles. "Establish fifteen knots down the deck."

"Aye, aye, sir." Then the officer of the deck commands: "Helmsman, make your course two-nine-zero, signal speed ten knots."

"Two-nine-zero, ten knots, aye." The engine room telegraph rings and *Boxer* heels easily to port turning to her new heading.

Boxer's air detachments are recovered without serious incident.

*

Boxer, off Makapuu Point, Oahu

First class radioman Cross steps forward on the bridge. "Captain, sir."

"Yeah, what's up?" Karl responds.

"A message from Marine Corps Base, Hawaii, sir." The radioman hands Karl a sheet of paper.

"Thanks." Karl starts reading. "Oh, Cross, stay here. I may need to respond." Karl reads: "The commander, Amphibious Squadron Five requests transportation to *Boxer* today to depart NAS Kaneohe 0800. Request meeting of all PhibRon Five ship captains in *Boxer* flag plot at 0900. Acknowledge." *Whoa. the general is really moving in.* "Okay, Cross, take down this reply: 'To ComPhibRon5. How many in your party?'"

Karl calls the quartermaster of the watch: "Hey Chief, Get me the exec and the air officer."

Rad1 Cross returns to the bridge. "I have a reply, sir." He hands the paper to Karl.

Karl reads: "The General and staff total 24 with usual baggage plus approx 500 pounds of equipment." *Hmm. One MV-22 ought to do it.*

Commander Johnson, the air officer, enters the bridge. "You called sir?"

Deploy

"Yeah." Karl slips out of his bridge chair. "We will receive our PhibRon Five commander today at about oh-eight-thirty. First, you need to send an *Osprey* over to Kaheohe to pick up Brigadier General Aaron Foote at the Ops building and bring him back here." Karl hesitates. "Send Cavallo."

"Aye, skipper. Anything else?"

"Yeah, I want to see Horse before he launches . . . er, and get Mats to straghten up the deck spot - make it look like a parade."

"Okay, Cross, take down this reply: To: ComPhibRon5: An MV-22 *Osprey* will meet you in front of the ops building at Kaneohe at oh-eight-hundred. Pilot is LtCol "Horse" Cavallo, our air detachment commander." Karl Pauses. "Then address this to the commanding officers of all ships in the squadron: 'Brigadier General Aaron Foote, Commander PhibRon Five will arrive *Boxer* at oh-eight-thirty today. He has requested the presence of the captains of all PhibRon Five ships in *Boxer's* flag plot at oh-nine-hundred, today. Acknowledge by name and ship."

"Lieutenant Colonel Cavallo reporting, sir." "Horse" announces with a salute.

Karl returns the salute. "As you were, 'Horse'. Do you know what your mission is?"

"Aye, skipper. I'm supposed to pick up General Foote at MCAS Kaneohe ops building at oh-eight-hundred."

"Right!" Karl eyes "Horse". "But remember. General Foote is a tough old infantry Marine so be sure you and your crew comport yourselves in accordance with the highest traditions of the Marine corps. You know what those are better than I do. And remember . . . the general is our combat commander . . . and first impressions matter. Oh, who will be your crew?"

"Sergeant Major Hanlon and Lance Corporal Perez, sir."

"Pass along what I told you." Karl pats Cavallo on the shoulder. "Safe trip, 'Horse'."

"Thanks skipper." Cavallo scrambles down the ladder.

*

"What do you need, Cap'n." Commander Flintly enters the bridge.

"General Foote is coming aboard at oh-eight-thirty via one of our *Ospreys* - oh, there goes 'Horse' now." Karl eyes Flintly seriously. General Aaron Foote earned the nick name, 'Rarin' Aaron', in the battle for Kotkai in South Waziristan, Pakistan, where then Captain Foote led his company house to house to clean out the insurgency and earning a spot promotion to Major. He wants a meeting with all his ship captains in flag plot today at oh-nine-hundred. Consider this a test. I understand he is a stickler for proper dress and bearing. I want you to announce the general's arrival to the crew and emphasize that we need to make an excellent first impression. The general will be with us for quite a while . . . er, I already told Oz to police up the flight deck and sharpen the deck spot. You and I will greet the general and his staff . . . oh, and bring Chief Williams with you. You and Williams will escort the flag staff to their quarters an I'll take General Foote to his." *Hmm. I hope all the ship skippers will be there by then.*

*

Karl watches as 'Horse' brings his *Osprey* to a smooth landing on the recovery spot just opposite the island. General Foote hops out of the open side door of the *Osprey* and heads for the greeting party in a comfortable trot, demonstrating his excellent physical condition. His staff follows at a brisk walk.

General Foote is a small man standing about five-foot-eight and, with his athletic build probably weighs in at about a hundred, fifty-five pounds. His black eyes peek out under his fatigue cap to punctuate his words.

"Captain Swenson." It was not a question.

"Aye, General." Karl salutes.

General Foote returns the salute and reaches out to shake Karl's hand.

"General, meet Commander Flintly, my exec, and Master Chief Williams." Karl steps aside to bring Flintly and Williams forward. "They will take your staff to their quarters . . . and your ship skippers are all here except Commander Eason of *Crommelin*. He'll be here by oh-nine-hundred." Karl gestures toward the island. "I'll show you to your sea cabin so you can freshen up before your conference."

"Great." The general seems pleased. "Blaisdell, I'll need you and your yeoman in the meeting so find out how to get there."

"Aye, aye, General." Karl thinks: *I guess Captain Blaisdell is the general's ops officer.*

*

General Foote stands behind a table at the front of flag plot, facing the commanders of all the ships in his Expeditionary Strike Force. "Welcome, gentlemen. I'm glad we had an opportunity to meet and talk a bit before we get to the meat of this conference." The general moves to the chart board at the front of flag plot. "I hope you all met Captain Ted Blaisdell during our short discussion period. If not, here he is, my seamanship coach." The general turns to accent a Marine Colonel standing behind him. "And this is Colonel Sam Gocio, commanding our MEU . . . uh, Marine Expeditionary Unit."

The reaction varied from a scowl here, a spontaneous laugh there, and the stoic. Captain Blaisdell takes his seat at the table and motions his yeoman to the chair next to his.

"I'm sure you all will appreciate the fact that I have an ops officer who has commanded warships, since I have not. Captain Blaisdell just returned from a two year cruise as CO of the guided missile cruiser *Shiloh* during which he spent a lot of time playing cat and mouse with the Chinese. Where we're going that experience will come in very handy. I'll lean on him a lot to plan our sortées and direct our maneuvering."

"May I have the op plan, Ted."

"Yes sir."

General Foote sits down and opens the document. "Gentlemen, I have orders to proceed immediately to the vicinity of the island nation of Taiwan and prepare to counter any moves the Chinese may make to threaten Taiwan." He turns a page. "We will be supported by the cruiser *Shiloh* and guided missile destroyer *Mustin* . . . **BUT** . . . there will be no aircraft carrier in the region. We'll be on our own for air defense." The general surveys the ship captains seated before him. "Now gentlemen, this information does not leave this compartment. **Do you understand?**" General Foote nails each ship captain with his commanding glare.

"Aye aye, sir." Is the unanimous response.

"Good." The general is only partially satisfied. "But I repeat: The content of our orders does not leave this space. Nothing about our destination is passed on to **anybody!**" I want to emphasize: We're just cruising west." He eyes each captain one more time.

The general turns another page. "Now, back to air defense. Swenson, I understand you have just six *Harriers* aboard." He eyes Karl for a response.

"Yes sir, General. We started with a mix of aircraft that could be generally responsive to most situations. We can probably get more *Harriers*."

"I've already ordered six more, bringing you up to twelve." Foote smiles. "If that is too many aircraft for *Boxer* you can transfer some helicopters to *Green Bay* and *Pearl Harbor* or, failing that, we'll just leave some of 'em here at Kaneohe . . . but keep all the crews. We'll need 'em."

Karl stands. "General, we only have four night capable *Harriers* so perhaps you could press your source for eight . . . all night capable."

The general gives a wry grin. "I think we can do that. All of the six we have on order are night models."

"That will certainly help, sir." Karl thinks: *Hell, I'd rather have more AV8Bs anyway.* "So when can we expect the other eight *Harriers*?"

"They'll rendezvous with us at sea on our way to WestPac so shuffle the helicopters today."

"How soon will we know whether we get six or eight *Harriers*." Karl is concerned about getting too many. "I'd like to know as soon as possible so we can off load the two day *Harriers* to Kaneohe and retrieve the pilots."

"Do it!" The general is emphatic. "I'll get eight!" Then: "Now, Captain Blaisdell will give you the line of battle and our basic maneuvering formation."

*

28
Protocol

Boxer cruising West

"A command dispatch from CinCPac, sir." The radioman hands the sheet of paper to Karl.

"Thank you Cross." Karl glances at the message as Cross stands by. "Oh this message is for General Foote. Deliver a copy to him and come back here in case I need to reply." Karl looks up at Cross. "You already acknowledged, I presume."

"Yes sir. And I delivered a copy to the general."

"Good. You're dismissed, Cross."

Karl reads. *Hmm. Let's see what the CinC has to say. Well, this is specifically to Commander Phibron Five. Perhaps I shouldn't be reading this. Oh well.* "The mission of US Ambassador Pearson George to Taiwan did not produce any softening and its continuation to Beijing was no better. Making things worse Taiwan last week petitioned for a seat at the United Nations as the Republic of Taiwan. The ambassador is in Tokyo for discussions on this regional crisis.

"Proceed to Taiwan in accordance with your orders, meet with the Taiwan defense minister for a situation update and report your intentions to this command."

Well, I better check with the general.

The Marine guard salutes smartly as Karl enters the anti-room to the general's office. "Good day, Captain."

Karl returns the salute. "I need to see the general."

"Yes sir." The Marine turns to enter the office and Karl can hear the voices. The Marine returns immediately. "Please go in, Captain."

"Good morning, General." Karl hesitates. "I'm not sure I was supposed to get the dispatch from the CinC. Should we tighten up that channel, sir?"

"Not to worry, Karl." Foote smiles as he sips from a glass of water. "Cross delivered it to me first and I told him to get you a copy. We're a team Karl. You'll know everything I know and we'll discuss the mission and its progress frequently. I need your broad experience." Foote puts down his glass and eyes Karl. "So what do you think?"

"Well, thank you for your confidence." Karl loosens up. "This situation is no surprise, sir. Chiang seemed adamant when he first announced Taiwan's independence and I just didn't expect him to back down. Especially with all the internal problems China has right at this moment. A perfect opportunity for Taiwan to split."

"But we've got to back up Chiang's aggressive move to independence." Foote leans back in his chair. "And when I say 'we' I mean PhibRon Five - you and me - and the rest of the sailors and marines in this little force." He pounds his desk. "And we're alone. Our *Harriers* are all the air defense we've got . . . and China's army is big enough to wipe our marines off any foothold we might establish." He sinks a little in his chair. "We have our orders. Now it's up to us to succeed."

"Yes sir." Karl was a little surprised by the general's burst of emotion. "But I've got an idea that might alleviate the air defense problem anyway."

The general leans forward in his chair, regarding Karl with some skepticism. "How would you do that, Karl?"

"Well sir." Karl pauses to organize his thoughts. "You may know that *Vinson* came out of moth balls about the same time as *Boxer* but she won't deploy for about another month."

The general scratches his head. "So what's that got to do with us?"

"So that means that *Vinson's* air wing should be just about ready for deployment." Karl leans forward in his chair. "We might be able to get one of their fighter squadrons sent out here to be based on Taiwan to support us."

"Ingenious, Captain." The general gives Karl a curious look. "But how do we make that happen?"

"I know *Vinson's* skipper. I met him when I relieved him of command on *Rainer* last January. Carbo is his name, Tony Carbo." Karl stops to think. "You could send a request through channels for a fighter squadron and I could pulse Carbo about getting one of his. What do you think?"

"I think it's a hell of a good idea." The general punches his interphone

Protocol

and calls: "Mahmoud, call Captain Blaisdell and tell him I need to see him ASAP."

"Aye, sir. I'll get him." The voice scratches from the intercom.

"I want to get Blaisdell in on this." The general regains his enthusiasm. "We can work out a strategy together."

"You called, sir." Blaisdell steps into the general's office. "Oh. Hello Karl."

"Have a seat, Ted." The general waves toward an available chair. "Karl's got a good idea for improving our air defense posture in case we get further entangled in the Taiwan situation." He looks to Karl. "Tell Ted what you suggested to me."

"Okay, boss." Karl turns to address Blaisdell. "I was reflecting on meeting a Captain Tony Carbo upon relieving him of command of *Rainer* back in January. Carbo was off to commission *Vinson* just out of the shipyard and the last I heard he planned to deploy in September. I thought, perhaps, we could borrow one of Carbo's fighter squadrons and base it on Taiwan to fly fighter cover for us if and when we get invoved in conflict with the Chinese."

"Sounds like a great idea but how the hell do you expect to pry one of *Vinson's* squadrons loose?"

"Well." Karl collects his thoughts. "We can to a pincers movement involving an urgent request through CincPac while I make a call to Carbo."

"Hmm." Blaisdell thinks. "How cooperative is this guy Carbo?"

"Uhh ... " Karl squirms a little. "You might have found the weakness in the plan. Carbo wasn't exactly impressed with the idea of a reserve officer - me - commanding a big deck at sea. What do you think?"

Blaisdell glances at the general. "Perhaps just leaving Carbo out the loop. With enough urgency a request through CincPac, by itself, might have a better chance."

The general sits back and smiles. "Sounds good to me. Now you two get together and draft a message for me to send to Cincpac."

"We can use my office if you like, Ted." Karl offers.

"Okay, Karl." Ted stands. "We'll be back with a draft, General."

"There's no hurry." Foote remarks. "Just make it good. We don't want to get carried away before we talk to the Taiwan Defense Minister.

29
Taiwan

USS *Boxer* off the north tip of Taiwan

A CH-60 Seahawk helicopter lifts off of *Boxer* and heads south. General Foote, Captain Swenson, Captain Blaisdell, and Colonel Sam Gocio, commander of *Phibron5* MEU (Marine Expeditionary Unit) are aboard.

"Hey Ted." The general shouts over the rotor noise. "What's the program once we get to Taipei?"

"We'll land at the helo port at The American Institute in Taiwan, where a U.S. Consul has just recently been installed. The military attaché, U.S. Air Force Colonel Charlie Sun, will meet us there." Blaisdell reports. "Colonel Sun has arranged an appointment with the Republic of Taiwan or ROT Defense Minister at oh-nine-thirty. He'll be with us for the meeting and will translate for us as necessary."

"Is this Colonel Sun Chinese?" The general queries.

"Second generation." Blaisdell calls. "Born and raised in Kailua, on Oahu, he wangled an appointment to the Air Force Academy from Senator Inouye in the early two thousands." Blaisdell refers to a small pocket ledger. "After a couple of tours flying AC-130 gun ships in Afghanistan he has been posted to various embassies in the far east. He speaks the Mandarin dialect fluently, just right for Taipei duty."

"Sounds like we're in good hands." Karl comments.

Minutes later, the Seahawk descends slowly to the helicopter pad atop the American Institute as a single observer, a tall, lean man in an Air Force blue uniform observes from a point near the door that opens to the stairway to the Institute offices.

The helicopter sets down smoothly and the rotor continues generating a breeze below its disk while the ground crew chocks the wheels.

General Foote leaps from the side door and jogs in the direction of Colonel Sun, followed by Swenson, Blaisdell, and Gocio. Colonel Sun opens the door to the stairs and signals the party to follow him down to his office.

Inside his office the colonel invites: "Coffee anyone . . . or tea? "You'll understand that most people here drink tea."

"Yes, Colonel. I understand that." General Foote smiles. "I'll have coffee, thank you." "Coffee here." Karl follows.

"I'll try the tea." Blaisdell glances at Foote for a reaction . . . none.

"Coffee." Gocio responds.

A small Taiwanese enters the office, appearing to be a messman.

Sun addresses the native in Mandarin, Then: "He got it."

"Well, gentlemen. The "Taiwans" will be very glad you're here." The colonel is expansive. "Let me fill you in on the situation quickly." He glances at his watch. "It wouldn't do to keep the minister waiting." He takes a drink of water and begins. "The Chinese target at this time seems to be Chin-men Tao, uh, Kinmen, same thing . . ."

The messman enters with drinks and passes them to the visitors and Colonel Sun.

"Colonel Sun speaks a few words to the oriental and signals him to leave.

"Okay." General Foote interrupts. "Which should we call it, Chin-men Tao, or Kinmen?"

"Either one, General, Kinmen is the English but you should know both terms."

"Thanks . . . I think." General Foote with sidelong glances at Karl and Blaisdell.

Colonel Sun continues: "The PRC . . . uh, Peoples Republic of China . . . began an artillery barrage last month from nearby Xiamen to which the Taiwanese Kinmen garrison responded in kind. It was almost like a naval battle between warships because it's less than ten kilometers between the two islands. Last week the PRC took the west end of Kinmen under cover of the artillery barrage causing numerous ROT casualties and occupied some of the caves there,. There have been a few PRC air attacks which have complicated the defense of the island. Most have been repelled by the ROT Air Force." Sun pauses for a sip of tea. "Worse than that, the Chinese have just last week driven the ROT garrison out of its base and up into the mountains at the east end of the island. The ROT Air Force was successful in slowing the PRC advance across the island and currently harasses the PRC forces pursuing the ROT garrison forces. The battle is active as we speak."

"Sounds like the PRC is doing whatever it wants using very effective air and artillery support." General Foote opines.

Karl interrupts. "What kind of fighter and attack airplanes does China have?"

"Well." Sun begins. "Their top fighter is the Russian built Su-37 *Flanker*, thought to be the equal of any of the current American fighters, except F-35. And their Su-30 MKK *Flanker* is in the same category but with additional attack capabilities. Their supersonic J-10 strike fighter resembles the Swedish JAS-39 Gripin, with its delta wings and canard surfaces but we don't see many of those.

"Where are . . . " Karl begins.

"Whoa! We better get moving. We can talk more later." Colonel Sun urges while checking his watch. "The car is waiting at the main entrance." He picks his cap off the hat rack and leads the group out of his office.

*

The Republic of Taiwan Minister of National Defense Yao Ching-jun greets the visitors with a deep nod of his head without leaving his overstuffed executive chair. Colonel Sun introduces the visitors in his clipped Mandarin dialect and each of the visitors bows upon hearing his name.

The minister responds and Colonel Sun translates. "The minister asks me to introduce his Commander in Chief of all Taiwan forces army General Peng Yan-gang." Bows all around.

"Welcome to   Taiwan, gentlemen. The Republic of Taiwan appreciates the United States support in the face of PRC incursion into ROT territory." General Peng offers in perfect English, then: "Minister Yao welcomes you to Taiwan and offers tea . . . ?" He looks to the visitors for a response.

"Okay." Foote frowns. "When in Taipei do as the Taiwans do . . . to murder a well known phrase." He bows slightly to the minister. "Tea please."

"Tea, thank you." Karl follows.

"I'll have the tea." Gocio orders.

"The same." Blaisdell conforms.

Before any more words are spoken the tea arrives on a tea wagon pushed by a young woman in traditional dress. She serves the tea.

Minister Yao is a dominating presence even in his large office and even thought his shoulders barely rise above the desk top and his black squinted eyes seem to peek over the desk top to view the visitors as they take their seats in a sumptuous red brocaded couch and chairs.

The minister speaks in measured phrases, giving Colonel Sun a break now and then to translate his message.

Sun speaks, haltingly because of the breaks in the ministers speech. "Minister Yao welcomes you to Taiwan . . . and expresses deep appreciation of the Republic of Taiwan for the force you bring . . . The forces of the Peoples Republic of China have already taken full control of our island of Chin-men Tao. . . and have put troops ashore on the west end . . . These troops threaten to take control of the island . . . Do I understand that you come with a force capable of preventing such an invasion . . . He's waiting for a response."

"Minister Yao." The general begins and Colonel Sun translates. "Our Expeditionary Strike Force brings six thousand Marines . . ." He hears Colonel Sun repeating his message in Mandarin.

General Foote thinks: *I guess I'll just talk slowly and when Sun stops talking, I'll start again.*

". . . supported by *Osprey* vertical takeoff transport aircraft, helicopters, and . . . air cushion landing craft, . . . all to transport the ground force to the target." The general takes a sip of tea and tries to conceal the frown. "Helicopter gun ships and *Harrier* jump jets provide fire support for the Marines . . . and the *Harriers* provide air defense . . . We will have enough room to carry and deliver a division of Taiwanese troops too . . . if we can work out a defined mission for them so we don't have to communicate except at the top level . . . The languages you know. The one shortage we have is air defense . . . I may be able to get an F-18 *Hornet* squadron to fly out and support us . . . Would you have a suitable base?"

The minister sits up a little and speaks. Sun translates. "You are a self contained strike force . . . but we surely will add support . . . troops and air defense . . . May I suggest that we can handle your air defense . . . and perhaps some of your close air support to your troops . . . and ours?"

"Air defense?" Karl's eyebrows go up. "What kind of air defense can the minister offer?"

Sun turns to relay the question to the minister.

"Minister Yao says that he has three tactical fighter wings flying F-16 *Falcons* and F/A-18 *Hornets* which will be placed at your disposal for this operation."

Karl thinks the offer sounds too good. "Do we have a language problem?"

Sun relays the question. Then: "The minister advises that over half of his fighter pilots are trained in the United States - F-16 pilots at Luke Air Force Base and F/A-18 pilots at Pensacola - actually, I knew that. Those pilots are fluent in English and the rest have some English capability."

"Oh, yeah." Karl snaps his fingers. "I met one of them at my daughter's winging ceremony at Pensacola last month."

Colonel Sun translates and Minister Yao smiles broadly as he responds. "He says he is very pleased that you met one of his pilots and congratulates your daughter . . . and you."

The minister speaks and Sun translates: "He suggests that you meet with the Four-ninety-ninth fighter wing commander at Hsinchu air base . . . Wait, he's calling someone."

Sun listens to the phone call and then to the minister. "General Ma Chia-wen, the commander of the Air Combat Command, is coming over. Be here in a minute. General Ma speaks very good English."

"That'll help." General Foote sighs.

General Peng offers a plan: "You will be relating directly with our air force and Marines and when your Marines land on Kinmen you will encounter our Army garrison, perhaps somewhat scattered by now. We'll arrange for meetings with appropriate units of the Air Force, Marines, Navy, and Army today and, if necessary, tomorrow."

The door opens and a smallish Chinese in the uniform of a Republic of Taiwan general enters. He bows deeply as he reports to the minister and again to greet General Peng. Colonel Sun translates. "Oh, he wants me to introduce you." Sun proceeds with the introductions in English.

Minister Yao speaks to Colonel Ma. Colonel Sun translates: "He is directing General Ma to work with you in planning and executing air defense during the operation to protect the ROT from PRC invasion."

"Gentlemen." General Ma greets the *Boxer* party with a deep bow. "Suggest we go Hsinchu base and you get acquainted with Four Ninety-ninth wing commander and staff. I go with you."

"Wonderful!" General Foote exclaims. "We can take our *Sea Hawk* helicopter. It's parked on the U.S. Embassy. Will you come with us?"

"Thank you." Ma is delighted. "I ready in fifteen minutes. I call Colonel Chen and warn him we come and start some other action." Ma hustles out the door.

General Foote reminds us of our other objective: "Colonel Sun, we will also need to confer with the General in charge of the Taiwanese ground forces that will participate, and perhaps the Navy."

Colonel Sun translates for Minister Yao and relays the minister's reply. "Minister Yao advises that ROC Marine Corps headquarters is on the Naval Station at Tsoying, near Kaosiung, on the southwest coast. He suggests you do the Four Ninety-ninth wing this morning and the Marine headquarters this afternoon. It will take you about an hour to reach Tsoying by helicopter from Hsinchu. He just ordered General Peng to arrange meetings with the Navy and Marines at Tsoying, and transportation. From there we will go to Army headquarters at Hualien-T'aitung."

*

Headquarters, 499th Tactical Fighter Wing. Hsinchu Air Base

General Ma leads the group in to the wing commander's office. "Good morning, Chen." There are bows, salutes, then a handshake and the general turns to the *Boxer* party. "Gentlemen, this Colonel Chen Wei-kang, the Four Ninety-ninth wing commander." The three Americans bow in the Chinese custom and General Ma waves toward the trio. "And here Marine General Foote, Navy Captains Swenson and Blaisdell, and Marine Colonel Gocio of Amphibious Squadron Five, standing off Taiwan North coast ready to assist our defense."

A very small, lean chinese in a white steward's coat enters, pushing a tea cart.

"Tea, gentlemen?" Chen invites.

Everyone accepts and all are seated.

Colonel Chen leans toward General Foote. "We thank you for your response to our emergency in the face of PRC aggression. How can we assist."

"We want to support Taiwan's effort to defend against the threat from the PRC." General Foote continues. "You've got the plan, Ted, go ahead."

"As you know, Colonel, we have our own little air force - twelve *Harriers* - which are best suited to close air support to our Marines and to air defense over the target and the ship." Blaisdell picks a sheet of paper out of his breast pocket. "Your *Hornets* can best be employed in high air defense over the target and forward combat air patrol in the direction of the expected threat and over nearby PRC air bases." He awaits a response.

Colonel Chen strokes his chin as he mulls Blaisdell's proposal. Then looks to General Ma for support as his national pride builds. "Sir, that puts our air force in a purely support role. this is our country. We should be in the forefront of the battle." Colonel Chen trembles a little.

General Foote is not surprised by this nationalistic attitude so he tries to show understanding of Colonel Chen's patriotism. "Sir, I understand your wish that Taiwan forces be in the forefront of this battle so I emphasize that your Marines will be first ashore as we land support forces on Chinmen Tao, your fighter aircraft will be first to engage incoming PRC air attack and may be the first to fire a shot in this battle. Our *Harriers* will focus on supporting the amphibious landing by your ROT forces backed up by our Marines." General Foote looks to General Ma for a response, realizing that he left out a key element of the attack, that U.S. Marines aboard *Osprey* transports will land inland of the amphibious landing to provide the second element of the pincers movement against PRC forces on the island.

General Ma looks to Colonel Chen, quizzically. Colonel Chen looks to General Ma for guidance. General Ma replies with a gesture unrecognized by the Americans.

"Good plan." Chen comments, reluctantly, it seems. "It uses the best attributes of our *Hornets* and separates command authority to avoid confusion." Then, abruptly. "Where do we go from here?"

General Ma shows an almost imperceptible smile.

Karl takes over. "Sir, You have a fighter director officer." He phrased it as a statement but it was really a question.

"Of course." was Chen's reply.

"May I suggest." Karl begins. "That we take your FDO back with us so that he and our FDO can work out all the procedures, protocol, and radio frequencies to make the whole operation run smoothly."

Chen sinks a little in his chair, showing a full acceptance of the plan. Chen calls to his aide in Mandarin Chinese. The aide immediately makes a phone call. "Just a moment, sir, Colonel Tina is on his way."

Karl resumes: "It is important that your FDO understand the protocol we have agreed to here before we take him out to the ship to confer with our Fighter Director Officer, Commander Forrester."

Both General Ma and Colonel Chen nod in agreement.

"Well." General Foote addresses General Ma. "Captain Swenson will take Colonel Tina out to the ship so I wonder if we could impose upon you for transportation to your marine headquarters at the Tsoying naval base."

"Transportation is all arranged." Colonel Chen reports. "Major Peng called from Minister Yao's office."

Lieutenant Colonel Tina Tseng-chang arrives and is introduced to the Americans and briefed by Colonel Chen with occasional interjections by Karl to assure a full understanding of the agreements made earlier.

"Time for lunch." Colonel Chen announces and all leave the office to walk to the officers' mess.

30
Kinmen Tao

Boxer Cruising in Taiwan Strait

At 0400 *Boxer* prepares to launch aircraft for a combined air strike and amphibious landing on the Taiwanese island of Kinmen Tao, formerly known as Quemoy. Taiwan Air Force fighters are on station as forward combat air patrol on a line toward PRC air bases in the PRC Fujian Provence. The cruiser *Cowpens* and Guided Missile destroyer *Russell* are just opening fire on charted PRC emplacements east of the Kinmen airport in support of planned amphibious landing on the beach facing Liaolo Bay. Four *Harriers* launched an hour earlier provide target combat air patrol. The Yokosuka based Cruiser *Shiloh* and Guided Missile Destroyer *Mustin* will arrive in about an hour to participate in the Kinmen bombardment.

"Captain?" A Marine sergeant calls as he enters the bridge with a sharp salute.

Karl turns his swivel chair to face the marine. "What's up Sergeant?"

"A Message from Captain Blaisdell, sir." He hands the message to Karl and turns to leave the bridge.

"Hold it, Sergeant." Karl calls. I may have to reply." He reads: *The feed from our ScanEagle-C UAV shows a surface force approaching the Matsu Islands. General Foote has diverted Shiloh and Mustin to engage the PRC force and requests that you launch four Harriers to support. Acknowledge!* "Take this message, Sergeant."

"Aye, sir, I'm writing."

"To Captain Blaisdell." Karl begins. "As you know, we have eight *Harriers* ready for launch to support our landings on Kinmen. The other four *Harriers* are on station over Kinmen as target CAP, uh, combat air patrol. Any reduction of *Harrier* force at Kinmen could jeopardize the success of the amphibious landing. Have you contacted Colonel Chen to get support from his 449th Wing at Hsinchu? He will eagerly give support, and he has more airplanes than we do. I suggest we wait two hours for our Kinmen strike *Harriers* to return. By then the initial amphibious assault will be ongoing and we will know the situation at the target so we should be able to spare four *Harriers* to support *Shiloh* and *Mustin*. With all due respect, Ted, I think the Matsu incursion is meant to divert our support forces to make it easier for the PRC to hold Kinmen Tao. Detaching *Shiloh* and *Mustin* just plays into their hands. We need their fire power at the beach. Advise. D'you get that Sergeant?"

"Yes sir." The sergeant turns and departs.

The speakers blare: "Tooee." The Boatswain's mate announces: "Now hear this. Air department, man your flight quarters stations for launching aircraft . . . Tooee Now hear this . . . "

The officer of the deck reports: "Fifteen knots down deck center."

Karl hails the officer of the deck: "Mister Washington. Advise the air boss to hold the launch until I get a reply."

"Aye, aye, sir."

The first *Harrier* achieves full throttle and, at deck officer's signal begins his deck launch.

The bridge squawk box blares: "Sorry skipper. Oz here. That one got off before we could stop the action."

Karl keys the squawk box. "That's okay, Oz. Go ahead and launch the rest of the first division. We have to hold four until I get word from the flag. Quartermaster, get me Captain Blaisdell on the phone."

The squawk box blares: "Hello Cap'n, Oz here. The four *Harriers* we just launched are formed up overhead. What direction should we give them?"

"Hold it a second, Oz. I've got Blaisdell on the phone." Karl takes the phone from the quartermaster. "Hey, Ted. We're holding four *Harriers* overhead and four on deck awaiting further orders but *Ogden* and *Pearl Harbor* should be landing the Taiwanese amphib force on Hu-ch'ien beach right about now while our *Ospreys* are dropping ROT special forces north of Yahg-chai to engage the PRC occupying force at their rear. Both landings need *Harrier* support now . . . Oh! You got hold of Colonel Chen, good . . . So we can release our Harriers . . . Good. Hold for a second, Ted."

Karl punches the intercom: "Hey Oz."

"Aye Skipper."

"Launch all Harriers and release all eight to the beach!"

Back to Blaisdell: "Hey Ted, are we holding *Shiloh* and *Mustin* at Kinmen? . . . Yeah, that'll help, thanks . . . well, I hope the Matsu threat doesn't develop cause any diversion would jeopardize the Kinmen operation . . . Okay. Keep in touch."

The squawk box blares: "Hello Captain, CIC here." Commander Forrester calls.

"What's up, Dan?"

"Colonel Tina at the four ninety-ninth reports their forward combat air patrol has engaged a formation of twenty-four *Flanker* fighter-bombers west of Kinmen Tao, sixteen at angels twenty-five topped by eight at angels thirty. "Tina believes the *Flankers* at angels twenty-five are Su35 MKC fighter-bombers capable of carrying laser guided bombs similar to our GBUs and the ones at angels thirty are Su27s armed with *Sidewinder* type air-to-air missiles, pure fighters." Forrester pauses. "We designate that 'Raid one'". "Oh, also, the four-ninety-ninth is launching twelve *Hornets* to attack the surface force."

"Well, that'll help." Karl pauses. "Oh, what's the status of our eight *Harriers* at the target?"

"Fan three has just relieved Fan one over Kinmen. Fan one's returning to Fantail."

"Thanks, Dan." Karl concludes. "Keep me informed."

*

Minutes later the *SeaHawks* are on station at ten thousand yards, spread across the target line.

Call signs are based on *Boxer's* call sign, "Fantail". Helicopter calls are "FanHawk" plus a number as in "Fanhawk-twelve" for *Seahawks* and "FanDrag" plus a number for the MH-53 *Sea Dragons*, and "FanO" for the *Ospreys*. Harrier calls are "Fan" plus one or two numbers reflecting the aircraft's place in the squadron organization, as in "Fan two-three" for the section leader in the four plane second division. Altitude commands are given using "Angels" plus a number connoting thousands of feet.

A Marine sergeant enters the bridge, faces Karl and salutes. "Captain, sir. General Foote urgently requests your presence in flag plot."

"Okay, Sergeant. Go! I'll follow you. Mr. Washington, you have the con."

"Aye, Captain." Lieutenant Washington salutes.

"Greetings, Karl." General Foote greets Karl. "We just got a surprise from Colonel Gocio at the beachhead. Ted will fill you in."

"Yeah. This is a real surprise." Blaisdell starts. "Sam reports that the Taiwan Marines have encountered suicide strikes using their own Amphibious Assault Vehicles captured during a pause in the fighting." Blaisdell takes a long breath. "They just drove the AAVs, packed with explosives, into an assembly of ROT Marines and detonated their unorthodox weapons. They caught the ROT Marines while assembled for a briefing on the next action after they had apparently killed all the PRC defenders or driven them into their caves, or tunnels, whatever. Many ROT casualties . . . and a few of our own."

"Suicide attacks?" Karl is startled. "We didn't think the Chinese were into suicide."

"No. But here's the kicker." Ted pauses as if for effect. "The Taiwan marines captured a couple of the perpetrators and you'd never guess what they got."

"Thanks. I won't even try."

"Another extension of ilDauli in Asia." Another pause, then: "Jemaah Islamiya!"

"Hey!" Karl counters. "I thought that bunch had faded away with al-Qaeda back in twenty-twelve."

"We all thought that." Ted responds." It sounds like the resurrection of al-Qaeda as il-Dauli is collecting allies like Falun Gong in China and Jemaah Islamiya in Indonesia and flexing its muscles all over the world ."

"That may be." General Foote injects. "But we have to figure out how to defeat them on Kinmen. Get to work on that, Ted."

"Aye, General. We'll have the prisoners on board within the hour and perhaps we can find out more about the strength of their force and their mission and objective." A pause. "It wouldn't surprise me if they want Taiwan."

General Foote inquires: "Do we have a casualty report, Ted?"

"Yes sir, General." Ted begins. "Overall we have an estimated seventy-five ROT marines killed and forty-five wounded and fifteen US marines killed and six wounded. One Osprey and one MH53 *Sea Dragon* down." Blaisdell refers to notes. "The *Osprey* pilot was able to make a hard landing and discharge his troops but the aircraft is a total loss. All were lost in the violent crash of the *Dragon* after it apparently took heavy small arms fire while descending to a clearing to deliver troops to the fight."

"We better ready the meds." General Foote suggests.

"We've already notified the 'Inspector'." Karl responds. "With all the detail we had and we'll update that as we go along."

"Who the hell is the "Inspector". General Foote queries, somewhat derisively.

"Just Navy lingo for the senior medical officer . . . whose other title is "Health Inspector".

"I get it." The General grimaces. "Squid talk."

Laughs all around.

"ALL HANDS MAN YOUR BATTLE STATIONS . . . ALL HANDS . . . . ." The bull horn sounds.

"What the hell is that for." General Foote cries.

"I'll find out." Karl announces on his way out.

On the bridge, Karl demands: "Mister Washington, what the hell is the GQ for?"

"Mister Forrester in CIC reports our *ScanEagle* feed shows a naval force approaching from the North, consisting of two cruisers and four frigate type escorts.

"Start zig-zag." Karl shouts.

"We just started a zig-zag and we've called *Cowpens* and *Crommelin* back from the beach."

"Well done, Mister Washington." Karl remarks, then: "Get Mister Barnes up here, ASAP, and make ready the *Phoenix* for launch as needed." Karl orders. "Quartermaster, get me the air officer on the phone."

Washington reports: "Mr. Barnes is on his way, sir . . . And Commander Johnson is on the phone."

"Oz, we may expect a missile attack within minutes." Karl warns. "What aircraft do we have on board?"

"Four *Seahawks*, two *Dragons*, and four *Harriers* just back from a support mission to Kinmen Tao."

"Okay." Karl thinks a second. "Rearm the *Harriers* for ship attack and launch them for possible attack on the PRC naval force. Perhaps we can use the *Seahawks* as radar pickets. Get me Commander Forrester in CIC."

"Hey Dan." Karl calls. "How do you evaluate the naval threat from up north."

"Aye, skipper, I think those "cruiser types" have guided missiles." Forrester reports.

"We're launching four *Seahawks* and two *Dragons*." Karl announces. "I hope you can use 'em for something."

"I'll use the *Seahawks* for submarine search across the target line and to double as radar pickets and we'll send the *Dragons* to Tsoying Naval Base for their security." Forrester sighs, then: "Hey skipper, CIC here."

Forrester calls. "FanHawk six reports an inbound cruise missile, range, about twenty thousand yards, altitude fifty feet."

"Thanks Dan." Karl calls. "Mister Barnes; alter course to one-one-zero, speed twenty knots, order the flag bag to display the maneuver signal at the dip, and order the *Phoenix* crew to stand by for launch. And advise *Russell* to maintain station on target line."

"Maneuver signal acknowledged, sir."

"Execute maneuver!" Karl calls.

"Two block maneuver signal." Mr. Barnes orders.

"Launch *Phoenix* on course one-one-zero, max speed." Karl orders.

"Phoenix away, sir."

"Now!" Karl calls. "Commence Anderson turn to starboard, new course two-zero-zero."

As Boxer lurches into its Anderson turn Forrester in CIC calls: "Fanhawk-four reports submarine contact."

"Karl calls: "Pipe the CIC communications up to the bridge."

"Fanhawk four here. Sub contact is a PRC *Han* class. That's an old model, kinda noisy but capable of an attack."

"Fantail here, can you attack?"

"Problem, Fantail. *Omaha*, our sub, is shadowing the *Han*. If we launch a homing torpedo it might attack *Omaha*. Oh-oh! Sonar operator just heard a large explosion." A pause. "The sonar operator has recovered his hearing and reports that the *Han* is gone. *Omaha* must have gotten her with a torpedo. Oh! We're seeing a big white dome of water a thousand yards to the East. Aha, now the dome has subsided and we see some pieces of wreckage."

"Lookout reports *Russell* firing on incoming." Mr. Barnes reports.

An explosion is heard. "It's *Phoenix*." Barnes exalts. "The cruise missile took out our *Phoenix* . . . as advertised." A cheer rises from the bridge occupants.

"Hey Fanhawk four, the cruise missile reported by Fanhawk six just took out our *Phoenix*. No damage to Faintail. What's goin' on there?"

"Fanhawk four here, approaching the wreckage, searching for possible survivors."

"Whoa!" Forrester shouts. "Now radar reports raid two, bearing three-six-zero, angels twenty-five, about sixteen aircraft." Now: "Fan two and three. Form up and vector three-six-zero, angels thirty, Buster."

"Fantail, Fan two, Fan three is with me now so I have eight. Wilco vector three-six-zero, angels three-zero, buster."

"Hey Dan." Karl calls. "Where is Fan one."

"All four *Harriers* of fan one have been refueled and rearmed and are just now climbing out on vector three-five-five to back up Fan-two on raid two. "Now we wait." Forrester sighs.

"Oh!" Forrester gasps. "Tina at the Four-ninety-ninth reports his fighters have cut raid one down to three *Flankers* over Kinmen."

"Fantail, Fan-two here, Tally-ho, twelve *Flanker*, angels twenty, and four more at angels twenty-five. Fan-three, break right, we'll break left to bracket the lower *Flankers* and we'll see what the top cover does."

"Wilco Fan-two, I've got the bandits in radar contact."

Now, Forrester: "Oh-oh, Tina reports they've lost seven of their first twelve at raid one and the rest are still in a dog fight with the *Flankers*. They've splashed nine of the fighter-bombers." A pause. "Fan-one, Fantail, what's your state?"

"Fan-one is on vector three-five-five, angels thirty, have bogies in radar contact at my one o'clock, over."

"Faintail here, that's raid two. Fan two and three are already engaging the fighter-bombers. You take the top cover."

"Wilco Faintail. Have top cover in radar contact. Fan 1-3, break right, fire missiles at will."

"Faintail, this is Fan two, Fan two and three are engaging raid two."

"Fantail, Fan one here, I have two bogies on my tube . . . Locked on . . . Missiles away!"

"Fantail, Fan three, Splash two *Flankers* but we just lost Fan three-four . . . "

"Fan two here, splash three *Flankers*."

"All Fans, Fantail here, disengage and separate from raids so *Russell* can fire Standard missiles"

"Faintail, Fan two and three are disengaging . . . Fan one disengaging after flaming one more *Flanker*. Forrester calls: "Skipper, I think a couple of the *Flanker MKC* are leaking through. Stand by for possible bomb attack."

"Now hear this." The boatswain's mate is heard on the bull horn. "Prepare for possible bomb attack . . . Stand by for . . . "

EXPLOSION.

Bull horn blares: "Bomb damage and fire at frame one-one-nine, port, and at frame seven-five, starboard . . . on the island. Fire details away!"

Karl calls: "Mr. Barnes, get us a damage and casualty report ASAP."

Barnes: "The bomb strike to the after port fueling station is burning out of control. Fire detail is on the way. Bomb damage to the island includes severe damage to flag plot and numerous casualties."

Forrester reports: Fan two reports pursuing bogies retiring to the north and Fan one reports four bandits flamed. Our *ScanEagle-C* now shows a large explosion on enemy cruiser. That must be *Omaha* attacking with torpedoes and/or missiles from *Shiloh*."

Barnes reports: "The fire at the after port fueling station is under control and casualties from flag plot are being removed to sick bay."

"Mr. Barnes." Karl calls. "We need a casualty report."

"Aye, sir. I'm working it."

Forrester reports: "Fan one has splashed three *Flankers* but Fan one-three is lost to an *Flanker* missile. Fan one is pressing bomb attack on the PRC cruiser. *ScanEagle* shows the PRC Cruiser retiring to the north."

*

Retiring from the battle scene, Karl gathers his communications officer, Lieutenant Wilson and "Spark" Flintly, the *Boxer* Exec in his sea cabin. "We need to get a dispatch off to CinCPac with copy to ComPhibPac, describing the battle and its results, detailing enemy losses and our ship damage, aircraft losses, and casualties. You and Wilson put that together, Spark." A pause. "I'll dictate the part about our command shuffle. We'll meet back here in an hour to finalize the text. See you then."

Karl clicks the intercom. "Beizholtz, come in here. I need to dictate."

"Aye, sir."

"This will be the last part of my report to CinCPac." Pause. "Finally, among the casualties in flag plot were Brigadier General Aaron H. Foote, commander Phibron Five and Captain Theodore S. Blaisdell, operations officer, both killed by the bomb blast. Such losses require a broad revision of Phibron Five command structure. I have temporarily assumed command of Phibron Five and Captain Flintly assumes command of USS Boxer. I await your instructions as we proceed to Tsoying Naval Base, Taiwan, for ship repairs.

31
Diversion

Aboard *Boxer* alongside a repair ship at Tsoying naval base

Captain Swenson sits in his stateroom reviewing recent events in his mind. *Well, we've helped the Taiwanese to recapture Kinmen Tao from the PRC, unfortunately sustaining some losses: most notable, General Foote and Captain Ted Blaisdell killed by a ship launched missile; a couple of V-22 Osprey lost after delivering troops and one Sea Dragon helicopter lost with all on board killed, the worst personnel losses on Kinmen Tao coming with the suicide attack by the Jemaah Islamiya using explosive laden Taiwanese Amphibious Assault Vehicles they captured during the battle for Kinmen Tao. The Taiwanese Marines cleaned out the infamous tunnel matrix with a combination of the new* NAPALM *and explosives, and our Marines drove the PRC troops into the sea. Our sea-air battle with the intruding PRC warships and air raids put most of our resources to work: Our submarine, USS Omaha, sank a Han class submarine; Our SeaHawks got off a few Penguin missiles against the enemy naval force; our Harriers downed fourteen Flanker fighters and scattered the rest of one of the PRC air threats losing three* Harriers *but recovering two of the pilots the next day, while the Taiwanese Four-ninety-ninth Tactical Fighter Wing at Hsinchu air base blunted an attack by Chinese* Flanker fighter-bombers *from the west. Now Vinson has arrived and is on station off Matsu where PRC forces still threaten. Soon Taiwan forces will be able to take care of themselves.* A knock at the door.

"Who is it?" Karl calls.

"Wilson, communications, sir."

What the hell can be this urgent. "Come on in, Wilson. What have you got?"

"Sorry to bother you sir." Wilson offers with a slight bow. "This dispatch from CinCPac is marked 'Urgent for all commanders at sea and ashore - EYES ONLY'. Something about ilDauli."

"Thank you, Mr. Wilson." Karl is dismissive.

Wilson pulls a paper out of his case. "Please sign this receipt, restricted distribution you know."

"Hah! Guilding the lily. I guess I'd better read it if it's that urgent. Okay. D'you have a pen with you?"

"I think they're protecting sources of such sensitive material, sir. Here's a pen . . . Thank you, sir." LT Wilson departs.

Well, I wonder what could be in here that warrants this kind of secrecy. Karl tears open the large envelope and extracts the contents. *Hmm. Top secret. Title: il-Dauli Movement.* "Sources in Indonesia report a bloody coup in Jakarta last week. Abdul Wahid al-Ali, Grand Vizier to Süleyman III, led the charge on the government center and has assumed control of Java with the help of Jemaah Islamiya and announced his intention to subject all of Indonesia to *il-Dauli* reign. Meanwhile, one of our patrol aircraft reports *ilDauli* naval units transiting the Strait of Malacca, perhaps to reinforce the ilDauli hold on Jakarta and support the expansion of this incursion. This is clear evidence that Süleyman III intends to extend the *il-Dauli* hold on China to Indonisia and perhaps beyond." *Well. We have our own evidence of that with Jemaah Islamiya right here on Kinmen Tao.* Hmm. Karl muses. *We'll have to get a message off to CinCPac on our Jemaah Islamiya contact today.*

*

"Captain!" The officer of the deck calls on the squawk box.

"Aye, Mr. Barnes." Karl acknowledges.

"An approaching *Sea Hawk* is signaling the desire to come aboard. Markings suggest the aircraft is from *Vinson*, sir."

"Yeah." Karl sighs. "We heard *Vinson* is in the vicinity." Karl muses: *But what's this? Some messenger with Op plans?* "Is the air department aware?"

"Yes sir. We have a ready deck. Wind is ten knots on our port bow. Commander Johnson has readied the air department. He needs clearance from you, sir."

"Well. Mister Barnes. Who are these people and what are their intentions?

"I am advised, sir, that beside the helicopter pilot, two pilots from VFA-24 of *Vinson* air wing are aboard. They're squawkin' friendly."

("squawking" refers to the IFF, Identification Friend or Foe to identify the aircraft as friendly or enemy on ships' radar).

"Sounds okay to me." Karl rubs his chin. "Tell the air officer to bring them aboard - and I want to see the pilot as soon as he is aboard."

"Aye, aye, sir. Shall I send him to your sea cabin?"

"Yeah. Tell him to knock."

*

The knock. "Come in." Karl orders. The helicopter pilot enters and salutes. "By your leave, Captain. I am Lieutenant Gross, HS-31, off USS *Vinson*. You wanted to see me, sir."

"Aye." Karl replies. "What brings you to *Boxer*, Mr. Gross?"

"Sir, I brought a couple of pilots from VFA-24 who wish to speak to you."

"'A couple?' Well, who the hell are they, son?" Karl's impatience shows.

"Lieutenant Chapman and Ensign Swenson, sir." Gross reports with a little cringe.

"Well then, bring them in." Karl spits the order with a suppressed smile.

Gross opens the door and the two VFA-24 pilots burst in, come to attention, and salute. Then Ensign Swenson rushes forward to embrace her father. "Whoa!? Karl reacts to the smooch. "Not very official behavior Miss Swenson." They both burst into laughter and hug again. Karl pushes Karen away and holds her by the shoulders at arms length, looking her up and down. "You look terrific, honey." He releases Karen and addresses the couple with a sly grin. "To what do I owe this surprise visit?"

The young lieutenant responds: "Lieutenant 'Chip' Chapman, VFA-24, here, sir. I wish to ask you for your daughter's hand in marriage."

"Hmph! That was sudden." Karl frowns. "What the hell's the rush, kids?"

Karen steps in: "We love each other, dad."

"Well." Karl frowns. "That's nice but you are in an environment not suited to family life . . . in any way." Karl pauses. "Why don't we sit down and discuss this rationally."

Chapman starts: "Sir, Captain Carbo has offered to give us our own stateroom."

"Do you mind if I don't believe that?" Karl challenges. "I know Captain Carbo and I know him to be a hard headed Academy grad who holds to the letter and the spirit of the rules he learned there. I can't imagine that he would encourage you considering all the pitfalls that come with such an arrangement. I guess I'll have to call him. The least he would have to do is to transfer one of you off *Vinson*. The Navy doesn't take kindly to having multiple family members serving aboard the same ship." Karl pauses to take a sip of water.

"But sir . . ."

"Dad . . ."

Karl raises his hand to quiet the two. "Hold it! Try this thought: You know that if you just stay in your present status you can enjoy being together in what civilians would call 'dating' without violating Navy regs or being separated by the transfer of one of you."

"But Captain Carbo wouldn't transfer one of us, dad." Karen pleads.

"Yes sir." Chapman eagerly agrees. "He encouraged our marriage."

"Well, I'll remind him of his duty." Karl smirks. "He won't like a reserve telling him, an academy grad, what his duty is but I can handle that." Karl mellows a bit. "Come on, lets be sensible. I like you, Mr. Chapman, "Chip", and I love my dear Karen, so I'd like to see the two of you marry in the quiet surroundings you'll find in shore duty - it won't be that long."

Karen and Chip sit quietly looking at the floor until they raise their heads and their eyes meet as a tear betrays Karen's emotion and Chip wraps her in his arms.

Karl tries to avoid any sign of his feelings. "Now, let's all do the right thing."

"I guess you're right, dad - as usual." Karen whispers through her tears, then looks to Chapman for a reaction.

"What can I say." Chapman sags in resignation. "I guess I'll just say 'thanks for the advice', sir. And on the bright side I sense that we have your approval to marry on our next shore duty."

"You sense correctly, son." Karl pauses as he considers the thought. "Of course, I'd like to learn a lot more about you. All I know now is that my daughter loves you and you are a Naval Aviator, both plusses. But how about your family, education, any other job or jobs you have had, and your attitude towards having a family?"

"Do we have time for this, sir?"

"I have all day, Chip." Karl smiles. "Proceed."

"Hmm, family?" Chip thinks. "Well, our family is Protestant - er, Episcopalian."

"You're gainin' on it, son." Karl comments. "We're Whiskeypailians too." A snicker. "another plus - And?"

"I was born in a little town in Michigan. You wouldn't know it"

"Try me."

"Saugatuck, on Lake Michigan."

"Oh, yeah." Karl enthuses. "We had friends in Grand Haven, only about forty miles North of Saugatuck. We visited them a few summers when I was in high school. They raced inland scows, a sloop rig, on Spring Lake. They were fast. I enjoyed going out with them. Are you familiar with the scows?"

"Yes sir." Chip liked the way the discussion was going. "We sailed a lot up there during the summer, mostly in the E class."

"Karen jumps in: "Hey. We've got a Cal 25 at home. We keep it in King Harbor down by Manhattan Beach. Great for sailing the Pacific."

"Okay." Karl responds. "We got to Saugatuck. Where do we go from there?"

"Oh! My grandfather was raised in New Jersey and married a Danish girl."

"Danish, huh." Karl comments. "That's close to Swedish."

"He worked for Ilfor, the U. S. partner in the Swiss Cibachrome line of photo printing equipment and supplies . They promoted him to manager of the Ilfor central region and shipped him off to Grand Rapids, Michigan. I knew him after he had retired and moved to Saugatuck. He had installed a complete dark room in his basement with all the Ilfor equipment needed to make great color photo prints from slides. He used to let me 'help'". Chapman makes quotation marks with four fingers.

*

A week later: Captain Swenson is in his office reviewing the plan for repair of the battle damage to *Boxer*. There is a knock at the door.

Karl responds: "Who's there."

"Wilson here, sir. Have messages for you."

"Come on in Wilson."

Wilson enters with: "Congratulations, Commodore." And hands the messages to Karl.

"Thanks, but aren't you a little previous, Mister Wilson."

"No sir. Just read the first dispatch."

Karl scans the first dispatch: *Hmm. Says here: 'One. On this date The President of the United States temporarily appoints you to the rank of commodore . . .'* Then comments: "I guess you're right, Wilson. Now what's in the other messages?"

"Here." Wilson hands the messages to Karl. "Here."

Karl scans the second message: *Well, here it is: 'One. In accordance with reference (a), you are hereby officially designated Commander, Amphibious Squadron Five reporting directly to the Commander in Chief, Pacific Fleet.* As he scans the rest of the message he picks up the third and begins scanning it. "Well, Wilson, I didn't expect this. It calls for my attendance at a 'Star' conference' at Pearl. Hmm. Sounds like the normal 'charm school' for new admirals and commodores. Thanks Wilson . . . And thanks for the congratulations. I guess you're the first to know."

32
Reunion

A week later at Marine Corps Base, Kaneohe, Hawai'i

Commodore Karl and Marcia Swenson sip a cocktail before ordering dinner at the Officers' Club while enjoying the beautiful view of the Pacific Ocean beyond the Kaneohe Klipper golf course.

Karl's cell phone rings. He opens the phone and sees that the caller is his daughter Ensign Karen Swenson. "Hi Karen, What's up . . . Oh no! Whoa Karen, We're in the Kaneohe O' Club dining room. Hold on while your mom and I take this out on the Veranda." Karl turns to Marcia. "Bad news from Karen. Let's slip outside."

"Okay, Karen, we're on the veranda and I have the phone on 'speaker'."

Marcia calls to the phone: "Hi Karen, what's up?"

Karen's tearful voice comes on: "Dad, you know Chip Chapman . . . He was . . . Gasp . . . I can't say it . . . Oh! He was, er, killed, sob, today . . . Sniffle."

Marcia absorbs the message slowly. "Oh! That's terrible. Your dad has told me about Chip and you . . . Ohh, you must be terribly hurt."

A messman approaches. "Would you like to order out here, suh?"

Karl turns a little irritated. "No! Just stand by. We'll be in shortly."

Karl chimes in: "How did it happen, Karen . . . Can you talk about it?"

"Dad . . . Sob . . . Chip's division, including me, was on patrol near Matsu when four Chinese *Flankers* jumped us. I caught a missile from one of them and bailed out."

"Oh! That's terrible." Marcia cries. "Are you hurt?"

"I'm okay, mom. Just a little shrapnel in my right arm and leg . . . I'm in sick bay right now. "

Reunion

"Is that good, Karl?" Marcia probes.

"A hell of a lot better than still being in her life raft."

"Then what, honey? Karl presses.

"I understand that Chip and the rest of the division shot down the *Flankers*. I landed in the open ocean and got in my life raft with no problem and it was just moments before Chip and the others were circling over me. That was reassuring considering the Chinese could be coming out to strafe me in my raft."

"That all sounds pretty good, Kaykay. Karl comments. "So what the hell happened to Chip."

"Well, after a while another one of our squadron's divisions showed up to relieve Chip and the rest of our division until the SAR 'copter arrived. But Chip stayed . . . To be sure I was protected, I guess. He finally left, by then probably very low on fuel. I'm told he . . . Gulp . . . ran out of fuel in the groove and crashed on the round down. His airplane fell back into the ship's wake and he was . . . gone . . . Sob."

Karl regroups. "Do you feel well enough to travel, honey?"

"I feel fine, dad, but I don't know how long they'r going to keep me here. Why?"

"Well, I'm here for a planning session, quote, for a week, and your mom came out to join me here at Kaneohe. Just get a week's leave and come join us. You need a break to heal your wounds . . . Both physical and emotional. Perhaps family can ease the pain."

"Hey! I've got an idea." Marcia calls. "Harm's unit is in Canada for R&R right now and his unit has orders to return to the Balkans to join 'KFOR', the NATO peace keepers in Kosovo. Perhaps he could get permission to come by Hawai'i on his way. We could have a real family reunion."

"Okay, Mush." Karl interjects. "You work on that. See if Harm can get here this week, while Karen is here . . . We hope. I've got a meeting at CinCPac tomorrow morning, early. No tellin' how long that process will take." Karl shifts back to Karen. "Okay, Kaykay, try to get back here, tomorrow if you can, keep your mom informed of your arrival details so we can pick you up."

*

HEADQUARTERS, PACIFIC FLEET COMMAND.

RADM Swenson approaches the reception desk and is greeted by a chief petty officer. "Good morning Commodore. Welcome to Pac Fleet. What brings you here, sir?

"I have orders to report to CinCPacFlt for and 'planning conference'." Karl unbuttons his blouse enough to extract a large manila envelope and hands it to the chief. "Here."

"Thank you, sir, I'll have these orders processed. Now, follow me."

Down a passageway to a door with a sign announcing: "CONFERENCE IN SESSION". The chief keys the key pad, the door lock clicks, and he opens the door and addresses the admiral in the room. "Sir, this is Commodore Swenson, Phibron Five, Commodore Swenson, this is Admiral Fredrick Frost, Commander in Chief, Pacific Fleet."

Admiral Frost is a tall man, about six foot, four, with short cropped hair, and a severe, almost pinched face. He shows an easy manner while clearly in command.

Karl advances to offer his hand. "Good to meet you, sir. I hardly know what to expect."

"Well, first, let me offer condolences to your daughter from me and the entire command staff for the loss of her friend Lieutenant Chapman in combat off Matsu Island and our sympathy for her own wounds. Have you talked to her?"

"Yes sir. Last evening just as Mrs. Swenson and I were sitting down to dinner at the Kaneohe O' Club. She's a little shaken but I think she'll be Okay. I suggested she take a week's leave and join her mother and me here."

"I'd like to meet her after she recovers a little." A fatherly smile.

Karl shows a smile of relief. "Thank you sir. Name a time and place and we'll be there."

"Now let me dispel any thought that this is a 'charm school' for a new promotion." Admiral Frost breaks wry smile. "Our purpose here is to outline a new mission for your Phibron Five." He turns to the two officers standing at the table. "Here are the primary movers of the concept for your next job, Captain Imo "Ziggy" Zymantz, my operations officer, and and Commander Earl 'Van' Vanderjagt, planning. No one else is involved, and will not be. We're holding this plan at the highest security level. Ziggy, give Commodore Swenson the broad outline of your plan."

Captain Zymantz has a appearance typical of some Balkans; very tall, about six foot, nine, and lean; the hawk like nose, long forehead, and a healthy shock of brown hair. As for Commander Vanderjagt, think of a guard on the Naval Academy Football team. Six feet tall, about two hundred thirty pounds, with a round pock marked face, a muscular neck, and cold gray eyes.

"Yes, sir." Captain Zymantz motions to a chair at the table. "Have a seat, Commodore."

"I'll stay with you for a while." Admiral Frost announces as he takes the chair at the head of the table.

Zymantz begins. "I think you'll find this concept quite bold. Its objective is to capture or kill Sultan Süleyman Third."

Karl is visibly shaken. "Whoa! That's a large order."

"But our plan **is** achievable. You'll see." Zymantz begins. We call it Operation Topkapi, or just OpTop. The first challenge is to create an opportunity to get Süleyman and the key to success is complete surprise."

"Yes." Admiral Frost interjects. "That means we must develop a diversion to cover the mission execution at Istanbul."

"Excuse me, sir." Karl turns to Admiral Frost. "At this point Phibron Five is a hell of a long way from Istanbul. I'd guess about three weeks at max cruise. Couldn't Sixth Fleet handle this a lot easier."

"Two problems with that." Frost notes; "Sixth Fleet has no Phibron at this time and won't have one for at least another year; and Sixth Fleet ops, even in its diminished state, is closely watched by *il-Dauli*, making it nearly impossible to succeed."

Zymantz continues. "Don't worry about the distance, sir. We have a diversion that can get us within striking distance and another that can cover the actual OpTop if it develops properly."

Karl muses. "So I guess the plan now constitutes an objective, capture Süleyman Third, and a tool, Phibron five. But it seems we've got a long way to go."

"The idea." Zymantz responds. "Is to take advantage of some natural disaster in the neighborhood of Istanbul to which Phibron Five will respond, with humanitarian aid, a U.S. NAVY mission with considerable precedent."

Karl raises his hand. "As I said, that's a long way to go from Taiwan. Not a quick response to a natural disaster, whatever it is."

Commander Vanderjagt enters the conversation with a smile. "We just take it step by step." He lays a chart on the table with South toward Karl. "Of course you are aware of the Somali pirates' continuing sporadic action in and around the Gulf of Aden, here." He uses his pointer to circle an area covering the Gulf of Aden and a large swath of the Indian Ocean. "These guys continue their piracy in this area with only occasional interference by individual nations through either hesitant naval action or financial countermeasures, heh, mostly ransom payments." With a knowing smile to Karl he continues: "Phibron Five could be ordered to intervene in this action at any time . . . at our convenience."

"Clever." Karl smiles. "That puts us within reasonable steaming time to the target. But what sort of authorization would we need to take action?"

Zymantz breaks a wicked smile. "None! As a matter of fact you wouldn't need to take any action at all to make this appear as a bona fide attempt to deter piracy. But once you get there it may be possible to obtain authorization to take out one or more of the pirates' bases; Eyl, the purported pirate headquarters; Hobyo; or perhaps Boosaaso on the North coast of Somalia. Meanwhile, you have been able to move to within reasonable range of our objective."

"Hmm." Karl muses. "Okay, so we got closer. What's next?"

"Do you know how many earthquakes they have in and around Greece?" Van inquires.

"I haven't the slightest." Karl confesses with a confused look. "Why?"

"About fifty per month, consistently."

"Per month?" Karl is taken aback. "That's pretty heavy. How do they survive?"

"Most of them are of pretty low magnitude, three or under." Van continues. "And in the last century the Greeks have built their buildings to resist earthquake damage so they survive these little shakes with little or no damage or casualties.

"So what's all this got to do with the OpTop?"

"Not much 'til you factor in the frequency of major quakes - those over six on the Richter scale." Van places a sheet before Karl. "Note that there have been ten quakes magnitude six or more in Greece in the last ten years - about one per year . . . And they haven't had one this year."

Karl scratches his head. "How does that affect OpTop."

"Here's how." Ziggy responds. "After PhibRon Five gets to the Gulf of Aden you can just bide your time alternately harassing the pirates and laying up at Djibuti, the only friendly port in the area." Ziggy spreads his arms. "And wait for the next significant Greek earthquake. It should take you about three of four days to get there with humanitarian assistance."

Karl nods and smiles. "We're close. What next?"

Admiral Frost develops a wry smile. "You deliver humanitarian aid to Greece in the daytime and snatch Sülyman by night." Frost gives his wicked smile. "The detail of the assault plan is up to you."

"But, sir." Karl pleads. "If I can't tell anyone how can I staff a plan."

"Wait for the earthquake warning and plan it during your transit of the Suez canal." Frost smiles. "You'll have three or four days. That should be enough."

"Okay." Karl nods. "But you will issue orders for each of our major movements with specific objectives for each phase, right?"

"Yes, of course." Frost nods toward Zymantz. "Ziggy will handle that, in accordance with the plan. And there will be no communications regarding the OpTop itself." He fixes all three with a firm stare. "Now we'll all go about our normal duties."

"Wait." Karl intercedes. "I hear there is a quiet prop-rotor being tested on an MV22 *Osprey* at Pax River. We'll need the best they have for insertion of our marines into Topkapi." A glance at Admiral Frost. "As Ziggy said 'surprise'. Our *Ospreys* are so damned noisy they couldn't surprise anybody in those close quarters."

"We'll work that problem." Frost responds. "Ziggy, get me the status and prognosis for the quiet *Osprey* program at Pax. We'll need a bunch of those propellers within the month."

"'Bunch' meaning twenty, sir." Karl interjects and Frost nods approval.

"Aye, aye, sir." Ziggy responds.

"Just one more thing, sir." Ziggy interjects. "I think you'll need a SEAL squad to pull this thing off. But you can't carry them all the way from Taiwan to Greece. They would definitely raise questions among your crews."

"Good thought Ziggy." Frost replies. "How can we handle that, Swenson?"

"Not to worry, Admiral." Karl injects. "Three or four of our marine platoons are trained and experienced in special warfare skills and our Colonel Gocio came from special ops. They can handle the caper at Topkapi, sir."

"Well, that was easy." Frost sighs. "Okay, Swenson, I'll get back to you about you and your family coming over for dinner."

Admiral Frost stands and all salute as CinCPacFlt departs.

*

33
Balkan Surprise

THE OFFICERS' CLUB AT MCAS KANEOHE

As Karen and Harm exchange news about their respective situations in the lounge, Karl returns from his conference at CinCPac and greets them both with hugs and an arms length view of each with an immodest demonstration of pride and love for them both.

"Kaykay, you seem to have recovered well from your wounds." Karl remarks.

"Yeah, Dad, I'm okay." Karen diverts her eyes. "But I keep thinking about Chip." A little tear wets her cheek.

"And you, Harm." Karl touches Harm's sleeve. "You got promoted again, congratulations, son."

"Thanks, Dad." Harm feels the chevrons. One chevron below Master Sarge. I'm workin' in battalion headquarters now . . . But look who's talkin'. The one with the wide gold. Congratulations, dad. I just knew you'd do it some way." Harm salutes.

Karen chimes in: "Let's hear from Harm. He must have some harrowing stories."

"'Harrowing' it's not." Harm responds. "'Boring' maybe. Confusing is more like it. Hey, we've got Kosovars, that covers everyone inside Kosovo borders, Serbs hold forth in certain enclaves in the North and South, and most other Kosovars speak Albanian. No wonder they won't talk to each other, they can't."

"I'm hearing that there is some talking going on." Karl nudges.

"Yeah, some." Harm scratches his neck. "I hear the U.S. Secretary of State . . . is it John Borden?"

Karl: "Yeah that's him."

"Well, I hear he has been doing some shuttle diplomacy in Pristina,

Kosovo; Belgrade, Serbia; and down in Tirana, Albania. Seems he's pushing some split-up of Kosovo between Serbia and Albania."

"How could that work?" Karl is flabbergasted. "What's in it for the Kosovars?"

"The rumor mill says Pristina's affinity for Albania is part of it, based on language, I guess . . . maybe access to the sea." Harm struggles to get out what he knows. "In Borden's plan, er . . . Serbia gets the Serb enclaves in Northern Kosovo, uh, around Mitrovica, Albania gets the rest of Kosovo, and Pristina gets easy access to Albanian ports for its commerce in all kinds of products . . . not to mention its heavy drug trade."

"Gad!" Karl exclaims. "I don't see how that could fly."

"Stranger things have happened in the Balkans, Dad. There's supposed to be a meeting in Pristina in a week or two. Apparently the Serbs and Albanians have agreed to meet, at least. We'll be there by then."

"Hey, you guys." Marcia asserts herself. "It's almost nineteen hundred - time for dinner."

34
Pirates

ABOARD USS *BOXER* IN THE INDIAN OCEAN

In the period following Karl's trip to Hawai'i he has returned to find all the ships of his PhibRonFive brought back to combat readiness; battle damage repaired, crew billets filled, aircraft losses replaced, and command staffs rebuilt. LtCol Horace H. Cavallo has been promoted to full colonel in the Marine Corps and brought into Karl's command staff as operations officer.

Col Cavallo, the "Horse" sits with Admiral Swenson in flag plot discussing the latest intelligence and orders.

"Hey Skipper, I don't understand what we're doin' here in the Indian Ocean."

"Watchin' the pirates, Horse." Karl replies with a wry smile.

"Yeah, but." Horse grouses. "There are ships here from every navy in the world. What the hell are they doin."

"Actually, Horse." Karl responds. "Some of them have actually taken action against pirates in certain circumstances."

"Yeah, but even if a pirate is high-jacking a ship around here, what can **we** do?" Horse grouses. "Between the UN restrictions and the constraints our state department puts on us we couldn't take action if pirates were acting right under our noses . . . And they know it."

Straining for a rationale, Karl finds a retort. "But you must remember that incident a few years ago when our Navy SEALs took out a small group of pirates in the act of commandeering a US flagged freighter and threatening to kill the captain."

"Yeah, I remember." Horse frowns. "But things have changed. Our restrictions have gotten tighter. What would we do if we found a US flagged ship being high jacked."

"I think we'd be authorized to take action." Karl replies, somewhat sheepishly.

"Well, here we are in range of the pirates' headquarters at Eyl with all the force we would need to take Eyl and cut off their supplies." Horse avers. "But I'll bet we don't get cut loose to do that."

"You're probably right." Karl thinks to himself. *Hmm. I know we should avoid entanglements like that. Such an action could deplete our capability for taking out Süleyman, our primary mission.*

*

A WEEK LATER - PATROLLING THE INDIAN OCEAN

A knock at Commodore Swenson's door.

"Come in." Was Karl's response.

The staff communications officer, Commander Phil Estes, a holdover from General Foote's staff, enters. Estes is a small man with balding hair and a sallow face. He approaches Commodore Swenson's desk. "Sir. We just received an encrypted message from CinCPac addressed personally to you. The transmission directed that, when decoded, the message be classified TOP SECRET and EYES ONLY. I decoded it myself." He hands the envelope to Karl.

"Thanks, Estes." Karl scans the envelope. "I guess I have to sign this receipt." It was not a question.

"Thank you sir." Estes departs.

"Hmm." Karl eyes the classification and thinks while he opens the envelope: *This can't be about OpTop. Admiral Frost absolutely forbade any communication on that subject.* "Oh! It's not about OpTop." Karl reads:

UNITED NATIONS ACTION ON PIRACY

Today, in a secret meeting at the United Nations, the permanent five members of the security council plus India and Japan, mindful of the increasing cost of interdicting Somali pirates over a broad area of the Indian Ocean, reversed their position on piracy.

Japanese Ambassador Ichihiro Hashimi suggested it is time to strike and hold the pirates' base ports to cut off supplies and new recruits. He argued that there was, currently, enough naval and amphibious power in the area to succeed and stop the Indian Ocean piracy. Further, he reminded members that the United States now has an Expeditionary Strike Group in the Indian Ocean which could lead an international force to strike known pirate havens along the Somali coast.

UK Ambassador Nigel Hopwood's motion for the inclusion of the Australian ambassador was seconded and passed. And he was called.

Mobilize!

French ambassador André Rémy objected to Hashimi's proposal on the basis that such an operation would place at risk those many hijacked crew members held prisoner in the pirates' enclaves. Countering, U.S. Ambassador George Washington Carver pointed out that U.S. Marines are trained in envelopment tactics which, on many occasions, have permitted the capture of insurgents while preserving the lives of their captives. He further noted that U.S. Secretary of State John Borden has received pleas from the Somali president for assistance in coping with the pirate problem which has ties to il-Dauli.

After some discussion, the "perm 5 plus India, Japan, and Australia" agreed with Ambassador Hashimi's proposal and U.S. Ambassador Carver did not hesitate to offer the commander of the U.S. Expeditionary Strike Group in the area as leader of an international force made up of willing members' naval assets. Karl takes a deep breath: "Wow! That's me!" Then reads on:

Expect specific orders from this command within hours.

Karl steps to the office door, opens it, and calls: Hey Horse, can you come in a minute?"

"Sure." Horse comes in and closes the door. "What's up skipper?"

"Karl, with a wry smile answers: "Your prayers have been answered. Read this . . . and note the classification."

"Okay." Horse moves to leave the office.

"No." Karl admonishes. "That document does not leave this office."

"Aye, sir. Then I'll just stay here and read."

"Good. Tell me what you think after you've read it." Karl picks up another piece of communication.

After a few minutes Horse reacts: "Wow. Big job, boss. Where do we start."

"First." Karl begins. "I expect our orders will spell out exactly what nations will be participating, name their designated commanders, and establish communication protocol." Karl pauses to think. "First, we'll have to find a meeting place accessible to all the commanders yet thoroughly secure, and a place that will not raise questions. I suspect that the extent of participation will be limited to ships from the 'Perm five' plus India, Japan, and Australia. The 'perm five' are China, France, Russia, the UK, and the USA." Another pause. "Think about that, but don't involve any of the staff at this time. I'll let you know when we get orders."

*

A few hours later. Karl is in flag plot discussing pirate sightings with his intelligence officer.

Commander Estes enters and approaches Karl. "I have two dispatches, sir. May we go in your office?"

"Yeah. Come on in."

Inside the office, Commander Estes delivers one envelope marked TOP SECRET and another marked CONFIDENTIAL.

"Thanks, Estes. Here's the receipt. You may go now, Phil."

Karl opens the TOP SECRET envelope, scans the contents, and immediately punches his intercom box; "Hey Horse, come on in here."

"Aye, sir" is the response.

Karl cuts open the CONFIDENTIAL envelope and reads the brief despatch: *Hmm. Subject: Temporary appointment . . . Pursuant to . . . etc . . . etc . . . President temporarily appoints you to the rank of Rear Admiral, lower half to rank from . . . well, this is a surprise.*

A knock at the door. "It's me Horse."

"Come on in, Horse . . . and close the door. Here, read this."

"Huh." Horse shrugs. "About as I expected. We get the UK, India, Australia, Japan, and I didn't think Russia would opt out. They're in. The Bear has interests in this region."

"Yeah, we can use them." Karl shrugs. "They just have a cruiser in the area but they have commando type troops aboard. They could spearhead an amphibious landing with British Commandos at Boosaaso and we can use them for bombardment if necessary."

"It seems to me that the Aussies should lead the operation at Hobyo since they have a good amphib capability." Horse suggests.

"Good idea." Karl mulls the thought. "And the two Japanese destroyers can support the Hobyo operation. What do you think.?"

"Makes sense to me."

Karl proposes: "Surprise! That leaves PhibRon Five to take the lead at Eyl. The info we have says that the pirates' main body is there . . . and the hostages are there too. Fortunately, we have intel that shows us exactly where they are held."

"Yeah." Horse agrees. "And Eyl is split into two parts, Dawad up in the foothills and Badey at the sea shore. We'll have to cover both of them."

"And once we rescue the hostages and pacify the town we'll need a force to take over the town." Karl shows a wry smile. "That's where the Indians come in. We put them in right after our marines land." A satisfied sigh. "Then after a few days we can retire to our Djibuti base and leave the Indians to run the town."

"Great idea, boss." Horse exults. "And we can put the hostages back on their ships to continue to their intended destinations."

"That's a good idea, Horse, I guess we can hope they will be in good enough shape to take over their ships." Karl thinks. "If not we can contact the ship's owners to get fresh crews."

"Okay, Horse." Karl exhales a big breath. "That's your plan outline. I'll need a plan by eighteen hundred."

"Aye, sir." Horse begins to leave the office.

"Hold it Horse!" We've got to find a secure meeting place where we can brief the plan to all the commanders."

Horse brightens. "I think the naval base at Diego Garcia is the place. I already contacted the commanding officer, a Captain Pace, and he was very receptive. He guaranteed that no one would know we're there."

"What secure facilities would we have?" Karl queries.

"The Air Force fiftieth space wing has a GPS station there." Horse replies. "It is a very secure operation, Captain Pace assured me."

"Sounds interesting." Karl mulls the idea. "But it would take us at least a day and a half to get there." A pause. "Here's a thought: We could host a 'Commanders Conference' on *Boxer*. (Quotations by Karl's fingers). Just a get-acquainted session, right?" "We just invite the participating commanders. A nice dinner in the wardroom followed by a conference in the flag plot conference room to assign operational tasks." Karl looks to Horse for a reaction.

Horse mulls that idea for a minute, then: "How do we keep **that** a secret, skipper?"

"We don't." Karl shows a wry smile. "We even invite our embedded corespondents to the dinner. They'll be excluded from the conference using the standard national security excuse and then they'll get a press briefing on the mundane elements of conversations that fit our surveillance mission." Karl smiles again. "You can do that. Right?"

"Aye, aye, sir. Can do."

"Okay, Horse. There's no time to waste. Get back to me by eighteen hundred with the outline of an operation plan for the assault using all the participants and a plan for the dinner and 'Commanders' Conference'. Heh." Karl is pleased with the progress. "Remember, your op plan must, at the least, identify prime targets and delineate specific assignments to each participant. A primary objective must be to avoid civilian casualties, if possible."

"Aye, aye sir." Horse gets up to depart.

"Whoa." Karl calls. "Here, read this." He hands the CONFIDENTIAL dispatch to Horse.

"Hmm." Horse reads. "Well, congratulations **Admiral.** And I think it's entirely appropriate considering you are now commanding an international task force."

"Thanks Horse. Now get goin' on that op plan."

35
Havens?

Four days later the international force, consisting of naval forces representing Australia, India, Japan, Russia, the United Kingdom, and the United States complete their movement at flank speed from their Indian Ocean patrol positions to their assigned assault positions as follows:

> At Eyl, the pirate headquarters and the location of most of the ships and crews seized by Somali pirates; Phibron Five and the Indian landing ship INS *Jalashwa* supported by the frigate INS *Brahmaputra* are positioned for the hopefully peaceful envelopment of Eyl.

> In the Gulf of Aden off the port of Boosaaso, a pirate haven harboring some seized vessels; the British LPD HMS *Bulwark* carrying a battalion of British marines and a commando contingent, with the Russian heavy cruiser *Peter the Great* in support.

> Off the town of Hobyo where some seized vessels are held; Australian amphibious ship HMAS *Kanimbla* carrying a battalion of Aussie marines and backed by Japanese destroyers *Harusame* and *Amagiri* stand ready to encircle Hobyo.

*

At 0400 the assault begins.

Off shore at Eyl, the U.S. Phibron Five and the Indian force eschew the usual pre-landing air strikes and bombardment in an attempt to succeed without unnecessary Somali casualties.

First, *Boxer* launches four command *SeaHawks* with Colonel Gocio in the lead aircraft and two air cushion landing craft for a beach landing at Badey on the coast. Minutes later, eight *Ospreys* with sixteen Marine platoons aboard depart *Boxer* for direct assault on the ships held by the pirates. Next, four CH-53D *Sea Dragons* depart Boxer to insert Marines on the hills West of the Daawad part of town to complete the insertion of three Marine Battalions and, finally, four *Harriers* are launched for a show of force over Eyl. Meanwhile, *Green* Bay (LPD-20) and *Pearl Harbor* (LSD-52) launch air cushion landing craft and MV-22 *Ospreys* to complete the insertion of a U.S. Marine regiment in and around Eyl.

Next, the Indian amphibious landing ship *Jalashwa* launches air cushion landing craft followed by two *Ospreys* to land a battalion of Indian Marines on the Eyl beach.

Upon arrival, the four command aircraft disperse over both Daawad and Badey and the captured ships to begin playing a taped message in Somali language: "Greetings, citizens of Eyl and pirates. Our mission here is peaceful. We wish no harm to any persons or property. In ten minutes you will be surrounded by one full U. S. Marine regiment with Indian reinforcements advancing on Badey. We wish only to reestablish the rule of law in Eyl, to free all hostages, and to repatriate all captured ships to their rightful owners. Any threat to the ships' crews will be met with deadly force but surrendering pirates will be handled in a civilized manner. Be warned; any fire directed a us will be returned with the full power of our armaments . . . Greetings, citizens of . . ."

As the announcement is broadcast, two marine squads rappel to the roof of the building identified by intelligence as the hostage holding point.

Simultaneously, British and Australian commandos are inserted into the ports of Boosaasa and Hobyo to take control of any seized ships they find in those locations, rescue the captured crews, and pacify the towns.

*

In *Boxer* flag plot at dawn, Admiral Swenson and staff listen to the radio traffic into and out of Combat Information Center (CIC): "Fantail, FanCom here." It was Colonel Gocio in the lead command helicopter. "Everything peaceful here now. Had one incident with some idiot taking a pot shot at us. Our response was as advertised, devastating. No more pot shots since. Water borne Marines are infiltrating the town from the South while airborne troops are moving in from the North, establishing check points on the roads as they come. Marines landed by our *Ospreys* have secured all the docks and are beginning to board the captured ships."

A pause. "Oh! My number four now reports that the Indian force met no opposition to its landing at the Badey beach and is now formed up for the infiltration of the town."

"Admiral." Horse calls." Spark Flintly advises that *Boxer's* brig is ready for any pirates that Gocio brings back and our hospitals are ready for casualties and/or Eyl citizens in need of care."

"Thanks, Horse." Karl responds. "How about humanitarian assistance, food and other needs, you know."

"*Boxer's* ready for that, skipper." Horse responds. "Well deck's loaded with everything from MREs (Meals Ready To Eat) to items of clothing and first aid items. They'll go via *Osprey* and CH-53 Sea Dragons as soon as the town is secured."

*

An hour later Col Gocio reports: "The Indian force has now arrived in Eyl and established command posts."

An hour later: "Fantail, FanCom one here." Gocio reports further. "I am landing with a translator/interpreter to meet my Indian counterpart Colonel Mahesh Paranjothi to arrange a partnership with the town's mayor for the security of the Eyl population and to plan the withdrawal of all U.S. Forces to leave Colonel Paranjothi in charge of town security and the continued surveillance of any remaining pirates."

"Horse" Karl inquires. "What reports do we have from the British and Australian forces?"

"The action reports are coming in now." Horse reports, handing the British report to Karl.

"Hmm." Karl scans the report. "Whoa! They got into a hornets' nest up there at Boosaasa, where, despite British peace overtures broadcast by their assault helicopters, strong resistance was mounted by weapons teams dug in around the port city. One *Sea King* helicopter shot down with some survivors and one landing craft severely damaged by coastal fire. Most firing was soon subdued by fire from the main battery of *Peter the Great* and from *Bulwark's* Close In Weapon System. Original casualty reports count nine Royal Marines killed and sixteen wounded." Karl sighs. "After a fierce battle with the pirates, the British force gained control of the port and the ships docked there, and are moving on the town in a pincers movement with Russian commandos in support." Karl puts down the report. "That spells trouble. Nothing said about the city government. The Brits may have to occupy the town for longer than we'd planned." Karl thinks: *We'll have to figure out a way to get out of this operation and get ready for a Greek earthquake.*

"And this came from the Australians. You'll like it better." Horse hands the report to Karl.

"Hmm. The report says that they enveloped the town of Hobyo with no opposition after playing our peaceful message. Hah! The only problem is that one of the hijacked ships was taken out to sea while the Aussie marines were taking control of the town. One of the Japanese destroyers gave chase and expects no problem retrieving it."

*

TWO DAYS LATER - BOXER OFF SHORE AT EYL

Karl is in his office reading dispatches. Horse Cavallo knocks and enters.

"Listen to this from *Kanimbla*." Horse fingers the report. "You remember the report from *Kanimbla* that one of the hostage ships had escaped Hobyo's harbor."

"Aye, I remember. But I understood the Jap destroyers were on the case."

"Yeah. The Japs caught up with the ship and boarded her." Horse smiles. "Ya know what they found?"

"Never guess."

"Yellow cake." Horse offers a quizzical smile. "That's nuclear material."

"Hmm. Karl frowns. "Was the ship flying an Uruguayan flag?"

"You got it skipper." Horse scratches his head. "How'd you know that."

"Some months ago there were reports that a merchant ship, made a port call at Lom, Togo, on the Gulf of Guinea. The ship was *Lago del Plata*. She's an Uruguayan flagged vessel owned by the British firm Rio Negro Shipping Company. When she left Lom she headed South. Recognizing the proximity of Lom to Niger, the UN suspected the transfer of nuclear materials and requested that member nations track *Lago del Plata* and determine her destination. Shortly thereafter *Lago del Plata* disappeared . . . completely. Well, now we know what happened to her. I'll bet the pirates didn't even know what they had." Karl mulls this over. "We've gotta report this to the UN through channels." He eyes Horse. "Get me a draft message to CinCPac ASAP."

36
Prep

BOXER AT THE NAVAL BASE AT DJIBOUTI

Col Horace "Horse" Cavallo, Phibron Five Ops officer; CAPT Steven "Spark" Flintly, *Boxer's* CO; Col Sam Gocio, commander of the Marine Expeditionary Unit (MEU); and LtCol Harold Sapperstein, *Boxer's* air detatchment commander are assembled with RADM Swenson in his office.

Karl begins: "The reason I asked you to come in is to brief you on a special mission we have been assigned." Karl leans back in his chair. "It's called 'OpTop' which means 'Operation Topkapi'. Does that ring a bell?"

"We-e-el." Spark Flintley is scratching his head. "I know Topkapi is the royal palace where the Sultan Süleyman third and his harem live." He glances at Horse, his face a question mark.

"Yeah." Horse agrees. "But what's that got to do with us?"

"Remember a couple of months ago I got called back to Pearl for an 'admirals conference'?" Karl grins and makes quotation marks with his fingers. "I thought it was charm school for new admirals . . . WRONG, Admiral Fredrick Frost, Commander, Pacific Fleet - CinCPacFlt - got me in a meeting with his planning wizards and they hit me with this mission . . . 'OpTop'."

Horse reacts: "Here we've been chasing pirates and knockin' down their bases for the last month and you didn't say a word."

"That pirate chase was a cover for getting us nearer the target. As you'll see, being here at Dibouti gets us even closer." Karl continues. "Admiral Frost demanded absolute secrecy until we get close." Karl smiles. "We're close so I'm going to brief you on the whole plan. Only the four of us will know the whole plan . . . And I want to keep it that way. You'll all have to do some preparatory training but make your training as generic a possible and still be applicable to OpTop. There will be no written plan - no paper. Remember, any breach of this secrecy can result in unnecessary deaths and certainly the failure of the mission. So Zip the Lip!" Karl eyes each of them in turn to emphasize the point. "**Understand?**"

Three heads nod. "Yes **SIR!**"

"First, the objective:" Karl pauses for effect. "Capture or kill Süleyman Third!"

Gasps all around. "Excuse me sir." Gocio begins. "That's **IMPOSSIBLE!**"

Karl smiles. "How'd I know you'd say that, Sam? But I know you and your marines can do it. I told Admiral Frost you have some marines trained and experienced in special warfare. Did I lie?"

"No sir. But that's quite a challenge."

"But you and your marines are up to it, right?" Karl gives Sam the eyeball to eyeball treatment. "Here's the plan."

"But sir." Sam persists. "Without any paper, how can we know how to proceed."

"It's a simple plan and I have some plan views of the target for you."

"That'll help." Gocio sits back. "I'm listening."

"Okay." Karl begins. "To start with you should know that some preparations have already been made: One; we just got new quiet prop-rotors for our *Ospreys*. The better to sneak up on the target; Two; CinCPacFlt staff has made a recording of a thunderstorm with characteristic lightning and thunder; Three; we have a water delivery system designed to simulate the rain of a thunderstorm; and three; we have humint at Topkapi to tell us when and if the Sultan is home at any time during our approach to the target."

"What's the thunderstorm for?" Horse inquires.

"To cover Sam's approach."

Gocio shows some pride in knowing that he will be leading an historic raid that could end the reign of Süleyman and perhaps even the fall of il-Dauli.

Horse interrupts: "Wait a minute, skipper. How the hell do we avoid the enemy's search radar?"

"Oh, I forgot to mention." Karl hides a smile. "We have electronics to cancel out his radar, effectively by absorbing the incoming signal. My freinds at Point Mugu dreamed it up and had a local contract electronics shop build us thirty of the black boxes. Spark, just have your crew install them in all the *Ospreys* and *Harriers.*" Then to Sapperstein: "Harold, you'll have to run some evaluation flights against the Djibouti radar."

"Aye sir." Sapperstein acknowledges. "But how about the SeaHawks and Dragons."

"We have just the thirty boxes." Karl replies. "You and Sam get together and decide how many and what kind of aircraft you'll need. I chose Ospreys and Harriers because of their speed. And do all of your planning in the flag conference room for security."

"Got it sir." Sapperstein glances at Gocio who nods his understanding.

Karl resumes: "The first thing we have to do is establish a cover operation. That will be a humanitarian mission for earthquake victims in Greece."

"Whoa." Flintley holds up his right hand, palm forward. "Where're you gonna get an earthquake?"

"The research CinCPacFlt staff has done shows a regular pattern of at least one strong earthquake over six on the Richter scale per year. That's been true over the past ten years." Karl shows the tabulation of Greek earthquakes. "So far, there has been no strong earthquake in or near Greece yet this year . . . We're waiting."

"So we just cool our heels and wait for an earthquake?" Horse shows his impatience.

"Not 'cool our heels' Horse." Karl gives Horse a stern look. "We've got a lot to do - mainly training." A pause. "Any natural disaster that requires humanitarian response will do." Karl thinks. "A devastating forest fire will do . . . or a flood, for example. Here's the scenario:

"As soon a natural disaster is reported in or around Greece we pack up and proceed at best speed to the Adriatic Sea via the Suez Canal. Once in the Adriatic we stay at the North end about two hundred miles West of Istanbul. From there we deliver humanitarian aid to Greece by day and conduct OpTop on a selected night."

"On that night we proceed at best speed to a position less than one hundred miles from Istanbul. Assault teams will be equipped with silenced Uzis and night vision goggles. At oh two hundred we launch six *Ospreys;* two with the assault teams, one prime and one to capture Abdul the Grand Vizier, if he is there; two as thunderstorm makers with sight, sound, and rain; two to carry the concrete barriers, one to be placed at the entrance to the palace guard bunk house and the other at the entrance to the third courtyard; and four *Harriers* to stand by with firepower in case Sam needs it."

Karl places a large plan of Topkapi palace on the table and uses a pointer to identify locations. "Sam, your assault team will rappel into the third courtyard, here, and move quietly and quickly to this building, here, neutralizing any guards encountered . . . quietly, and contine to the sultan's chambers, here. You'll immobilize Süleyman Third and his companion, if any, with chloroform and ties." Karl looks to Gocio. "Who will lead your second assault team?"

"Major Ramos, sir . . . Oscar Ramos."

"That's good." Karl continues. "Meanwhile, and I mean simultaneously, one *Osprey* is placing his concrete barrier at the bunk house gate, here, to prevent the palace guards from entering the action. And the other is placing his barrier at the entrance to the third courtyard, just in case."

Sam, you must move quickly to get the sultan and companion, if any, to the courtyard to be hoisted into the prime *Osprey*, followed quickly by your assault team."

All *Ospreys* will retire at best speed and recover aboard *Boxer*, followed by the *Harriers*. Any questions?" Karl sits back to hear comment and questions."

"Uh . . . " Horse starts. "What about Abdul the grand Vizier? He's the muscle behind Süleyman three . . . and probably the brains too."

"Good thought, Horse." Karl thinks. "We should take him out too, if possible. See if our spook knows where he is. Major Ramos and his team can take care of him. His quarters are right here, off the second courtyard."

Okay." Karl continues. "Meanwhile get a training cruise organized to execute ASAP. Sam's got to get his marines familiar with the target territory, our *Osprey* crews need to practice putting those marines into a small courtyard and retrieving them . . . rapidly, placing concrete barracades accurately, and checking satisfactory operation of the thunder, lighting, and rain machines, and all air crews need to test the effectiveness of the stealth electronics. Sam, there should be some space along the shore North of here where you can build a simulated target environment, putting the materials in via *Osprey*."

"Where would we get the materials, Boss?" Gocio asks . . . with trepidation.

"My god, man." Karl exclaims. "You have quite a few Sergeant Majors. Any one of them will know how to kumshaw what you need."

"Yes sir." Gocio cringes.

*

BOXER AT SEA IN THE GULF OF ADEN

"You'll be interested in this, Admiral." Estes hands a print-out to Karl. "It's Associated press reporting a major earthquake in Greece."

Karl receives the paper, concealing his excitement. *Hmm. A magnitude 7.2 quake up around the northern Greek city of Thessalonika.* "Well, earthquake in Greece. That's interesting."

"Thanks Estes." *Hmm. This will require humanitarian aid. We're equipped, but a long way from Greece. We might get orders.* "Be on the lookout for anything from CincPacFleet."

"Aye, sir."

Karl keys the intercom. "Hey, Horse. Come in here."

"What's up boss."

"Read this." Karl hands the AP article to Horse.

"Hmm." Horse scans the article. "Orders?"

"Not yet." Karl eyes Horse. "Get our OpTop crew together ASAP. I want to review our readiness for both humanitarian aid and OpTop."

"But Sam is still on the beach with his marines, sir."

"Get him back here, on the double." Karl shows urgency. "I expect orders for humanitarian aid any moment now . . . That'll be the signal."

*

Thirty minutes later in the conference room Karl starts: "You've all heard about the earthquake in Greece I presume."

"Yes sir." Was the unanimous response.

"Okay Spark." Karl eyes Spark Flintley. "Do we have a good supply of aid items for the earthquake victims."

"Aye, sir. We have a maximum load for all available *Ospreys* and *Sea Dragons*; water, food, blankets, warm clothing, tents, et cetera."

"And both *Green Bay* and *Pearl Harbor* are loaded with similar items." Horse interjects.

"And how are things with the marines, Sam?"

"Well, sir, we got our simulated target laid out and partially built . . . uh, sufficient to get a good feel for what we're up against. My marines know what to do and how to do it." Gocio pauses. "I would recommend that all *Ospreys* carry the thunderstorm noise and that we synchronize them to all play at once for better saturation."

"Do we have enough storm sound boxes?" Karl wonders out loud.

"Yes sir." Sapperstein chimes in. "They sent us twelve of them."

"Okay, Sam. How'd it go rapelling into the courtyard and placing the barracades."

"Those *Osprey* drivers can drop a squad of marines into the courtyard in just a few seconds and they placed the barracades right on the money." Gocio shows his pride.

"Well, then. how do the rain machines work."

"The two *Ospreys* were able to sprinkle the courtyards and buildings with a variable intensity rain shower, somewhat sychronized with the lightning and thunder." Gocio looks surprised.

"Good." Karl looks to Sapperstein. "How about the stealth electronics, Harold?"

"Worked great skipper. I sent two flights of two *Ospreys* and two *Harriers* each into the Djibouti radar, the first flight equipped with the stealth and the second without. I watched the radar in the Djibouti tower and their radar never had a blip on the first flight but showed plenty of return on the second flight. As you know the naked *Ospreys*, with their huge prop rotors make a big, bright blip on a radar screen. So I think the stealth boxes are going to work fine."

Karl thinks. "How can you be sure. The Istanbul radar will have a different operating frequency."

"There is a setting for the radar operating frequency and the Istanbul radar is one of the choices." Sapperstein smiles with satisfaction. "Your Point Mugu freinds did a good job."

A knock on the conference room door. Horse opens the door a crack to see Estes with a manila envelope and admits him.

"A dispatch from CinCPacFlt, sir." Estes hands the envelope to Karl and leaves.

"Thanks, Estes." Karl draws the sheaf of paper out of the envelope. "Yep. Orders for a humanitarian mission to Greece." Karl scans further. "Says 'Proceed at best speed to the earthquake effected area in and around Thessaloníki in Northern Greece to provide humanitarian assistance.' That's perfect. It's going to take us almost four days to get there by my calculations. And we'll have to observe speed limits in the Red Sea, if any, and in the Gulf of Suez. The canal itself will cost us some time so we have no time to waste. Set course now for Bal el Mandeb to proceed through the Red Sea at 'best speed' and on to Suez." Karl pauses. "We'll have to obey whatever speed limits are in effect, Spark. Do you have that covered?"

"Aye, aye, sir." Flinley departs for *Boxer's* bridge and Cavallo calls flag plot to advise the other ships of PhibRon Five of the orders and the course change coming.

37
Day And Night

FOUR DAYS LATER: PHIBRON FIVE ARRIVES IN THE NORTHERN AEGEAN SEA

Horse Cavallo reports: "Admiral, we have reports of widespread structural damage to housing and some damage to buildings in Thessaloníki, some towns are deluged by flash floods, and hundreds of people are without shelter and in need of warm clothing and blankets."

"Pretty bad." Karl comments. "Is there any other aid in the area?"

"Well." Horse responds. "The Greek Department of the Interior is doing the best they can with the resources they have - mostly providing minimal shelter and food."

"Do we have any advice or instruction from our embassy in Athens." Karl inquires.

"They did send a welcoming message with encouraging words." Horse begins. "They have a crew of staff people in the area, mostly to survey the situation and advise aid agencies. That's where we got the information we have."

"Sounds like we better expedite our aid operation."

"Yes, sir. *Boxer* is about to launch all six of our CH-53s loaded to the gills with all kinds of supplies for the refugees, each destined for a particular area of reported need." Horse pauses to check his notes. "Our *SeaHawks* are dedicated to antisubmarine patrol and we have a division of *Harriers* on top. You never can tell. We're holding the *Ospreys*."

"Sounds good, Horse." Karl smiles. "Is there more we can do?"

"Yes sir. *Boxer*, *Green Bay*, and *Pearl Harbor* have just launched their CH-53s with supplies and they have a total of five air cushion landing craft loaded with goodies for launch as soon as we move in a little closer."

"How about OpTop." Karl gets serious.

Day And Night

"Right now, we're waiting for a report on the situation from our guy in Istanbul." Horse checks his notes. "All the OpTop *Ospreys* are equipped for their individual parts in the operation, and Sam Gocio continues to drill his teams on their mission, including the *Osprey* pilots."

*

0300 at TOPKAPI PALACE

Lightning . . . and thunder three seconds later appears to be coming from over the Sea of Marmara south of Topkapi. Two minutes later: lightning, with almost immediate thunder just south of Topkapi. Three minutes later; rain starts over Topkapi amid another spate of lightning and almost simultaneous thunder as the rain intensifies and the prime *Osprey* arrives over the third courtyard and drops a squad of marines led by Col Gocio. Guards come out of their shelters to be met by Gocio's squad firing their silenced Uzis. As the secondary *Osprey* drops Major Ramos and his squad near the entrance to the Grand Vizier's quarters the concrete barriers are placed; one at the gate to the guards' quarters; and one at the Gate of Felicity, the entrance to the third courtyard. In the process, all three Ospreys are fired upon by guards in their courtyard unable to get out because of the barrier. All three *Ospreys* return fire to silence the guards' weapons.

The Sultan and his companion, both sedated, are hoisted into the prime *Osprey* followed immediately by Col Gocio and his squad. Meanwhile,

Major Ramos and his squad find that Abdul, the Grand Vizier, is nowhere to be found.

Upon the agreed signal all six *Ospreys* retire at best speed to the south over the Sea of Marmara and the Dardanelles and thence to *Boxer*.

*

THE NEXT DAY ABOARD BOXER CRUISING THE ADRIATIC SEA

Horse Cavallo is discussing the capture of Süleyman III and his wife Aleksandra with Karl. "Well, boss, now that we've got 'em, what do we do with 'em."

"But we lost Abdul." Karl shows regret. "Do we have anything on them."

"Yeah." Horse replys. "He an his wife Svetlana have been seen in Sevastopol, Crimea, Svetlana's home. They're well protected there." Karl pauses. "Regarding the prisoner disposition, think of it this way." Karl thinks out loud. "Admiral Frost has my report in which I requested an early resolution and orders for the disposition of the prisoners. He and his planning staff must have thought of this eventuality. I expect orders soon."

Horse thinks a moment. "We can't safely hold them in *Boxer's* brig for very long sir. Those *il-Dauli* types will be after us pretty soon."

"Good thought, Horse." Karl thinks. "We'd better get out of the confined Adriatic and out into the Med. That's probably on the way to where we will deliver our prisoners anyway." Karl snaps his fingers. "Oh! I almost forgot about our humanitarian mission. How's that going?"

"Oh yeah." Horse pulls a small sheet of paper from his shirt pocket. "We've delivered all the relief supplies we had and local Greek relief efforts are pretty well in place now, but *Green Bay* and *Pearl Harbor* still have personnel ashore."

"Okay, get our personnel back on their ships on the double and set course for Crete and then eastward to the wide part of the Med." Karl thinks. "Oh, and advise our embassy in Athens of our intentions."

"Aye, aye, sir." Horse acknowledges. "And we'll augment anti-sub and combat air patrols." Horse scratches his head. "You know, this might take a while. The TV tells me that the UN, the U.S., and the world court in the Hague all claim jurisdiction over the prisoners. I hear the U.S. would rather the world court take them."

"We'll see."

38
Epilogue

PACIFIC PALISADES, CALIFORNIA

RADM Karl Swenson is back home on a one month leave. The scene is the patio of the Swenson home. Karl and Marcia enjoy the sunset with a scotch and rocks.

"Hey honey." Marcia starts. "Well, Süleyman Three is on trial at the world court in the Hague and his il Dauli seem seriously diminished since you and your 'PhibRon' put them out of business. You're a hero you know."

"Don't I know it." Karl bristles. "TV shows, interviews, book offers, what's next. I just want to relax. That's what this month's leave is supposed to be about." Karl shifts in his chair. "Correction, Mush: Süleyman Three is not on trial . . . yet. Hell, seeing the past World Court trials he could well die before his case is decided. Think Radovan Karadzic the Bosnian Serb boss."

"What happens to you now?" Marcia quiries.

"Hmm." Karl thinks. "Boeing has shown interest in taking me back as Vice President, Western Region. I'd like that. But I don't have a clue about what the Navy might want me to do."

"Well, your cruise was quite successful." Marcia glows. "Who knows, you could end up in some Navy policy position."

"In Washington?" Karl sneers. "You certainly wouldn't like that."

"Hmm." Marcia sips her scotch. "Our family is pretty fragmented now . . . Harm back in Victoria to finish his education and raise a family with his dear Katja, and Karen climbing the ranks in the Navy."

"Yeah." Karl smiles with satisfaction. You know that the young Lieutenant Swenson's going to the Top Gun school up in Fallon."

Marcia takes Karl's hand. "Washington might be a welcome diversion."

Karl chokes on a sip of scotch. "Whoa! That's a switch. But be careful what you wish for. The Navy might just make it come true."

"What d'ya hear about Abdul, the Grand Vizier?"

"Silence." Karl spreads his hands. "Just melted into the Crimean population, it seems. His wife, Svetlana, was born and raised there so they have a lot of help." Karl sips his scotch. "Too bad. I think Abdul was the brains behind il Dauli. Süleyman was just the charismatic front man. We probably got the wrong guy."

ACKNOWLEDGEMENTS

RADM Roger E. Box, USN, Ret., Commander 6th Fleet ca. 1990

Col Robert H. Lilac, USAF, DoD Director Military Foreign Sales

CAPT Robert Ford, USN, Commander USS Belleau Wood ca 2005

CAPT T. J Culora, USN, Commander USS Boxer ca 2005

Col Gregory O. Stanley, USAF, Commander AMARC, ca 2003

Mr. Herbert E. Sweatman, Director Navy Office, AMARC, ca 2003

CAPT Lee H. C. Little, Commodore Training Wing six ca 2005

BIBLIOGRAPHY

Clot, Andrew & Reisz, Matthew J, (Translator), *Süleiman the Magnificent*, Saqui Books

Friedman, George, The Next 100 Years, Doubleday

Severy, Merle, *The World of Süleyman the Magnificent,* National Geographic, November,1987

LaVergne, TN USA
10 December 2010

208143LV00002B/3/P